Unravel Me

Katherine Bitner

IBSN: 979-8-9870948-2-2

Book Cover Design: Katherine Bitner

Developmental Editor: Andrea Halland

Copy/Line Editor: Aspen Brown

Contents

I dedicate this book to my mom, who taught me to never settle for anyone who doesn't love you for exactly who you are.
And if you haven't found that person yet, there are always book boyfriends.
(May I present to you Rhett Anderson)

Author's Note

This book was born out of my love for all things Southern..the accents, the food, and the warm Carolina summers. This book will make you laugh, cry, and feel all the feels. However, a few elements may be triggering to some. I take that very seriously, so if you'd like to be for-warned please see content warnings below:

Unravel Me has cursing, alcohol consumption, illegal drug use, toxic parental relationships, parental death (off-page, in the past), cheating (not by the main characters, off-page), and brief physical violence. It also has sexual content that would be appropriate for readers 18+.

Playlist

For all the proper story vibes.

1. Take Me Away – Morgan Wade

2. All I See Is You – Shane Smith & the Saints

3. Old Money – Lana Del Rey

4. Champagne Problems – Taylor Swift

5. Boons – Zach Bryan

6. Cowboy Take Me Away – The Chicks

7. Margaret (feat. Bleachers) – Lana Del Rey

8. Smaller Acts – Zach Bryan

9. Cinnamon Girl – Lana Del Rey

10. Lose You to Love Me – Selena Gomez

11. Darlin' – Houndmouth

12. In Your Love – Tyler Childers

CHAPTER ONE

Audrey

The champagne bottle wobbles dangerously on the edge of the marble side table, and I lunge forward, catching it just before it can crash to the ground. But it's too late. Sticky champagne splashes across my white silk minidress, the one my maid of honor and I had carefully chosen for my engagement party next weekend.

None of that matters now.

I glance down at the ridiculously expensive pink bottle. Three hundred freaking dollars. That was nothing to Jackson though. He loved buying expensive things simply to prove he could. He bought this one after I landed a large client at work a few months ago, but we never ended up celebrating.

What a damn waste.

I meet my gaze in the mirror, staring at my pitifully swollen hazel eyes surrounded by streaked mascara. The mascara that Penny, my maid of honor and best friend, assured me was hurricane-level waterproof. You know, because I needed to look polished and fresh through my upcoming engagement party, where there would be tear-jerking toasts and emotional Kodak moments. The idea makes me shudder with a humorless laugh now.

Perhaps my tears of heartbreak are stronger than tears of joy.

The sharp clicking of my new Louboutin's is the only sound in the apartment as I amble into the bathroom. Setting the champagne bottle on the counter, I lean into the mirror, contemplating my next move. Thirty minutes have passed since the phone call that turned my world upside down—that's long enough to get over a five-year relationship, right?

I can't think in the deafening silence of this bathroom, full of products and monogrammed robes. The only thing reminding me I'm still alive is the pounding in my head from crying, so I lift the opening of the half-full bottle to my lips, tipping it back gently so the brut bubbles can drown out my impending sobs.

Merely four days ago, I stood right in this spot, kissing my handsome fiancé goodbye.

Less than two hours ago, Penny and I were video chatting, and I was showing her my outfit all put together. We were all laughs and smiles, gushing about the upcoming engagement party that's been in the works since the moment Jackson Tippins slid that four-carat ring on my finger on New Year's Eve.

The party was going to be like a wedding in itself, with a large guest list, and a lakefront venue that was to die for. I'm not sure what's more nauseating to me, the fact that my heart is shattered into bits, or knowing the backlash I will face when I cancel the engagement party—*and the wedding*. My throat restricts as I step back, hitting the wall, and slide down into a puddle on the floor.

The feeling of needles across my chest takes over, as I picture my parents' disappointment when I tell them the news. Undoubtedly, Evelyn Elson, my mother, will be cold, and offer small jabs of backhanded sympathy—her forte. My father, *the* Samuel Elson, will insist I'm being too rash. He'll want to fix this like he fixes everything; by throwing money at it. He's always been more concerned about preserving our family's reputation—and canceling the wedding would be more disgraceful than anything. Including *why* I'm canceling it. He'll be adamant this can be remedied, not unlike a PR disaster at my father's investment firm.

I take another sip of champagne, mumbling what I will end up saying to my father.

Sorry, Dad. I know you loved Jackson (more than me). Sorry, I know you have a deep business history with the Tippins family.

Of course, my parents will expect that nothing on the surface changes. I'd have to remain poised, continue performing well at work, and keep my social circle free of gossip—AKA never disclose the truth. My mother will most likely remind me it's okay to mourn, but only for the appropriate amount of time. That amount of time will be predetermined, and when the time is up, it will then be socially acceptable to reenter the dating pool; which she'll enthusiastically encourage since I'm not getting any younger.

Shaking my head with the bottle to my lips, the only thought running through my mind is *this is not how it's supposed to be.*

This was the derailment I never saw coming, and truthfully, I've never felt more naive.

Two more large sips of bubbly roll down my throat. A familiar tightness follows, and instead of screaming like I want to, I kick my new heels off and watch them skid across the bathroom floor into the glass shower wall, as an angry grunt ripples past my lips.

If I shut my eyes, maybe I can pretend this was all a bad dream, and when I eventually wake from this slumber, I will still be the soon-to-be Mrs. Tippins. But when I close my eyes, feeling the cold marble floor beneath my clammy palms, all that flashes before me is the life Jackson and I had planned, now washed away like a flood.

An annoying buzzing pulls me from my self-loathing trance as my eyes dart across the room to my phone.

Penny's beautiful, glowing face lights up the screen. Our blissful video chat earlier had been abruptly cut short with Jackson's call. I never did call her back like promised.

I only answered Jackson's call because it had been unexpected. He had reminded me earlier today he'd be unreachable tonight; busy schmoozing clients or whatever he did to work his way up to VP at twenty-six years old. It was expected. He often has week-long business trips in cities all around the world. But then again, he hadn't meant to dial me tonight. That part was a mistake—it was *all a mistake,* he assured me.

However, mistakes that continue for six months can hardly be considered *mistakes* anymore, can they?

Silencing Penny's call, I shakily text her from the bathroom floor, letting her know I'll call her later. When later is, I don't know. Especially if I keep drinking this champagne, which is starting to taste like water.

I sit for another minute before I can't take the silence any longer and nearly leap from the floor. This apartment no longer feels like my safe space, but more like the walls are caving in and pulling the air from my lungs, so I grab the champagne bottle, leaving my phone on the floor, and drunkenly stumble to the foyer. Slipping on my fuzzy, pink slippers, I rip open the front door, and step into the quiet, empty hall.

CHAPTER TWO

Audrey

Jackson wanted to live somewhere impressive, a building with history and prestige, so the Brecken Building became our home; complete with our renovated apartment that could be a spread in *Southern Living* magazine. Jackson's mother, Vivianne, helped decorate it. She took me with her on a weeklong escapade right after we moved in, bringing me to exclusive member only showrooms where her interior designer met us. We picked out everything from the pillows to the floral arrangements. Everyone who enters our home comments on how beautiful it is and they aren't wrong. But as I stand in the hallway, peering back into the foyer, I see everything in a new light. I could leave here right now, and someone else could move in, and besides my clothing, nothing would indicate that this place is mine. Nothing here reflects who I am. Everything was chosen for the sheer purpose to impress. From the chef's kitchen to the bookcase full of trinkets, not books, it's like I could disappear in a poof, and it would be fine. But even if I had the chance, I wouldn't know how to make this space truly mine. This home symbolizes the life I was promised, one that is perfect and safe; beautiful and planned. Everything in its place.

This place, my life, was built around me, *without me in mind.*

With my eyes locked on the metal door at the end of the hallway, I walk with haste, pushing it open and clomping up the stairs. Fresh air hits my face as I step onto the apartment building's rooftop deck. It's been renovated recently, giving the feel of an upscale resort with lounge chairs, gas firepits, tables, and a lush array of plants that make you temporarily forget you're in the city.

As always in North Carolina, the air is humid, but I don't mind the heat that encases me as I shuffle towards a lounge chair.

But before I sit, I flip on the lights, and a zigzag of Edison bulbs illuminates the space above me. Swaying slightly as I sit down, I tuck my long, chocolate brown hair behind my ears and set the champagne bottle on the ground beside me. With my head resting back, I gaze up at the sky, wondering how in the world I got *here*. Drunk, alone...and falling for a man who couldn't keep his hands to himself. It takes only seconds before I begin to fidget, though, every nerve buzzing from both the alcohol and anger raging through my veins.

A fat, hot tear rolls down my cheek as I swipe it clumsily away.

"Fuck you, Jackson," I say aloud, louder than I meant, and am startled as someone clears their throat nearby. Sitting up abruptly, I glance in all directions, noticing a man I didn't see before. His back is to me as he leans against the railing, a cloud of smoke billowing above him.

"I'm sorry, I didn't realize anyone was up here." I stumble over my words, heat creeping up my neck as I smooth my white dress.

The man turns around to face me, leaning his back against the railing, eyes piercing me. "No need to apologize. I was just about to head out anyway." His voice is gravelly, a thick southern drawl rolling off his tongue. Not an accent you hear often in this city full of transients.

I try to shove the champagne bottle behind the lounge chair with my foot, but when I look up, he glances away quickly, a smirk on his lips. A glowing cigarette dangles between his lips, and I bite my tongue, resisting the urge to tell him there's no smoking allowed up here. He doesn't strike me as someone who would care about those kinds of rules, and right now, I'm not sure I do either. He remains half in the shadows of the dark night, but I stay mesmerized as he releases a roll of smoke, snuffs out the cigarette, and tosses it in the trash can.

Maybe it's the alcohol racing through my body, or maybe I just have nothing left to lose, but no part of me feels worried about being on this dark rooftop, alone with a strange man. In fact, I stand up and take a step towards him.

It's not like the conversation in my head is a pleasant one, so I smile weakly, and steady my voice.

"Do you live in the building?" I ask, already assuming the answer is no. The Brecken Building isn't huge, and I know every tenant in it, especially the ones close to my age, and he can't be much older than thirty.

He smirks, shaking his head a little. "No, ma'am. I just finished up a job in apartment six. Mrs. Lawson," he says. I nod. It checks out. Laura Lawson is a wealthy, albeit grumpy woman who is constantly renovating her already impeccable apartment. She is also continually complaining about it.

"That makes more sense," I reply as his eyebrows shoot up, giving me a view of the palest blue eyes I've ever seen. Almost silver.

"What gives it away? The boots?" he asks, and I turn red, looking down at his loosely laced, work boots.

"Oh shit, no, I wasn't implying anything..." I backpedal, slapping a palm to my forehead. "It's just there are only twelve apartments in this building, and I know mostly everyone. I've never seen you around, but you could've been someone's boyfriend, or son, or—"

He cuts my rambling off. "It's okay." He lets out a small chuckle, his voice soothing. My heart starts to slow its hammering. "You don't need to explain yourself."

I purse my lips together. I really hope I didn't offend him. God, I need water and a painkiller, and certainly a break from drinking for at least a month.

He doesn't say anything else but doesn't leave either. He turns his back, looking over the railing out at the city, and I take this chance to get a better look at him. A worn-in white shirt, frayed jeans and work boots. Paired with broad shoulders, arms rippled with thick muscle, and a lush head of hair. I can't peel my eyes away.

The lights overhead are a bit blurry, reminding me how drunk I am. Good thing my years of etiquette lessons are ingrained in every fiber of my soul. I've had plenty of polite conversations over bottles of wine at dinners and events I didn't want to be at.

Mystery man turns back around as I stand there like a drunk fool and rakes his eyes slyly over me, landing on my feet.

"I would add, though, my choice of shoes is more practical than the bunnies you have on your feet." He crosses his arms over his chest, a teasing smile on his face. My jaw drops as I scoff, peering down.

"Okay, okay, in my defense, I had gorgeous Louboutins on with this dress, but I figured stilettos weren't really practical for late-night rooftop decompression sessions."

"I don't understand a single word you just said, but it sounds like you need one of these more than I do." He pulls the carton of cigarettes from his pocket, extending it towards me. Without hesitation, I pulled one out. Jackson was allowed as many cigars as he wanted, but if I so much as touched a cigarette, he would throw a fit. All the more reason to do it.

I place it between my lips and he closes the gap between us, bringing a lighter up, his eyes locking with mine as I suck in. His head could rest on top of mine, and he smells like fresh cut wood. As I inhale my legs grow wobbly, and I have to rip my eyes away from his, heat rising in my chest.

I let the toxic smoke fill me, chasing away feelings of guilt. Yes, he's attractive, but I'm not kissing him; it's just a cigarette. He flicks the lighter closed, dropping it in his pocket and steps back, giving me space. I can hear my best friend assessing him in my head.

Strong jawline, check. Pretty eyes, check. Dirty blonde hair women would kill for, check. His hair was a little messy and curled up at the nape of his neck.

"I'm not a smoker," I say, my voice thick as I blow out a puff away from him.

"Right," he mumbles with a flicker of amusement in his eyes.

"It's been a long night, that's all. I know this is bad for you." I wiggle the glowing cigarette towards him. He bows his head, stifling a laugh.

"I'm guessing your long night has something to do with Jackson?" he asks, and I snap my neck to look at him, lips ajar.

"Wha—"

"*Fuck you, Jackson,*" he mimics my line from before, and I can't help but let out a yelp of a chuckle, even if nothing about this is even slightly funny.

"Oh right, you heard that."

"Hope he's not the one responsible for the ring on that finger of yours." He nods towards my hand, and I glance at the heavy stone on my finger.

"Thank you for reminding me to take this off as soon as possible." I bring the smoke back to my mouth, disgusted with myself and needing it all the same.

"I'm sorry for oversharing. I think I had a bit too much champagne."

That's an understatement.

"You call that oversharing? Darlin', where I'm from, everyone knows everything about everyone. Hell, I don't even know your name, so don't apologize to me. Done nothing wrong that I can see." He runs a hand through that dirty blonde hair, his forearm flexing, showing off a splatter of tattoos inside his arms as my eyes unwillingly land on his face.

My own flushes and I lean on the railing beside him.

"My name is Audrey." He doesn't reply, but I continue. "And I'm in this ridiculous outfit because I was planning my engagement party two hours ago."

"Congratulations?" he asks, facing me.

"Thank you, but it's actually off." I inhale a sharp breath. "I found out my fiancé, *Jackson,* was cheating on me. He has been for months actually...it started before he even asked me to marry him."

I look up as sudden tears cloud my vision, and shame envelops me like a cloak. The man's —who still hasn't told me his name—eyebrows knit tightly together, and he hesitantly moves a bit closer to me.

"Well, fuck you Jackson, indeed," he says gruffly, and I laugh, but it quickly turns to sniffling, and I tuck my face away from him, embarrassment building in my belly.

"Thank you...I'm...I'm sorry. Crying in front of a stranger was not on my list of to-dos tonight."

"Audrey," he starts, and my stomach clenches in response. He says my name like he's known me for years. "Remember what I said about apologizing? Stop it. You have every right to be pissed and cry or whatever the hell you want to feel. That's fucked up. Excuse my language."

I nod, the voice in my head louder than this kind stranger. "Maybe I'm naive. Maybe this is just how men are. No offense," I add, glancing his way.

"Sadly, you're not wrong. Not all of us, but a lot of guys don't know a good thing when they have it. But that doesn't excuse what he did."

I bite my lip, unsure what to even say to this stranger who knows my most vulnerable secret.

"Don't take this the wrong way, but if I just ended my engagement, I'm not sure I'd be so...composed?"

"Ha!" I throw my head back, laughing through the tears. "I chucked my phone into the wall, creating a hole, and drank an entire bottle of champagne. Trust me, I'm barely holding it together," I shot back, but he smirked at me, releasing his grip on the railing.

"You shared something with me, so I'll even the playing field, okay?" He muses and I nod, yet again having nothing to lose. And oddly enough, standing here with this stranger is better than being alone with my thoughts.

"When my Mimi found out my Papa was deep into gambling again, after he'd sworn he'd stopped, she solved it by grabbing her shotgun and giving him two choices. Leave before she could shoot him or change his ways. He lived to be ninety years old. They stayed married, and he never gambled again."

I snort in disbelief, but his face stays the same.

"Oh, you're dead serious, aren't you?"

"Of course, I am."

"So, are you suggesting I wait for my cheating ex-fiancé to get home and threaten him with a weapon?" I ask, amused, and he laughs, scrubbing a palm across his five o'clock shadow.

"No, I'm just saying there's a lot of ways to deal with shit in life. And you gotta do it in the way that's right for you."

I shake my head as his pocket chimes, and he slides his phone into his palm. "Well, duty calls."

I cast my eyes away, not asking for an explanation he certainly doesn't owe me. A guy like this probably has a family, or a girlfriend waiting for him at home. He doesn't need to spend any more of his Saturday night on a rooftop with a crying rich girl.

"I should go, too." I snuff out what was left of the cigarette. He nods, an unreadable look on his face as we both turn towards the door. Avoiding eye contact, I pick up my empty bottle and focus my gaze on the stairwell door as I attempt not to stumble while I walk. Nausea bites at my stomach.

He follows me down the steps, keeping a respectful distance as we enter the hallway of the sixth floor together.

"The elevators are right down there." I point past my door, down the hallway. "But of course, you already know that since you work here," I add, and he flashes me a charming smile.

"Thank you, take care."

"You too. This is me," I add, buying time for reasons I can't articulate. I stop outside my door, my hand hesitating at the keypad.

My gaze rests on his back a heartbeat too long before I quickly type the code into my door. His footsteps sound down the hallway, getting further away, and without hesitation, I pause and holler after him.

"Thank you for letting me vent."

He stops, peering back at me over his shoulder. "You're welcome."

"Oh, I didn't catch your name." I wait, my breath hitched in my chest.

"It's Rhett." His lips pull up to one side as he nods his head at me.

Rhett.

"Well thank you, Rhett. Have a good evening. Or night."

"Goodnight, Audrey," he says, and as soon as he disappears into the elevator, my shoulders sink and I drag my feet through the threshold of my apartment, alone again.

Chapter Three

Rhett

I crank down the window of my truck and turn up the radio, letting music drown out the noises of the city as I pull off the brick lined street. The Brecken Building fills my rearview mirror. I'll be happy to never come back to this pretentious neighborhood, at least not for a while. The people around here pay well, but not all of them treat me with dignity. I've got thick skin, but it gets old quickly.

My phone lights up on the worn bench seat next to me, and I thumb open the notification as I idle at the red light. Just another alert from my security system telling me motion was detected on the front porch. My dog again—probably slipped out the back door. For the second time this week.

She won't go anywhere; she just doesn't love being alone. I thought she'd get used to it by now. It's just us for the foreseeable future, I keep reminding her. Girl doesn't listen.

The streetlights pass by in a blur as I merge onto the freeway, the smell of gasoline coming through the car vent. This drive is routine, I could do it in my sleep. I know each curve of the roadway, shifting the old gears without a single thought.

Except for the thoughts about Audrey. The way her hazel eyes shined with tears; unnecessary embarrassment etched on her face. The way the cigarette sat between her full, pink lips.

I'll never see that girl again. I don't need to be thinking about this shit.

But seriously, what the hell kind of loser cheats on a girl like that? On their fiancé?

Not that I've always been a star boyfriend or date. Hell, I've never even come close to being engaged. My longest stint lasted just shy of a year and we were eighteen.

The timing in my life also hasn't been impeccable, but I'm glad I decided to take a load off on that rooftop before driving home tonight. I hope Audrey is passed out in her bed by now. She definitely drank enough champagne to sleep for two days.

Reaching for the old, yellowed dial, I tune the radio to a new station. Classic rock, just like my old man used to blast decades ago from this same seat. My friends harp on me for not upgrading the stereo system in this old truck, but I like the simplicity of old things.

As I'm pulling off the road onto the gravel lane that leads home, I think of her again, a pang in my tired chest, wondering if she is okay.

My boots hit the grass outside my truck door, and I snatched my lunch cooler and canteen off the passenger side floor.

If I was a betting man, I'd say her asshole ex is already on his way back to her with a dozen roses in tow, an expensive gift, maybe a surprise trip to somewhere she always wanted to go, ready to beg her to get back together—that's what rich guys do, right? And maybe she'll say yes and brush this all under the rug, and live happily ever after.

And I'll just be a stranger she'll forget by tomorrow afternoon.

Woof!

My eyes dart up, catching the shadow of my eighty-pound dog lazily getting her butt off the porch, crossing the yard and waltzing up to me.

"Again, girl? When you gonna learn to not nudge the door so hard?" I ruffle her long hound dog ears, and she follows me happily to the backdoor. I make a mental note to fix the latch on this door as I pull it open, flipping on the light over my kitchen island.

A stack of mail and a pan of what's probably zucchini bread sits on the butcher block counter. Tell-tale signs my mom was here again; she can't go a day without making something from her garden and dropping it off. Retirement has her going stir-crazy.

Tossing my lunch cooler and canteen in the sink—it's tomorrow's problem—I rifle through my mail. Nothing important, as usual.

"Think we got time to catch the end of the game?" I ask and Mabel perks up her ears. She doesn't follow me into the bedroom, where I strip out of the dirty work clothes I've been wearing for twelve hours now. I kick off my worn-out boots, and they land near my bed, my gaze holding onto them for a beat longer.

Who the hell wears pink slippers on a rooftop deck? That's just ignorant and unsafe.

Cranking the shower spout, I also push open the window above the tub. The exhaust fan and my AC simultaneously stopped working last week, which is a death sentence in the Carolina summer, but they will have to wait for a fix until another day. And another paycheck.

Clean, but tired as hell, I grab a tin of assorted nuts from my pantry, and kick back on my sofa. The newest thing in my house. My sister convinced me it was time to say goodbye to the bachelor pad furniture and nearly forced me to buy this tan, slipcovered sofa. The cover is machine washable, she touted in the showroom, reminding me it was essential with my stinky dog who finds herself sleeping on this sofa every afternoon.

Like she can read my mind, she hops up next to me, circling three times before plopping down, eyeing the snack in my hand.

I toss her a peanut, turn on the TV, catching the end of the Braves game.

It doesn't take long before she's snoring next to me, and my eyes grow heavy. Right before the blue walls of my living room turn to black, my thoughts flash back to the girl in the white dress.

CHAPTER FOUR

Audrey

"One moment, I'm coming!" I yell out, my voice echoing through the apartment. The pounding on the door ceases, but the pounding inside my head does not.

Cradling the back of my neck with my palm, I squint against the bright sunshine pouring through the living room bay window. I attempt to roll my neck out, but it's still stiff as hell, along with the rest of my body. That's what happens when you fall asleep intoxicated, face down on top of the bed. I'm too old for this.

As soon as I swing the front door open, Penny's jaw drops. Casting my eyes to the black and white checkered stone floor, I extend my arm out, inviting her inside.

"I know. Don't say anything," I warn as I head into the equally bright kitchen. Penny's hot on my trail, looking exceedingly fresher than me.

"I got here as soon as I could. I've been worried sick. How are you holding up, honey?"

Penny came straight from the airport to my place, even though I told her not to. I knew she wouldn't listen to me though, and I'm kind of grateful she didn't.

"How was San Diego?" I ignore her question, opening the glass front cabinets and grabbing two matching coffee mugs. "The wedding looked beautiful. Was that Balboa Park?" Penny is a wedding photographer, and her work takes her everywhere.

"Oh, the drama was endless. The mother-in-law was truly unhinged, and I promise to fill you in later but do not ignore my question."

I bite my lip, casting my eyes away from Penny.

"After your cryptic text last night, I moved my flight from 10 a.m. to 6 a.m. for you, so we are going to talk about what the hell went down." She plants herself on a barstool at the long kitchen island, props her chin on her elbows, and stares at me with the intensity of a stalking jungle cat.

Without answering, I shrug, grab my water bottle from the counter, and chug it all.

"Holy shit, how hungover are you?"

"I don't know...however hungover you get after drinking an entire bottle of Dom Perignon." I winced, moving to place the mugs under the hot espresso spout. I swear I still smell champagne, like it's oozing from my pores.

"Okay...then let's start at the beginning." Penny's face is tight, her words slow and deliberate.

After I finish making our cappuccinos, which feels like it takes an ungodly amount of time, Penny follows me into the living room, and we sink deep into my linen sofa. I get in one sip of the delicious frothy espresso before reality hits me like a ton of bricks and tears sting the back of my eyes. I hate crying in front of people. I already met my quota for the year by crying in front of a stranger last night. But I remind myself Penny has seen me at my worst. She was my roommate all four years at the University of North Carolina, after all.

I pull my legs up under myself and clear my throat. "Okay, I'm only going to relive this once and only once. Because I will have to rehash every demoralizing detail for my mother sooner rather than later."

"I won't make you repeat it, I promise." Penny holds up her hand like a Scout's honor and I muster up a tiny laugh.

"Jackson accidentally dialed me last night. During sex—"

"Wait, wait, wait! What do you mean—" Penny jumps straight up off the sofa, nearly splashing espresso on her shirt. Squeezing my eyes shut, I hold up my hand but she is enraged. "I'm going to kill him, Audrey. I will literally get rid of his body. Okay?"

"That's a lovely offer but please don't." I scrunch my nose at her, and she throws her hands in surrender, sitting back down and smoothing her blond ponytail around her shoulder.

"Okay, go on. I'm sorry." Penny grabs a velvet pillow and places it on her lap, like it's a giant stress ball. But first, I reach for the remote on the coffee table, and point it toward the window, lowering the shades a bit. Hangovers and morning sunshine do not mix.

Deep breath.

"I'm just going to start. I heard everything...their names...I can't go into detail. It was awful. It was the worst twenty seconds of my life," I mumble quietly, a pit forming in my stomach just talking about it.

"I'm in complete shock...I'm so sorry. Do you know who it was?"

I nod reluctantly. "Yeah, it's Kelsey." This time, Penny slams her mug on the walnut coffee table and jumps up, red creeping up her neck.

"Kelsey? *The* Kelsey who works directly under him?" Her nostrils flare as I nod slowly. "The girl who came to your housewarming party with her annoying attorney boyfriend?"

"That's the one."

"How freaking cliche of the bastard. He is screwing his coworker? May as well get a tattoo that says 'stereotypical douchebag' across his forehead!" Penny paces my living room, looking like she wants to smash something. I drop my face into my palms and inhale slowly, before lifting slightly to look at my fuming best friend.

"I can't believe I'm saying this...but in all honesty, I'm not even mad at him anymore." I carefully choose my words as Penny balls her fists, her eyes widening. "Perhaps it's because deep down, I'm not surprised."

She nods, still pacing in front of the fireplace.

"How did the phone call end...did you call him back?"

Tears sting my eyes as Penny rushes to my side, wrapping her arms around my hunched shoulders. "At first, he denied it, but after less than two minutes of me begging him to be honest, he was. He said he was sorry, and without even prodding, he admitted it's been going on for six months." I rub my hands down my legs again and again. "He *sighed* after telling me, like it was a weight lifted off his fucking shoulders." Penny's brown eyes grow wide in horror as she waits for me to continue. "I calmly told him it's over, and all he said was *I'm so sorry* but that was it." Snot ran down my face as I wiped my nose across my robe sleeve like a child. Tears run down both our faces now, as Penny empathizes with me. "We exchanged a few texts right before I passed out, but he barely had anything to say to me."

I shake my head, leaning on my best friend's shoulder.

"The worst thing is he didn't even fight for me. I wouldn't have gone back, but am I not worth fighting for?" Lifting my head to look at Penny, she takes my face in her palms, forcing me to look at her.

"You are worth so much more than he could ever give you."

"I just don't understand. We've been planning a life together since we were twenty-one. Five whole years. And he threw it all away." A shrill chuckle escapes my hoarse throat as my shoulders hunched further. "The wedding is planned. The renovations on the house he insisted we buy are only weeks from being complete." My chest constricts as I rattle off the failures heavy on my heart. "I feel like he ripped the rug out from under me, and everything is crashing down. All the plans we had...all the plans *he* made for us." Glancing down at my empty ring finger, I ball my hand into a fist. "All I know is the engagement ring sitting on my nightstand represents the end of everything, not the beginning."

Penny squeezes her arms around me tighter, handing me a tissue from her purse.

"And now, I have to call everyone and explain to them the engagement party is off, the wedding is off…that I fell for a no-good cheat, and I have to…" My voice trails off as she grabs my hands, bringing my spiraling thoughts to a halt.

"Audrey, listen to me. You are allowed to feel all the things you feel. Hell, I want you to be madder than you are but that's a different topic. Jackson screwed up everything. But life is not over. Just imagine if you didn't find out about his true identity until it was too late."

"Yeah…no, I know you're right."

"And stop worrying about everyone. I'll help you get the message out and cancel things. Jackson Tippins doesn't need protection. He did this. And you are a newly single woman, who will now be free on October twenty-first."

Groaning, I comb my fingers through my greasy hair.

"Promise me, on October twenty-first, we will have an anti-wedding celebration. Get drunk and carve pumpkins or something."

Penny laughs and nods.

"I could never survive without you. Seriously. Can we just be single, and buy a beach house, and shun men forever?" I add and she hugs me.

"Of course, babe."

"I don't know how I'm going to get through this week, Pen. I have to call my parents…and deal with Jackson face-to-face eventually." I look around my home, my heart ticking up with every racing realization. "Oh my god, I cannot live here with him."

The last thing I was planning on doing this week was picking up the pieces of my suddenly shattered life.

My best friend pulls out her phone, typing furiously, a stern look on her face. "One step at a time, Aud. First things first. Let's get brunch. Afterwards, you'll call your parents, and I will contact the wedding planner.

Everything will be okay. One day at a time." She squeezes my leg.   "And you can move in with me, okay? I insist. It will be like college all over again."

"As much as I love you, I know you like your space. I can find a place."

She grips my shoulders, forcing me to face her. "I *insist*. You can stay with me as long as you need. I'll help you find the cutest bachelorette pad ever when you're ready, no rush." She hands me another tissue, and I dab my puffy eyes. "I'm shooting a wedding almost every weekend this summer anyway, so you'll practically have the place to yourself."

I swallow the lump in my throat as I muster up a weak smile.

"Thank you. I'd be so lost without you."

"What are girlfriends for, if not for picking up the mess men leave behind?"

CHAPTER FIVE

Audrey

Two hours later, Penny hugged me goodbye outside of our favorite brunch spot, making me promise if I felt overwhelmed today, I'd give her a ring. She embodied older sister syndrome to her core, but I loved her dearly for it right now.

On my walk home, all ten blocks, I mentally prepared myself for the call with my parents. Penny and I already talked it through at brunch, but she could never truly understand what it meant to be the only daughter of Evelyn and Samuel Elson.

At brunch, with the liquid courage of a mimosa or two, I had also sent a text to Jackson letting him know I'd be breaking the news to my family. Which meant by five o'clock today, everyone would be made aware that the nuptials were off. His response came as I was walking into the Brecken Building.

Jackson: People call off weddings for many reasons, it's no one's business what transpired between us. No need to air dirty laundry. I'll be telling people we had a mutual agreement to end things civilly. I trust you won't do anything to tarnish our family names.

God forbid, I let the world know the real Jackson Tippins.

I let out a laugh that ricocheted off the marble walls of the lobby. Laughter was the only response I could summon up—it was the only one that made sense in this absurdity. I was past crying; it only made my head hurt and my eyes red.

I'd never *air our dirty laundry* because the backlash from his family wouldn't be worth the three minutes of joy. He knew that, too—he knew I only had one choice. To let it go. Because Jackson Tippins *always* wins. Men like him always do.

But there's two people who would get the truth, and they were a phone call away. I prepared myself by filling a glass with sparkling water and propped my phone on a stand on the dining table, sitting up straight in my chair. I run my fingers through my long, chocolate brown hair in a poor attempt to look put together and straighten my plaid headband. I don't need any additional reason for them to criticize me. I've become quite good at playing the part of a successful, sophisticated, and dignified daughter the few times of year I'm forced to speak with my family. Lately, with my mother's talons in wedding planning, it's been more like a few times a month but that will all be over soon. Very soon.

I hit 'Evelyn Elson' in my contact list and wait while my heart hammers in my chest. She picks up the video call on the third ring and dread fills my veins.

"Audrey, I wasn't expecting to hear from you." My mother looks at me but is quickly distracted by whatever is in front of her. It appears she is sitting in a golf cart, a visor on her head, and a wall of evergreen trees paint the horizon behind her.

"I didn't realize you were busy. I can call back later, Mom." I'm ready to hang up, when she vigorously shakes her head, bringing her focus back to me.

"No, your father is finishing up now." She waves her hand at my father, beckoning him over. Samuel Elson appears on the screen, both of them looking tan even though summer only just began in Connecticut.

"Audrey," my father addresses me unenthusiastically, visibly irritated that I've interrupted his Sunday game, but before I can answer, he continues talking. "Is Jackson there? He hasn't been returning my calls this weekend, which isn't like him, nor professional and—"

I cut him off with a polite smile and wave. They both freeze on the phone and my mother's tiny grin falls.

"That's why I'm calling, actually. I need to speak with both of you." My stomach dips as my father's peppered eyebrows knit together.

"Oh? Is he okay?" My mom feigns concern as her fingers touch her dainty gold necklace.

"I am not sure, he isn't with me either...but if this isn't a good time to talk, I can call back later." I rush as cold sweat pricks my neck.

"You have your mother worked up and we have already paused our round so come out with it, Audrey." Samuel Elson uses the same voice for me as he uses in the boardroom, and even five hundred miles away his iron grip had me in a chokehold.

"The engagement party is off," I begin as my mother's lips fall open, and I squeeze my eyes shut for the next bit just to get through it. "Because the engagement is off." My mother gasps on the other end of the call.

Deep breath. I peel my eyes open, only to momentarily wonder if the call is frozen as they gawk like a deer in the headlights. The sound of golf carts puttering by, and murmurs of other golfers play in the background until my mother's face crumbles.

"I don't understand Audrey, what did you do?"

Of course, by default, it's my fault.

I quickly rehash the events. Not the part about the sex phone call of course, that would be too humiliating. I tell them all they need to know.

That Jackson was an unfaithful man, and he admitted it, and there were no intentions to rectify the relationship. I made it clear it was unforgivable in my book, and my mother nodded, swallowing hard. My father on the other hand is stoic. For a moment, I wasn't even sure he was still listening.

"This puts me in a very uncomfortable situation. You know how involved Elson Enterprises is with The Tippins Group and—"

I bite my tongue, fighting the tears back, fighting the sob violently rippling through my body. My father learned I was betrayed, and I'm clearly shaken; and all he can think about is the business implications.

I compose my face, nonetheless, swallowing hard several times. "Dad...Jackson made it very clear this would stay under wraps. You now see what kind of man Jackson really is...it's up to your discretion if you want to do business with someone like him," I add harshly, angry it has to be said at all.

My father bobs his head, though his face stays strained. Anyone else would be shocked that this is how my parents would handle a broken engagement, but I was numb to it. After all, this was the Elson way.

Everything was transactional, *everything* was business.

If Jackson didn't come from a family like mine, I would've questioned his intentions with me, but when we met five years ago, I already knew who he was, and he already knew of me. Beyond the surface level, I believed he was the kind of man I was supposed to end up with. Marrying him would ensure I kept the deep-seated legacy going. He came from great wealth and power; he understood business and built an ego long before he was old enough to understand what that even meant. Marrying him meant things wouldn't change for me. I'd live a life just like my mother had and her mother. Jackson was the perfect match. It didn't matter if I never had butterflies with him or if we rarely spent more than a few days together in a row; he checked the boxes on paper. That's what mattered to my parents. Love was not mandatory for a successful marriage to them.

"This is very unfortunate, and I know you must be devastated right now," my mother adds, almost as an afterthought. "I will work on the correspondence to the guests. In your condition, you will be too emotional. This needs to be concise and—"

"Handled with utmost privacy and care," I finished my mother's sentence. "Thanks," I add through gritted teeth, but they don't notice.

"Have you seen a write up on assets?" my father asked, and my lips parted, eyes furrowed, unsure what he even meant. Annoyed, he continued, leaning closer to the iPhone screen. "The house, Audrey. Who will get the house in Forest Hills?"

Burn it down. I don't care. That's what I wanted to say.

"I don't know Dad, we haven't discussed it. It's in his name, so I'm assuming *him*."

My mother clucks her tongue like it's despicable for me to not have an answer.

But that was the last thing I wanted to think about. How could I live in a house where we had planned a future together? What would I do in an eight-thousand square foot home by myself? Was I supposed to just walk through the kitchen and pretend I hadn't thought about Christmas parties with Jackson or which rooms would make the perfect nursery? Now, it all seems like a silly dream. Like I was just daydreaming to escape the truth in front of me. Deep down, I think I knew Jackson was never the man I thought he was. He just knew how to play the part long enough to keep feeding me slivers of hope.

"I believe this week also marks five years at work, correct?" my father asks, jarringly changing the subject like this was another run of the mill conversation for us. All I can do is bobble my head, while chewing my lip.

"It's time for a promotion, then. You're nearly twenty-seven, you don't want to be mid-level forever. Ed's a smart guy, but you need to assert yourself and take what you deserve. Elson's are not doormats. Remember that."

My boss and father were old friends, fraternity brothers from Brown. The only thing more disappointing to my father than this marriage not happening was that I hadn't followed in his footsteps and attended his Ivy League alma mater. My brother, Andrew, had of course. We were four years past that now, but it's hard to not see all the disappointments add up like tallies on my skin.

We end the call moments later. While logistically it appears everything will be taken care of, everything will be okay, and I will keep going on the path I have been set on from birth; a deeply unsettled feeling falls over me.

Because this life I've been conditioned to live no longer feels like a good plan.

Or maybe it never really had.

CHAPTER SIX

Audrey

I didn't sleep well last night. The cream-colored Egyptian cotton sheets I picked out for our apartment a year ago felt like they were strangling me, and as the elevator climbed to my office on the eighth floor I nervously adjusted my collar until I was pretty sure I'd permanently stretched out the shirt. I pretended to be busy with something important on my phone as I walked past reception and into the safety of my office; a tiny gray room that smelled like synthetic air freshener and was void of natural light. At least it had a door that shut.

And the moment I was alone, I kicked off my heels and dropped down into the leather swivel chair at my desk, already mentally spent.

My shirt's too tight around my neck, my skirt feels itchy, and I forgot my emotional support water bottle in my kitchen. Not to mention my evaluation with my boss is in three minutes—not nearly enough time to run across the street for the cappuccino my body so desperately needs.

Trying to find the positives, I think about what I can cross off my long mental to-do list. Both Penny and my parents worked on canceling the engagement party and informing the guests. God bless Penny, who also asked that no one reach out to me right now. Even if she hadn't requested that, I knew I wouldn't be hearing from the Tippins family. Surely, I was public enemy number one. Jackson had probably spun some tale, casting the blame on me.

I was just a pawn in his life, nothing more.

It was a miracle I had arrived at work looking half-polished, with a fresh blowout and dewy face, because I was reminded, yet again, by the alert on my phone for my meeting that life goes on. Even with a shattered heart, I had business to attend to.

Steeling myself, I breathe in deep, roll my shoulders, and walk across the hall. Put on a brave face—*the Elson way.*

"May I?" I knock lightly on Ed Pierce's open door, and he beckons me in with an unreadable expression. I sit in the stiff leather chair in front of Ed's mahogany banker desk. It's similar to the one Jackson has in his study, and I wonder if this is who he'll turn into. A man who avoids his family by marrying his work. A man who never smiles and who speaks in textbook terms. A man whose tie is too tight and his gut too large.

Despite him being my manager for nearly five years, Ed and I don't have much of a relationship. The first year I worked under him, I was interning as a senior in college. After all this time though, I'm still nervous sitting in this seat even though there is no reason to be. I show up eager to please, have an excellent repertoire with the clients who are double my age, and play the part this financial corporation expects of me.

In all five years here, I never once questioned if this was what I wanted to do or where I was meant to be. This is just what I do, and here I am, knowing it's time to wager my promotion. It's a checklist, a timeline, something predictable.

The last steady thing in my life at the moment.

"Your end-of-quarter numbers are above projections, as you already know." He gets right into it, offering a compliment that sounds like he's reading from a script. He clicks his mouse a few times, eyes no longer on me.

"Three new clients this month, correct?"

"Yes," I reply robotically, nodding along.

"Miss Elson, if you keep this up, you're going to be a director in five years by my predictions," he chuckles, but the words suck the wind out of me, and I have a hard time finding the humor in it.

Another *five years*. There's nothing good about that amount of time. Nothing at all.

The room is starting to feel small and hot, the lights too bright. My mouth goes dry, and a slight ringing echoes in my ears.

"Where do you see yourself in five years?"

My eyes refocus, finding Ed's, and I suddenly can't form words.

If someone had asked me last week, I would have said in five years, I'd be happily married to Jackson Tippins. We'd live in the exclusive Forest Hills neighborhood in our stone house, which we would've turned into a family home. I'd be thirty-one and maybe even be a mother by then, if that was in my cards. But now, as I sit at this desk, feeling smaller and smaller by the second, the answer escapes my mind.

"Are you listening, Miss Elson?"

At that, I perk up, clearing my throat.

"I apologize, Mr. Pierce. I am not feeling my best today, but I'm here." I plaster on the fake Elson smile, sitting up straight on the edge of the chair, tucking my hair behind my ear.

"I'll make this quick then. With your record, if you keep putting in the hours you are, I believe you have real potential. This hasn't been announced yet, but the New York branch will be adding a position that would start in Q-four, end of September, really. They want you, Audrey."

He pauses and all I manage to say is "*Oh*."

"It would be a step up, with a sizable pay increase as well. I don't make it my business to learn about my team's personal life, but I know you're to be married this year. However, I would advise you to consider this offer." He smiles smugly, adding, "You'd be closer to your family again as well."

My heart flutters in my chest, and I rub my palms on my thighs. I don't correct him about the marriage that isn't happening anymore.

"Wow, I wasn't expecting that. I don't know what to say."

"I don't need an answer right now, but I'd urge you to consider it seriously, Miss Elson. Let me know by Friday before they open the position company-wide."

Offering a small smile, I nod and scoot my chair back, eager to get out of here before I pass out.

"Thank you, I will consider it carefully."

Back at my desk, I ignore my rapidly growing inbox of unread emails and instead find myself browsing real estate listings. New York City is only an hour from my parent's house in Connecticut, but it's far enough I could have my own life there. A fresh start. Away from this mess. Besides, a promotion would keep my parents happy for a while, maybe even make them forget about my imploded engagement.

Until now, I'd never seriously thought about a life in the Big Apple. But after the abrupt end to my chapter in North Carolina, maybe it's time for something new. A way to ensure I don't make the same mistake twice.

By the time I'm home that evening, I'm functionless from the bouts of mental gymnastics I had to perform all day just to stay focused. Stripping off my constrictive business clothing, I put on my softest loungewear and fall back onto the sofa. I flip on the TV, grab my Kindle, and phone. I want every distraction so there's no chance of self-loathing, or reminders of the work I didn't accomplish today. As I settle on rewatching my favorite comfort show, my phone buzzes.

> **Jackson:** I'll be home Wednesday evening—just wanted you to be aware. See you then Drey.

Slouching back on the sofa, letting the cushion swallow me, I toss my phone without following up to that unwelcome message. There's nothing I could possibly say in response.

Normally I'd be planning a dinner out for Thursday night to one of his favorite places, maybe even inviting some of Jackson's friends to keep him entertained. But the thought of socializing turns my stomach, and there's a small, satisfying relief in knowing I'll never have to play host to Jackson's circle again.

CHAPTER SEVEN

Audrey

Tuesday morning began the web of lies. Lie number one: I told Ed I was sick and needed to work from home. 'The flu', I told him. Lie number two: when my father called to ask me if I was promoted, I said yes. Technically, I was offered a promotion, one I'd been entertaining in my head. The third lie, or omittance of truth, was that Penny knew neither of these things, thinking I was doing fine. I told her I was busy with work, and I'd love to see her on Saturday for a girl's night. I suggested something low-key, like movies and wine.

I didn't love the lying; in fact, it ate me up inside. But the truth was beyond painful right now. My emotional state could only be described as *whiplash*. One moment I was walking past the dresser, seeing the Tiffany's picture frame holding our engagement photo, and bursting into tears. The next, I was scrolling apartment listings in New York, blasting angry music so loud the historic walls in the living room shook. The worst though, was sitting on the sofa, numb.

Tuesday night, in the middle of another restless slumber, it dawned on me that if he cared about me, if Jackson ever truly loved me, he would've booked a red-eye flight home Saturday night. His absence was the answer I had always feared.

Wednesday morning greets me like an ice-cold slap to the face, even though it's a hot June day. I yearned for time to slow down because I still had no idea what I would say to Jackson when he walked through the front door tonight.

My kitchen, which once smelled like fresh cut flowers, was taken over by the copious amounts of takeout food I'd ordered in the last forty-eight hours. And I had not replied to a single work email since last week.

I contemplated baking, perusing the internet for new recipes. I didn't have the appetite to eat anything, but baking usually helped me get out of my own head. And Jackson had no ground to shame me for my favorite hobby anymore. But by the time I found a recipe, it was late afternoon, and the reality that I'd have to face my ex-fiancé soon crept into my bones and took over.

I closed my laptop, concluding work for the day from my dining table—if you can call what I did *work*—and slipped into the shower, attempting to quiet my mind. I attempt to scrub the worry from my skin, using every product within reach and when that doesn't work, I sit at the vanity in my bathroom, and blow my hair dry. I spend an hour there, doing a complete blowout like I am going somewhere nice. My chocolatey, brown hair cascades down my back, my pale legs poking out from under my silk robe as I sit staring at myself while my stomach ties itself into vicious knots.

Padding into my walk-in closet, I pull my prettiest silk pajama set from the hanger and slip it on. I apply lotion slowly to every inch of my five-foot six frame but can't manage to look at myself in the mirror as I do.

I hate this.

I hate how nervous I am to see Jackson. I hate that I'm desperate to appear *fine*, unscathed, when he had sliced me open mere days ago. I hate that I put on his favorite perfume behind my ears and on my wrists when the idea of him even touching me viscerally repulses me. And I hate that when my mother called me earlier today to tell me the plans for Labor Day weekend this year, a party at their Hamptons home, I feigned excitement. Like it was a normal Wednesday, like my world wasn't crumbling or that her and my father didn't burn me, too.

At 7 p.m. on the dot, rustling keys sound from the front door, and it opens with a woosh louder than I ever noticed before.

Fuck, fuck, fuck.

With my feet frozen to the tile floor in the kitchen, I watch in horror as my tall, polished, ex-fiancé snakes his way into the apartment. With one arm held tightly against my body and one hand propping me up on the counter, I wait like helpless prey.

It's nearly eighty degrees outside, yet Jackson dons a pullover, khakis, and loafers. His chestnut hair is perfectly coiffed back. I can picture it; I've watched him get ready a million times. I know how he places his comb on the counter, how he brushes his teeth, how he sings Frank Sinatra in the shower when he is in a good mood. And right now, he looks like he could sing. He's polished, like he'd just woke up from a solid eight-hour sleep. His eyes flit over me and a slight frown tugs on the corner of his lips.

Almost like he forgot I'd be here, that I live here too.

"Audrey." Jackson's voice was cold, like he's addressing one of his subordinates at the office who disappointed him. *How dare I even exist in his universe.*

"Jackson."

Nothing could've prepared me for this moment. This conversation.

When he left, I believed there was love between us or a semblance of love. Now, I see a man I don't even recognize. A stranger in my home. And I have so many questions, but I know for a fact that I don't really want to hear the answers to any of them.

When Jackson used to get home from business trips, I would be over the moon to hear my name on his lips again, vying for any ounce of admiration from him. He gave it sparingly, but I cherished it like a fool.

"How are you?" he asks, the tension thick in the air between us. A tightness clawed at my chest.

"I'm fine," I bite out, adding, "I've found a new living arrangement and will be moving out next week. Thought you'd like to know."

Jackson shifts from one leg to the other, taking his hand off his rolling luggage.

"Oh—wow." He lifts his eyebrows. Did he expect me to fight for him when he should be the one groveling at my feet? But I remind myself this isn't a movie. This is real life. My life.

And the men in my life don't fight for me and *never* expect a fight out of me.

It wasn't as if I thought he'd show up with flowers and tears in his eyes, but part of my heart still aches as I stand here, feet from him in the apartment that I desperately tried to make a home.

"Well, I figured a clean cut would be best. The sooner, the better."

"Yes, yes, of course. Where are you going?" His green eyes meet mine, no evidence of sadness in them.

"Does it matter?" I sigh, crossing my arms in front of my chest. I'd never tell him it was Penny's. I know he was never overly fond of her, and he doesn't need more ammunition to aim at me. "I'm out of here, that's what you wanted, did you not?" I start to turn, taking one step away from him.

"Drey, please…" His fingers feather across my shoulder and tears rush to my eyes at his touch.

"What?" I snap, clenching my jaw so tight, I wonder if I cracked my teeth.

He furrows his brow, but we hold each other's gaze. A small, nearly inaudible sigh leaves him as he slips his hands into his pockets.

"For what it's worth, I *am* sorry. I didn't plan it this way…I take full responsibility."

A million thoughts race through my mind, but none make it past my lips. Nothing suffices, nothing would get through to him. It would be wasted energy, of which I already am low on.

When I don't respond, he steps back, grabs his suitcase, and rolls it into the bedroom. I wait until the bedroom door clicks shut behind him before I back up to sit at the island, staring into space, praying for a numbness to come over me. I wait, and wait, and wait.

From behind the bedroom door there's faint rustling, drawers opening and closing. He's been in there for a while. Maybe he's texting Kelsey, giving her a play by play of his pathetic ex-fiancé.

Ten minutes later, the heavy wooden bedroom door swings open slowly. Jackson steps out with two large bags at his side; the expensive luggage we used for our European trips. He hasn't changed clothes, probably desperate to get out of here as quickly as he can. He pauses in the doorway, glancing up at me. I had pictured this moment, anticipated it all week. I don't know exactly what I thought would happen, but I never thought it would be like this.

I never thought he'd be so cold or that I'd be counting down the minutes until the door shut behind him, getting him out of my sight.

It's not so hard to let someone go when you realize they were only ever a projection of who you wanted them to be.

"I'm staying with my parents until you're out of here. Please let me know if you need movers, I can make arrangements with the same company that moved us in."

I shake my head, holding back a humorless laugh. "That won't be necessary."

"If you change your mind, let me know," he replies, almost gallantly. Pinching my lips together, I peel my gaze from him and he sighs. "Goodbye, Audrey."

"Bye," I replied on autopilot.

I let him walk out of the apartment without so much as a scolding.

That night, while I lay awake in bed, the empty spot next to me becoming familiar, I decided to do something. Pushing back the covers, I pad to the dining room where my work laptop remains. The apartment is still, the lights dim other than the light over the stovetop casting a warm glow. Tucking one leg under me, I sit at the dining chair and open my browser.

Before I can second guess myself, I type out an email which has the power to change everything for me.

Ed,

Thank you for considering me for the senior level opportunity at headquarters. I've thought about it carefully this week and am happy to say I would love to accept the position.

Best,

Audrey

The clock reads 2 a.m., so I close the laptop, sitting a moment in silence as the decision weighs on me. Going to sleep alone without a ring on my finger isn't what's led me to writing the email. I'm not sad Jackson's gone.

I'm sad I've wasted time living out *his* plan.

Maybe it was time I tried to figure out what *my* plan was.

It was only June, so I had four months to prepare for the move to New York. Ed said initially the paperwork and details wouldn't even be ready until August; it wouldn't be set in stone for a while. But that was good, it gave me time to figure out how to break it to Penny that I was leaving. And to tell my parents I was coming back up north.

There was nothing left for me in this city, and I knew I needed to find myself or whatever it is you do after your world turns upside down.

How would I ever move on if I was constantly being suffocated by the ghost of my past?

CHAPTER EIGHT

Rhett

I rolled out my shoulders as the sun was setting at my back. There was only another hour tops of daylight, but I was just about done anyway.

I'd been hunched over the engine of my 1983 F-250 since I got home from work, already having polished off a few beers, and my best friend was on his way with more.

When his car rolled down the driveway, I peered around the hood.

Kylan, or Ky as I've been calling him since we were ten, walked up, a six pack of some new craft beer in his hand, wings in the other. We were too old to be living like bachelors, but at this point our Friday night tradition has been going on for so long, neither of us were going to say shit to each other about it.

"Damn man, weren't you working on this thing last Friday, too?"

I paused, scowling from under my greased-up baseball hat. He knows how I feel about this truck, even if I'm fixing some shit on it every weekend.

"She just needed some fluid. Routine maintenance." I tightened the cap and lowered the hood gingerly.

"That's why I went electric." Ky nodded towards his new car that probably cost more than what I made last year.

"Yeah. You know that'll never happen. She's good as gold." I slapped the hood and whistled for my dog.

Ky makes good money, lives in a new-build condo on the edge of town and is happy working behind a computer screen for most of the day. He might be my best friend—a brother to me, really—but we couldn't be more different.

He thinks practically. To him, the truck I've been driving since I was in high school is just something that eats time and money. But to me, it's the last piece of my dad I have. He taught me how to drive a manual in it. I picked up my first date in that truck at 16, hell—I lost my virginity in the damn truck bed. My mom gave me the keys to it the day after my dad's funeral, almost thirteen years ago, and I'll be driving it 'til it's turned to dust.

"The game starts in a few; you got the screen up?" Ky asks and I nod, following him to the back yard.

We settled in, stretching out on the outdoor sofa and chairs, the big screen secured to the side of the house. In reality it was simply a white tarp I found at the thrift store, but I recently splurged on a projector so now I had an outdoor theater. A redneck version. It was cool for watching games though, and I knew the moment my six-year-old nieces saw it, they'd freak out too.

"Dude, did you see Beck's wife is pregnant?" Ky asked, and I knocked a beer against the wooden coffee table I made, the cap landing somewhere into the grass.

"No shit?" I didn't look at Ky but saw him nod from the corner of my eye. For such a quiet guy, he sure gets all the gossip immediately. Almost quicker than my mom.

"Well, good for them." I take a swig of beer and lean back, trying to focus on the baseball game but I can't. "So, I guess we are the last two lucky bastards?" I chuckle but Ky doesn't.

"Last ones standing. We'll see if they all show up tomorrow."

I gaze over to my best friend and scoff. "They'll show up. It's your birthday."

We've watched our friend group dwindle down over the past few years. Everyone's gotten married, had a kid or two, moved closer to the city for work. Our Friday nights used to be a group of five of us, shooting the shit around the firepit in my backyard. I couldn't really be mad; everyone was going their own way. Family came first, I get it.

But now it's just Ky and me. While I know he secretly worries he will never find a wife and have kids, something he's always wanted, I don't worry, which equally annoys him. Maybe that's my issue, I'm pretty content with where I'm at, with what I have. Sure, a partner would be nice, but I spent my early twenties angry at the world and a straight up asshole in my love life.

I spent plenty of Saturday night's getting into fights, drinking too much, and bringing home women I had no intention of seeing again. It took hitting rock bottom, spending a night in the county jail, and my mom begging me to straighten up my act to turn shit around.

Five years ago, I also started taking my carpentry business seriously, bought this foreclosed farmhouse, and have been turning things around little by little.

"You won't believe who I saw coming out of the gas station on the corner of Main yesterday," Ky starts again.

I reached for a wing, being eyed down by my bloodhound who would probably kill me for the basket of chicken.

"Who?"

"Johnny Kent."

My head whipped so fast towards Ky I nearly choked. "You're fucking kidding me? I swear if he even comes within a hundred yards of Desi's house, I'll run that fucker out of this town."

"He looked washed up as hell, man. I doubt he was here for anything but to collect money from his parents. He keeping up his end of the deal?"

"According to my sister, he is," I grunted.

"Good." Ky threw back the rest of his beer, then walked into the house to use the bathroom.

I shook out my legs, ripping off a piece of chicken for my dog, who swallowed it in a millisecond. My mind raced thinking about Johnny—the low life who knocked up my sister six years ago then skipped town. He never met my nieces or spoke to my sister again. I was there to pick up the pieces, making sure those girls never went without a father figure in their life. Five years ago, I ran into him in a bar and overheard him saying some choice words about my sister, Desi.

That was the night I ended up in county jail, Johnny right in there with me. Both of us with black eyes. Not my most proudest moment, but since that night he hasn't missed a single child support payment. I can't say I regret it, though I promised my mom and sister I'd never do something like that again, and I've kept my word.

It takes a lot to provoke me now. But I'll always defend my family.

That's not something you can shake out of me.

Ky came back out, nearly tripping on the loose back steps. "Dude, you want to tell me why your back steps are a death trap when you literally have a woodshop with every tool fifty feet away?"

"You sound like my sister." I shook my head, eyeing the rotted wood steps. "I fix and build crap all day. The last thing I want to do is fix things in my house. I'm going to get to it eventually."

Ky looked at me like I was delusional. "You got long legs anyway, jump next time," I added, and we both laughed.

"You're a fucking idiot." Ky cracked another beer as I pulled a cigarette from my front shirt pocket. A habit I was trying to kick. I was down to two a day.

"And yet, here you are, hanging out with me."

He had nothing to say back. We fought like brothers, but I knew Ky would do anything for me. And vice versa.

It's why I agreed to go to the Bourbon Barrel tomorrow night for his thirtieth birthday. The bar was a bit too loud and rowdy, even for me. But he wanted to leave his twenties with a bang, so I agreed.

It's not like I had anywhere better to be on a Saturday night.

Chapter Nine

Audrey

I tried to avoid looking at the clock all day, but my self-sabotaging instincts kicked in and at quarter to six, I let myself lament. In a parallel universe where I was still engaged, toasts would now be starting at the lakeside venue of my engagement party. My parents would've raised their champagne flutes, saying something sappy for the sake of their public image, and I would've been tucked into Jackson's side, wearing the white silk dress that is still sitting in a puddle on the floor in my closet. I'm pretty sure I should burn it at this point.

The self-pity that was festering in my bones was starting to annoy me, though. And it wasn't like I was reeling with options of people to reach out to. My so-called 'friends' disappeared the moment Jackson and I split. Their loyalty had always been to Jackson, and deep down I knew that all along. Penny, of course, was the outlier, but she had met some guy at the wedding she was photographing last night. She said he was a European athlete and only here for one night so naturally I didn't hear from her all day. I couldn't blame her; she was out living her best single gal life to the fullest.

It's also been *near* radio silence from Jackson. He texted me and said his lawyer would be reaching out soon about the house in Forest Hills. *His* lawyer...because there was no *our, us,* or *we* anymore. It's like the last five years were figments of my imagination.

Though on the surface of the life we lived together, nothing had changed this week. The bills were all paid, the housekeeper showed up yesterday morning like she does every Friday, and the groceries were delivered this morning. Just like it was another routine Saturday morning in the Brecken Building.

My parents had also been very—dare I say—chill about everything. I was expecting more persuasion to mend my broken engagement, even if I made it clear it was unfixable. Every time I opened my front door to grab deliveries or let the housekeeper in, I half expected to see my mother with her stern face staring straight back at me. Their silence over the matter was almost more unnerving, but I wasn't about to test my luck and wake a sleeping bear.

Just a few hours ago both my phone notifications and the apartment were so silent, I thought I might truly go mad. I didn't want to listen to any more self-loathing thoughts about how much I truly messed up, so I put on my sneakers and walked. I was only a little walk away from a row of boutiques, so I popped into the stationary store.

I moseyed around, feigning interest in items I had no use for just to avoid being talked to. There was a beautiful little leather notebook with a brass latch which last week's version of me would've bought to write grocery lists in, but now it all seemed trivial. I picked it up, though, to fan through the blank pages.

What could I write about now? My failed engagement? Being the family black sheep? I could write about running away from the pressures of home and then it catching back up to you in a different life. I went from needing to be perfect for my parents and the society they shoved me into, to needing to be perfect for a man who didn't respect or love me enough to fight for me.

I set the notebook down, abruptly walked out of the shop and straight home.

Penny is supposed to be here any moment for our agreed upon evening. Grab a bite to eat, then back to her place to chill and have drinks.

The doorbell chimes, but the door opens moments later as I sit back on the sofa.

"I'm in the living room!"

"Oh my god, Audrey, I could've been anyone. You could get murdered that way."

She comes in hot, bringing her big personality and strong floral perfume into the living room. I look up at her from my pathetic stance on the white, down-filled sofa.

"Okay, first, you need to stop listening to those true crime podcasts. Only you and Jackson have the door code. And second, I thought we agreed we were wearing loungewear."

I glance down at my college sweatpants and glare at her outfit; a wrap-around, preppy mini-dress and heels.

Penny doesn't set down her purse, clearly riding a different energy wave than I am.

"Okay, change of plans."

The blood rushes to my head, and the toile wallpaper on the wall behind her starts to swirl as I spring to my feet.

"Not feeling Mediterranean food anymore?" I joke, picking at my manicured nails and then stop. They are the only put together thing about me. I need to make them last.

"Oh no, we are still grabbing dinner. I've been dreaming about spanakopita, but we are going out tonight. I can't watch you roll around on the sofa any longer. You're starting to make me really sad." Penny's lips curl up into a mischievous grin.

I shove my hands in my hoodie pocket, glancing at my sweatpants then back at my best friend.

"I'm still in mourning, you brat."

"No, you're in self-destruction mode. Jackson sucks, this sucks, but I'm not going to watch you waste away in here. I'm not saying you need to find a new man tonight...but you need to keep living, okay?"

"I don't know..." I moaned, kind of wishing I would've locked my front door and pretended I wasn't home.

"Let's make a deal. Let me take control, just for one night. If it goes horribly wrong, I will let you go back to sulking and eating takeout every day. But if it goes well...you promise to remember life isn't over, and you pick yourself up." She stares me dead in the eye. "He may have derailed your plans, but he didn't take your crown. You're still Audrey Elson. And tonight, we are going out."

"Okay," I squeak out. "But can I be anyone but Audrey Elson? I'm really sick of her."

"You can be anyone you want, babe." She smiles, whipping her blond hair behind her back.

"Okay. Let's get this over with," I add, and Penny jumps up and down squealing. Her pink glossy lips break into a huge smile, which makes me smile but then realization hits. This city isn't that small...but the circle of people and the places we frequent are.

"What? Why that face?"

"I don't want to run into *him* or his friends. We can't go to any of the usual spots."

I knew for a fact Jackson was out living his best, little ego-filled, trust-fund-baby life. His Instagram stories were evidence. Last night it looked like he was at his own bachelor party, and that was the last straw. I finally got the guts to block him once and for all.

"Okay...." Penny was thinking, pulling out her phone, her fingers moving fast. "Leave it to me, I think I have an idea. We can go somewhere totally new. Somewhere I know for a fact Jackson nor any of his asshole friends would go."

I couldn't lie and say the idea of going somewhere new thrilled me. I was a creature of habit and familiarity.

But look how much that's done for me.

Penny insisted we get ready at her house, but before we left my apartment, she instructed me to shower, so I did without reluctance. I also didn't fight it as she ransacked my closet while I blew out my hair, deciding on big bouncy curls. She held up various pieces of clothing, nodding and biting her lip, throwing items into my overnight bag. Twenty minutes later, my best friend and savior grabbed my hand like I was a lost toddler and guided me out of my sad apartment.

She was right about another thing—spanakopita did solve a lot of problems.

CHAPTER TEN

Audrey

After dinner, we went to Penny's to finish getting ready. It was quarter to eight and she still hadn't told me where we were going. She threw down clothing options for me to wear on her bed.

"Penny, I am not wearing your rhinestone cowgirl boots!" I swipe them to the side with my foot. There was an obvious theme evolving here with the outfits, and I wasn't sure I was on board with it.

"We're going to a *casual* place. Your Soren Devereaux little black dress will not do here. You don't want to stand out like a sore thumb, do you?"

I picked up tiny denim shorts and a lacy black corset bodysuit she paired underneath.

"I'm concerned that wherever we are going *this* outfit *won't* stand out." I held up the bodysuit, something that was definitely from one of Penny's bachelorette trips to Nashville. Not that I didn't think I'd look good in it...but I was someone who liked to be understated. By all means, I actually did want to blend in.

"Audrey, please try it on for me. This isn't *just* us going out. This is your *'fuck Jackson, I'm a new woman'* redemption night. It's your debut into society as a single woman."

"I already did that eleven years ago at the Windsor Country Club." I smirk and she shoves the rhinestone boots back towards me.

Penny slips on an equally flashy outfit. She pulled it off though, looking like she belonged in a country music video. I put on the outfit, standing in front of the mirror in Penny's bedroom.

"Okay, the ride is about to pull up, you ready?" Penny asks, scooting up next to me, primping her hair.

"First night out as a single woman...since...junior year of college?" I ponder. Penny nudges my side.

"Yes, ma'am. Loud and proud! You are single and *free*. All our Pilates classes are paying off too, do you see your ass? You look like sex on a stick."

"Penny!" I hit her shoulder with my clutch. I look like Barbie going to a honky-tonk. If Barbie had long brown hair and hazel eyes.

As we slide into the backseat of the cab, the driver gives us judgmental once-overs. Penny promptly pulls a flask out of her purse and takes a swig. The driver's eyes meet mine in the rearview mirror, and I internally cringe.

"What the hell is that?" I whisper. I never was good at breaking rules.

"Here, finish it." She shoves it into my lap and fixes her gaze straight ahead. There was no use fighting it anymore because clearly as soon as I slipped this body suit and bedazzled cowgirl boots on, the night was going in a direction I had no control over.

My mind had been in overdrive, analyzing every minute of the past five years of my failed relationship all week. For just one night, I wanted it to all stop. I wanted to let loose and forget about the rules, and expectations, and just have fun.

My lips brush the metal tip, tasting vodka. I cough spastically as it rolls down my throat and cap the empty flask, shoving it back towards Penny.

"When did we get so old?" I ask, remembering all the fun times we had in our college days.

"We are *not* old! We simply got busy with life, and men, and careers."

"I've missed you." I look at my best friend, thinking about how eventually I'd need to tell her I was moving after this summer. But even the thought of the conversation crushed me.

"Don't get sappy on me!" She grinned, pulling me into a hug in the backseat of the taxi.

"Where are we going? I think you can tell me now," I whisper, and Penny hesitates as she pulls out her phone, glances at Google maps, and promptly shoves it back into her purse before I can see anything.

"We'll be there in thirty minutes."

I gape at Penny. "There is nothing but farms thirty minutes east of the city."

"That's not true. Because there is the Bourbon Barrel."

"Elaborate," I demand, and she does. Apparently, twenty miles east of the city is a new honky-tonk called the Bourbon Barrel.

She reassures me it will be fun, so I swallow the lump in my throat and take a deep breath.

"Hey, would next Friday be too soon to move in? It gives me a week to pack."

"Of course not. I already cleared out the guest room."

"Okay, thank you. Jackson offered to get me movers—"

Penny gesticulates wildly. "*Oh*, how heroic of him! Where does he get off? Man, he sickens me." She pauses, her eyes narrowed at me. "Why aren't you pissed off?"

I shrug. "I don't want to waste any more energy on him."

"Fine, but I still get to hate him, okay?"

"Be my guest."

The car slows as we pull into a gravel parking lot in front of a large industrial building shaped like a barn. String lights illuminate the parking lot, full of groups of grinning people leaving their cars and walking into the oversized entrance doors. Even with the car windows shut, I can hear music blasting from inside.

We thank the driver, get out, and Penny grabs my hand, squealing.

"You ready?" She pulls me along, as fast as one can run in cowgirl boots, to the front door. Keeping my eyes forward, I try not to notice all the eyes on *us*. I was used to people looking at me, not because of who I am, but because of whose arm I was hanging from. The Tippins family demanded a lot of attention wherever they went in this city, even statewide. I was used to people watching me, waiting for me to screw up, so they could swoop in and marry Jackson Tippins—or his fortune.

But here, I think Penny and I were getting looks for completely different reasons.

"I feel ridiculous," I leaned over to whisper to her as we showed our IDs to the doorman.

"Of course, you do...because you're finally not living in someone else's shadow."

Way to cut to the core. Damn, Penny.

The lights grow dimmer as we walk in, and the whole view comes into play. There's a rather expansive and impressive bar, the liquor wall nearly two stories high. A large wooden dance floor sits in the middle of the barn-like structure, and a mechanical bull in the back corner amasses a rambunctious crowd.

Not my scene, but here I was.

"If I'm going to make it through tonight, I need a drink *stat*." It's me who grabs my friend's arm this time, and we beeline to the bar.

We wiggle our way through the patrons who are completely unaware they are blocking the bar. In particular, a group of guys who tower over Pen and I, all with drinks in hand, talk loudly. If they were to back up even an inch, we'd be crushed.

"I've never seen so many fine asses in jeans before. Why the hell didn't I come here sooner?" Penny whispers in my ear, licking her lips, and my eyes go wide. She isn't *wrong*, though.

"Excuse me, I need to get through, please." I tap on the shoulder of the guy directly in front of me. He doesn't budge. So, I lean closer, slamming my palm on his upper arm, noticing how soft his faded green shirt is. People behind us are closing in, making the space tight.

"Excuse me!" I yell, slapping his shoulder *hard* this time. He casually peers over his shoulders at me, turning slowly, and as I get a whiff of musky cedar cologne, my gaze meets his. Icy blue eyes I would've recognized anywhere.

CHAPTER ELEVEN

Rhett

I can hardly believe my luck but I keep my composure, a slight grin on my face, even as my heart pounds against my ribcage. Rooftop girl. She stands out here, truly breathtaking. I notice a few guys around us eyeing her up. But her eyes are locked on mine, her lips hang open like she's just seen a ghost.

The song that was playing fades out, starting a new country song I've been hearing everywhere. A group of people on the other side of the bar cheer—like I said, this place gets rowdy. Not a place that normally draws the city crowd.

"Audrey, right?" I lean in closer, drawn to the gold flecks in her eyes as they catch the light, sparkling up at me. Every nerve in my body is electrified, and I can't remember the last time I felt a pull like this.

A blonde woman next to her wedges in closer, nearly between us, her eyes flitting back and forth from Audrey and me.

"Hi, I'm Penny and this is my friend Audrey. My *single* friend Audrey." She holds out her hand, and I stifle a laugh, shaking it. Audrey's face turns even whiter.

"Nice to meet you, Penny," I reply, trying to ease the tension.

"Penny, this is Rhett." Audrey smiles tightly at her friend.

"Uhm...nice to meet you?" Penny muses, gazing at me with narrowed eyes. More people pile in behind them, and I stand up straight, not about

60

to let the girls get shoved around. I haven't had any altercations for five years now. But something about the way she is looking at me makes me feel like I have no control.

"I met Rhett last weekend, uh…on…" Audrey struggles to finish the sentence, and just like last Saturday night, I feel the familiar urge to step in and rescue her.

"We met on the rooftop. Audrey let me crash her party of one." I wink, teasing her, and Penny looks even more confused. I guess she didn't mention us. Not that I mentioned her either. She only lived in my head all week.

"I didn't share my champagne with you, so it was hardly a party." She rolls her eyes, her long eyelashes batting flirtatiously. Even if she doesn't mean to.

"Well darlin', maybe I can change that. Where's your drink?" I ask her and she makes a show of her empty palms.

Good, something I can easily fix.

"Well, we were trying to get a drink, but a group of large, rowdy men were blocking our way." Penny raises her brows, flirting her way into the conversation. Blondes aren't really my thing, but I always like sassy brunettes.

"How dare they. Let me make it right." I swivel in my spot in front of the crowded bar, bring my fingers to my lips and whistle loudly over the music. A bartender catches my eye, blushing and leaning towards me, cupping an ear in my direction.

I turn to look at the girls, who are watching me eagerly.

"What's your drink?"

"She'll take a vodka tonic. Make it two," Penny pipes up as I nod, turning back to place the order. I get myself a double whiskey, neat, and pull a toothpick from my pocket—a nervous habit for when I want a cigarette. I let it dangle from my lips and hand them their drinks.

Audrey keeps her eyes on her friend but when I scan the crowd around us, I feel her eyes raking me over. It fills me with heat, and I know if I keep drinking these whiskeys, I'm going to be a man in trouble.

The mass of people near the bar makes it hard to have a real conversation, and when Ky taps me on the shoulder, telling me he and the guys are migrating towards the dart boards in the back, Audrey swoops in, eager to go as well.

"Go with your friends. I'll see you around, yeah?" she offers, a small, flirty smile on her face, and I nod. She's so polite and reserved, I still don't know what she's doing here.

I watch them walk away into the crowd.

But she's crazy if she doesn't think I'll be looking out for her tonight. Not that I doubt her and Penny can't hold their own. I just know the guys in this town.

None of them are good enough for Audrey.

Except, in my buzzed, delusional mind maybe myself.

CHAPTER TWELVE

Audrey

My body is buzzing as we push our way through the crowd, and I've only had two sips of vodka. I follow Penny to a high-top table tucked against the wall on the opposite side of the bar from Rhett and his friends. My mind reels, unable to believe he's here again.

"Okay, you have about thirty seconds to tell me how you know that cowboy Casanova?"

I shake my head, sucking down my vodka soda in an ungodly short amount of time, buying a moment to find the right words.

"Like he said...we met last weekend on the rooftop of my building."

"I'm going to need a little more to go on," she demands, leaning over the table. We have to talk loudly to hear each other, so I quickly look over my shoulder, praying he's not right there.

"After *the* phone call, I went up to the roof, the bottle Jackson got me in tow, and low and behold, Rhett was up there. He does some type of work, I'm not sure what, but he was working on the apartment below mine. You know the rude, older woman Mrs. Lawson?" Penny nods, her eyes wide as she leans in intently, chewing her lip. "Anyway...I was crying, and I drunkenly told him my sob story." I bite the grin trying to spread on my lips, because something about that night, standing up there, sharing a moment like that, a cigarette between us...it felt more intimate than I'd been willing to admit to myself this past week.

"And then he walked with me back to my apartment. That's it. Tonight is just a wild coincidence. I mean, there's probably only one decent bar this side of town, and so of course, a guy like him would be here."

"A guy like what?" Penny pushes.

"A guy *not like Jackson*. I don't know, Pen!" I begin to feel flustered and look away from my best friend who is nonetheless trying to peer into my soul. She won't find anything there to uncover, other than a very lost person whose boots were not properly worn in.

We agree we need refills, and Penny needs to reapply lip gloss, so she goes to the bathroom, and I stand up to get drinks.

As I weave back towards the bar, I find myself scanning the crowd. My pulse quickened as I quickly clocked faces. I wasn't sure if I was trying to find those blue eyes or hoping to avoid them. Nothing was clear right now to me.

But one thing made my shoulders relax—I could almost guarantee not a single person in this establishment was friends with Jackson Tippins. And not a single guy in here looked like him. This crowd couldn't be more different; a stark, deliberate escape. I'd said I wanted to be anyone but myself tonight, and for the first time, it almost felt possible, wrapped in the smoky haze of the Bourbon Barrel.

I find an empty spot near the end of the long bar; the smell of liquor, leather, and cologne filling my senses. An enormous pair of bull horns hang above me on the wall, and I silently pray they don't fall on me as the live music nearly rattles everything in here.

After I order drinks, I shift my gaze cautiously down the bar, taking in my surroundings. I haven't stood at a bar like this in a long time—and most certainly never in an outfit that sat on my body like paint. Jackson had a shortlist of exclusive bars and speakeasies he liked to frequent when we went out, the kind you had to be a member of or know someone to get into. And you never waited at a bar, the drinks were brought to you.

This was kind of freeing and as the thought crosses my mind, a small smile pulls on my lips. Just as the bartender hands me two drinks, she gazes flirtatiously at whoever is standing behind me.

"You here with Kylan?" she asked the person I couldn't see, and I grabbed my drinks, turning to leave.

"It's his birthday. The big three-oh, so we had to get him properly obliterated." The same gravelly voice that seemed to follow me everywhere wrapped around me, freezing me in my spot with my back against the bar, chest against him.

Rhett's chest is nearly eye level, and I can't help but notice the way his short sleeve shirt is unbuttoned halfway down. It's not like the two-hundred dollar ones Jackson wears. It looks like something a mechanic would wear and just enough chest is showing so that I have to pull my gaze purposely away. But not before I got a peek of a tattoo that stretches across his impressively thick chest. My neck grew hot, and I exhaled slowly.

For five very long years, I had trained myself to not look at anyone but Jackson. And it wasn't very hard. I was loyal to the man I loved. Something that I now realize was pointless. It was easy to feel proud to be Jackson's other half...back then at least. The cloak of naivety was lifted from me, and nothing made me squirm quite like being attached to that man in any capacity. Even the label of 'ex-fiancé' felt like a heavy burden to bear.

"You should try the snake eyes next time." Rhett's blue eyes were solely focused on me, and I grasped the drinks harder.

"I don't know what that even means..." I let out a breathy chuckle as he moved to lean on the bar next to me. I could move now but I don't. His forearms flex, his legs nearly touching mine, and I can see down his loose shirt. Unspeakable thoughts about the contents under that shirt enter my mind, but I quickly snap my eyes back to his, thankful for the loud music or else he might hear the thumping of my heart.

"Snake eyes—it's a signature drink here." He winks at the bartender who was only half paying attention to Rhett as she fills a beer. "It's a mix of tequila and…" He snaps his fingers and shrugs playfully. "You know, I won't even pretend to know what else. It's good. It will put you on your ass if you're not careful, though."

I crinkle my eyebrows at him.

"And you think I'd enjoy something like that?"

Rhett pauses as he traces the outline of my mouth with his eyes. "I won't pretend to know a thing about what you'd enjoy."

I swallow hard, my brain going fuzzy, my naval growing hot.

"I need to get back to my friend." Penny was probably already being swept off her feet by someone.

Rhett bows his at me, and I push the butterflies circling my stomach out of mind as I cross the bar, searching for a blonde. I sip my drink, relishing in the bitter taste of the vodka tonic on my tongue.

Penny and I sip our drinks, liquid courage lacing our veins. Once they're gone, along with half my nerves, she reaches for me, pulling me towards the dance floor.

"I don't dance, you know that!" I yell as the lights dim, and the stage lights start to flash.

"Come on! One song, for me?" Penny beams at me and my sigh is drowned out as the song picks up in volume. I'll dance. For her.

I did the bare minimum, shuffling in the crowd to the music I didn't normally listen to but by the second song I'd loosened up a bit, and Penny convinced me to stay out there. Penny, unfortunately, was one of those people who could get a whole crowd going. She was contagiously fun, her laugh and smile eating away at my resolve.

"Don't look now, but you have an audience," Penny whispers into my ear. I didn't listen, my self-control was gone with the second drink. I meet his gaze across the floor.

"He could be looking at anyone. I don't even really know him!" I yell back, but my heart starts beating irregularly.

"Well, he seems hell bent on changing that."

"Do I need to remind you I just got out of a relationship?" I yell back and she nods enthusiastically.

"Exactly, you're out of the relationship. Time to have some fun."

I wouldn't even know where to begin.

My thoughts are interrupted by the song ending as we exit the dance floor and make our way to the bar to order our final drink. My ears are ringing, but I'll give it to my best friend…it was nice to let loose and not care what everyone around me thought.

"What will it be?" the bartender asks.

"Two snake eyes, please."

Penny raises her eyebrows at me.

"What? I heard it's their signature drink here." I shrug. "I figure we will never be coming back, so we may as well try it."

We get our drinks and assess the place. For such a large venue, it was beginning to feel incredibly small. Penny pulls her phone out, recording something for her social media, and I wave at the phone, flashing a smile, but Rhett catches my attention over her shoulder.

He's leaning against the metal bar table, one large hand wrapped around a sweating bottle of a beer, and I'm drawn in as he laughs. His jaw is chiseled and square, and his dark blond five o'clock shadow is begging me to drag my lips down it. His hands are large and rough looking, and I want to feel them on my skin.

A sharp pang of guilt hits me, and my eyes drop instinctively to my bare ring finger. The absence feels louder than the music pounding around me. I wonder when it will finally sink in— when I'll truly accept that I'm no longer tethered to someone, no longer part of a pair.

"You okay?"

"I should be driving home with Jackson right now." My throat is tight as I reply. "We had a whole day planned tomorrow for brunch with my parents at the country club, and then we were meeting with the baker for cake tasting. I really wanted that lemon cake." It sounded so trivial and stupid even as I say it, but tears form in my eyes, and I swallow a large gulp of the snake eyes drink, letting it burn my throat.

"No, no, no." Penny takes my face between her hands. "You have to let go of what could've been. If you don't, you'll never open yourself up to what could be. You have a whole life ahead of you, and you don't want to miss out on it by looking in the rearview mirror. Got it?" She forces me to nod my head.

"Wow...that was really profound for you being several drinks in."

"I can't watch you be sad anymore. You deserve all the happiness in the world, Audrey."

I choke back the remaining tears. They will have to come back another time.

"No crying in rhinestone cowgirl boots. It's the law."

We both laugh at the ridiculousness of this whole night and turn our attention to the dance floor, peering around as the lights change again.

"What the hell is this place?" I ask no one in particular. Cheers erupt from different corners of the bar, followed by a chorus of hollering that drowns out the music. Penny and I inch closer to the edge of the crowd as dozens of people spill onto the enormous dance floor, everyone arranging themselves in lines. *A freaking line dance, this can't be real.*

"Hey, your boy can dance, too," Penny whispers to me, nodding towards Rhett who's right in my line of sight. Like he did it on purpose. He's laughing at what some guy said next to him, moving effortlessly in his fitted Wrangler jeans and cowboy boots. He steps like he is sure of himself, like he doesn't have a care in the world, and my gaze softens as I watch.

The lines of men and women all dancing take a few steps towards the front of the dance floor where Penny and I are. She taps her feet and claps while I stand there completely still.

Though, it only takes one wink to break me from the spell...or put me in a new one.

"If you don't take him, I will," Penny says and I jerk, looking at her, forgetting for a moment she was even standing next to me. Suddenly, everyone stops dancing, as they all grab a partner from the audience. Penny is scooped up instantly, setting her drink down on the table behind us, but I stand there, wishing I could dissipate into thin air when a large, outstretched palm appears in front of me.

Rhett tips his head, flashing his icy eyes up at me under unfairly thick eyelashes.

"Darlin', may I have this dance?" he asks, and without hesitation I set my drink down, and slowly place my hand in his. I move in a trance as his grin grows wide, and he wraps an arm around my waist, pulling me into him. The song continues, but we don't move quickly like the other pairs. He laces his fingers in mine, and I feel every movement, every muscle in our hands as they touch. His grip around my waist is warm and strong, and I fear if he loosens it, I'll fall right over. I can't bring myself to meet his gaze as he spins me effortlessly across the floor.

Looking at him would be an acknowledgment that whatever was stirring in me was real.

"Where'd you learn to dance like this?" I muster up the words after the silence begins to feel awkward.

"Watching my parents. They danced together any chance they could get," he replies before unexpectedly spinning me out, and this time I do look up at him, not expecting a vulnerable answer like that. Amid the swirl of blue eyes, bright lights, and tequila in my veins, I'm not fully convinced it was really me—Audrey Elson—dancing in a honky-tonk bar with an impossibly handsome man who called me "darlin'." All on the night of my engagement party.

"That's really sweet," I finally replied.

"You enjoying your night?" he asks, as he pulls me and spins me around, away from a rowdy group of men who were about to run into me. He puts his body between me and them without missing a beat.

"That's a loaded question."

"Oh yeah?" His eyebrows knit together, and we stop dancing as the song fades out.

"I wasn't supposed to be here tonight."

I'm unsure how much more I want to say about the matter, but Rhett's lips twitch, and he leans down closer to me.

"I disagree...I think this is exactly where you were supposed to be." Then he dips me, pausing with his face inches from mine. My heart stops, and I tighten my grip in his hands, but I get the impression that I'm a feather in his arms.

Rhett's eyes dilate, his lips part, and then just like that, I'm back upright on my feet, his arms at his side.

Penny's arm loops around my shoulder, filling the space Rhett was just in.

"Thank you for the dance," I say, my voice barely above a whisper as I tuck my now messy chocolate strands behind my ear. "You should go join your friends." I smile and absently wave him towards the group of guys eyeing me, but Rhett hesitates, biting his bottom lip in a way that should be illegal.

"If you insist." He reaches for my hand and pulls it to his lips, planting a gentle kiss before nodding to Penny and walking back towards his hooting and hollering friends. My hand burns hot after he drops it.

"I hope you at least got his number."

I turn to shush her. "Stop, it's nothing. He is just a really nice guy."

"Whatever you say, *darlin'.*" She mocks him, but I ignore it, unable to think beyond what transpired during that two-minute song.

Penny and I stayed for a few more songs, and I continue to wait for my heart rate to return to a normal pace, but it never does. Penny got us pulled into a group of people and we mingled mindlessly with a few guys. I didn't feel like making small talk as they asked us what we did and where we were from. *The city. Finance. Yes, really.* I was quickly bored and couldn't keep my pesky eyes from wandering about the bar, looking for a particular face that had started to feel familiar.

We didn't run into Rhett for the remaining time, and then suddenly it was closing time, and time to leave. Penny requests an Uber as we made our way out into the night.

"Holy shit, you can really see the stars out here," I drunkenly mumbled, my head cocked back, arm linked with Penny's as we swayed on the sidewalk.

Loud laughter captured my attention, and I turned to see a group of guys with Rhett at the center. A cigarette dangling from the lips that I couldn't stop thinking about.

It's the tequila talking, of course.

A beautiful girl comes up to him and pulls him into a friendly hug. I avert my eyes, knowing I have no right for the tightness in my throat as her hands linger on his forearm. She was pretty, in a pair of bell-bottom jeans and crop top.

"How's your mama?" she asks with an accent as thick as his.

"Oh, my god I would kill for red hair like hers. Do you think it's natural? I want to tell her how beautiful she is," Penny mumbles, sloppily holding onto me a bit too tight.

I shush her and take a step back into the shadow of the building while we wait for the ride. Lots of people start pouring out into the parking lot but I'm still focused on him.

Rhett exhaled his cigarette smoke away from the southern belle and flashed that charming smile. "Oh, she's doing good..."

"You tell her I said hi!"

"Will do, she'd love to hear from you."

"And how's Miss Mabel? Your mama was going on and on about her at the farmer's market."

Rhett's smile grows even larger, and he does that boyish thing where he blushes and looks away. "Mabel is as crazy as they get, but you know I've got a thing for those wild girls." They both laugh, an inside joke she must be privy to. Maybe everyone knew Rhett's reputation but me. Of course, I couldn't know. I don't belong here. I don't belong in *his* world. That was just a three second, drunken daydream.

"You ain't kidding, you sure do. Well, I'm glad you have her. I was beginning to worry about you up there at the farm all alone. As was your Mama."

"She is convinced I'm going to die alone in that house, but I'm perfectly fine now that I have my girl."

She laughs and hugs him again. "Give Mabel a big hug and kiss from me."

"I will. Take care." Rhett tips his head and stomps his cigarette butt on the ground beneath his boot.

It may as well be my heart.

"The Uber is here!" Penny exclaims and as she slides into the back seat, I look back one more time at Rhett, who finally sees me. He almost looks like he is going to say something, but someone else comes up to talk to him, so I take my shot and climb in after Penny.

"I had so much fun. We are definitely coming back," Penny announces as we pull out of the lot, and I use every fiber in me not to turn around to see what wreckage is left in that parking lot. Because this is the last time I'll be seeing Rhett. I would make it a point to avoid this town.

"Count me out."

"What? What are you talking about?" My best friend swivels in the dim backseat of the SUV.

"He has a Mabel."

"A what? Is that a disease?" Penny gags.

"He has a girlfriend, Penny. I heard him talking to that beautiful redhead all about Mabel."

"What the hell...I'm so sorry..."

"He hit on me all night, right? I wasn't imagining that, right? I thought there was a spark. Of course, he has a girlfriend. I'm beginning to truly believe all men are the same."

"Wait, you have spent the whole evening avoiding him, and telling me it's nothing, and now you're heartbroken?"

"I know. It just felt good to be wanted...I haven't felt that in a long time. But I'm done...I can't handle any more rejection."

I'm leaving this state soon anyway.

My best friend consoled me the rest of the car ride, through her drunkenness, to the best of her ability.

But as I was falling asleep in bed an hour later, after washing the glitter off my chest, and peeling the skin-tight bodysuit off, I cried.

At least it wasn't about Jackson this time.

Chapter Thirteen

Rhett

I circle the block for the third time, cursing this damn place. Mrs. Lawson casually told me to pick up the check from her, but I knew she was about to leave the country for the summer, so I didn't want to miss my chance. It wouldn't be the first time I was stiffed by one of the rich pricks in this part of town.

She also didn't believe in paying in anything but cash or check, which wasn't what annoyed me. It was that I had to pick it up from her on a Friday morning downtown, where the parking was slim. And even slimmer for a truck like mine.

But I needed the money. On the fourth loop around the block in the historic neighborhood with narrow brick-paved streets, I spotted a parking space. With my blinkers on, I inch forward when a large SUV cuts in front of me, sliding crookedly into the spot.

"You've got to be fucking kidding me right now!" I yell to no one but myself. Out pops a blonde chick with two enormous coffees in her hand. She kicks the door shut behind her, talking to someone through earbuds, not even looking in my direction before she struts across the street into the Brecken Building. A car behind me lays on the horn, so I do what I haven't done in a long time—crank the window and stick my hand out, winding up my middle finger.

Like I said, I hate this city. It brings out the worst in me.

Ten minutes later, after finally finding a spot several blocks away, I made it to the building, buzzing Mrs. Lawson's apartment. Tilting my head back, I peer at the six-story building, thinking back to the night on the rooftop. Thinking about the dance with Audrey at the Bourbon Barrel. My biggest regret was not getting her number. She drove away before I could get the chance. Maybe it's for the best, there's nothing a woman like Audrey could possibly want in a man like me, right?

Mrs. Lawson buzzes me in, getting me out of the hot, humid sun, and I take the stairs, needing to get some of this pent-up anger out. My lungs burn by the time I get to the fifth floor, and I'm sure I'm red in the face when she invites me in. Mrs. Lawson—which is the only name she ever let me call her—thanked me again for the work in her custom walk-in closet and handed me an envelope with a check that would be enough to sustain me for a few weeks. Enough to get a new A/C unit. It made up for the way she talked to me—like I was an uncultured swine.

Well, it sorta made up for it.

Eager to get back to the peaceful lull of Roseville, and with the envelope tucked into my pocket, I pull my baseball cap down and take the steps back down. But as I reach the lobby, the elevator doors ding, drawing my attention to the most beautiful woman who wore a scowl that could kill.

"You've got to be kidding me," Audrey says clear as day, running a hand across the top of her ponytail, and I can't help but cock my head back and let out a husky chuckle.

"If you're stalking me and going to murder me, just get it over with, okay?" She stops moving, a hand truck stacked with uneven boxes teetering against her.

"Wow—of all things, that's not what I was expecting you to say," I reply, but she continues to glare at me. Even in her annoyed state, she looks impossibly attractive.

She turns her attention back to the dolly, groaning under its weight, her teeth gritted, anger fueling each push.

"I'm not stalking you. I was in the building to pick up my last paycheck." Drumming my fingers on my thigh, I rack my brain to say something else. But Audrey is paying me no attention as she steadies the dolly that appears way too heavy for her and starts walking backwards towards the door.

"Let me." I reach out a hand, but she shakes her head, jaw tight.

"No, thanks. I got it," Audrey snaps back.

I don't know what the hell I did, but regardless, she's made me feel like a jackass. I also can't remember the last time I cared what anyone thought of me, maybe that's why my heart feels lodged in my throat. She's pissing me off in a way that's confusing as hell.

Stepping behind her, I hold open the door, biting my lip as she yanks her uneven boxes over the threshold. "Thanks," she mumbles as she heads straight towards the big black SUV that cut me off.

Of course. The blonde was Audrey's friend from the bar.

I watch in complete horror as the hand truck shakes back and forth, the boxes threatening to fall off. I could leave her there, but I would never do that. I may be an asshole, but I'm a gentleman. So, I light a cigarette, inhale, and watch her wave her foot under the bumper, prompting the trunk to open. She hulks a box into the trunk and my eyebrows shoot up.

She is determined as hell; I will give her that. But it's like watching a trainwreck...and I gotta intervene.

She reaches up, aggressively tightening her long ponytail, and her chest heaves with the efforts, while she also expertly avoids eye contact with me.

"Let me," I said again, taking a few strides towards her and lifting the next box into the trunk. Audrey bites her lip and gazes across the street.

"I overpacked that one." She points to the bulging cardboard box with probably an entire roll of packing tape keeping its contents in.

I want to blurt out '*no shit*' but I withhold and put it in the trunk while she holds her scowl.

"You have a body in this one?" I joke, pulling my dangling cigarette from my mouth.

Her long lashes blink rapidly. "No, it's shoes." She nearly hip checks me. "Now watch out please, before the trunk decapitates you." I ducked out of the way just in time as the trunk door came down.

"By the way, cigarettes are known carcinogens. Have you thought about giving them up?" she asks curtly.

That's fresh, coming from her.

"I hear liquor can kill, too."

She shoots me a glare that makes me wish I could swallow my words.

Between the parked cars, the tension is as thick as the humid air around us. She clearly wants me to move out of the way, but I'm hell bent on getting my answer. Even though I'm much bigger than her, I don't doubt she could put me in my place.

"Did I do something to upset you?"

She laughs without smiling. "You don't even know me." Audrey grabs the top of the dolly, trying to push it past me but I grip the side, stopping her in her tracks.

Her cheeks blush and hazel eyes dilate as they meet mine.

"You're right. I *don't* know you, but can't you see I was trying to?"

Audrey cocks her head back.

"Here's the thing, Rhett. It's hot as hell today, and I'm running on four hours of sleep. I've spent all morning arguing with movers who clearly didn't show up. So, now it's just me and my friend moving all my stuff out of my ex's apartment." She puffs out an angry breath, leaning into me. "And you know what I really don't have time for in my life? Cheaters. So, if you could kindly move aside, and stop showing up everywhere, I'd really appreciate it." Her words could slice, but I narrowed my eyes, doubling down, because I was anything but a cheater. And even though she is clearly pissed, all I want at this moment is to turn her day around. Don't ask me why. There's something about this girl that won't stop pulling me like a damn magnet.

Audrey white knuckles the side of the hand truck, so I release it, stepping aside to let her through.

"I'm sorry you didn't get more sleep, and I can't change the weather, but I *can* help you move boxes."

"What?" she snaps.

Shrugging, I repeat myself. "Don't pretend you don't need help." I smile, which I thought would help but she forcefully shoves the dolly across the bumpy road. Like an ass, I follow her, fully aware the odds are not stacked in my favor right now.

"What would *Mabel* think of you helping me?" Audrey spat out and now I was genuinely confused. I don't remember ever talking to her about Mabel. I mean, I had a handful of whiskeys at the Bourbon Barrel, but I have a pretty good memory of that night. It's been replaying in my head all week.

"Well darlin', I think Mabel would be okay with it. Last I checked her plans involved sleeping all day."

My answer somehow only angers Audrey further, and she whips the dolly onto the sidewalk. With a vicious scowl on her pouty pink lips, she stares me dead in the eye, making my heart skip a beat.

Probably not her intention.

"Don't *darlin'* me. And like I said, I have no time for two timing cheats—"

"Wait a minute." I think I know what's happening and if I'm right I'm going to lose my mind. Cautiously raising my hand, I slip my phone from my back pocket. I have to bite my lip, so I don't laugh as I scroll to a photo of Mabel and hold it up silently to show Audrey.

The tightness in her face drops so quickly I actually feel kinda bad.

"So, Mabel is a..."

"She's a two-year-old bloodhound," I replied coolly.

Audrey's cheeks turn bright pink.

"Right. Well, I'm sorry, but you can see why I'd think that. Nothing has really gone my way lately, and I'm beginning to think I only attract complete jerks into my life." She gestures around, and my stomach sinks with heaviness as I recall the first time I met her on the rooftop. She was trying so hard to hide her tears, carrying that champagne bottle like a lifeline. I wanted nothing more that night than to find the fucker who did that to her.

"Don't sweat it, it's an honest mistake. Mabel would be flattered, but I won't be telling her. The ego of a hound is already through the roof," I comment, and she gives a tiny nod. "But hey, if you'll let me, I'd be happy to help." I put my hand to my chest. "I have no plans until five."

Why don't you just scream that you're a single guy with way too much free time?

"Do you know how to use a dolly?" She glances up at me, still clearly reserved, but I swear to god, my knees buckle.

CHAPTER FOURTEEN

Audrey

I slyly wick the sweat off my brow as Rhett strolls into the lobby, pushing the dolly ahead of me. His baseball cap sits low on his head, his hair curling up under it, and he takes up a lot of space in the lobby. Not only because he's jacked. It's the way Rhett commands a presence that I can't quite decipher. I'm not sure what was making my stomach churn more at the moment; that I would now be returning to my apartment with Rhett in tow—or as Penny referred to him, Red the Prick—or the fact that for the last few days, I have been truly bothered by a girlfriend who never existed.

The made-up girlfriend of a man who wasn't mine.

I want to dunk my head in cold water and promptly hide inside the utility closet for eternity, but instead I steel my stomach, and trail behind Rhett into the elevator like nothing was wrong. Like my life lately wasn't a rollercoaster.

"So, getting out of dodge, huh?" he asks as I hit the number six button.

"Come again?"

Rhett chuckles, readjusting his hands on the dolly, my eyes drawn to them. Ten minutes ago, I never wanted to see his face again. Now, watching his hands wrap around the handle, I could barely compose a thought.

"Are you leaving town?" he clarifies, but I shake my head.

"Oh, no. Not yet at least. I'm moving in with my friend temporarily."

"Penny?"

I tilt my head. "You remember her name?"

"I remember everything," he remarks, and it sends a tickle down my spine.

The elevator dings and there stands Penny in my doorway, with a strained look on her face as she struggles with an enormous box. As soon as she notices the tall drink of water behind me, she stops wrangling the box and silently mouths *what the fuck* to me.

Gritting my teeth in warning, I shake my head ever so slightly.

"Look who I ran into outside," I muse, smiling at them both.

Penny tilts her head, daggers aimed at Rhett. "How convenient. And odd."

"Rhett offered to help us move some boxes down." I pointedly give Penny a *ceasefire* look.

"Wow, *how* generous of you. What a true gentleman. Helping all women, everywhere—ouch, Audrey!" Pinching her arm, I nudge her back into my apartment, beckoning Rhett to follow.

"We are going to continue taping up some boxes in here, if you want to take the boxes from the hallway down to my car."

Rhett nods, scanning the inside of my apartment.

"Do you have another moving truck coming?" he asks, and I stop fidgeting, gazing up as he leans to peer down the corridor into the kitchen.

"No, just my SUV. Why?" I bite my lip.

"Your place is pretty big. I just wasn't sure what all you were taking," he adds, and I nod. Because I understand exactly what he is saying and probably know what he is thinking. This apartment is enormous, and full of *stuff*. The built-ins that frame the fireplace are full of decor, gathered treasures from travels, and books. None of it's packed. None of it's coming.

"Actually, I'm only taking what's already packed up in the living room."

Rhett nods now, scanning the haphazardly placed row of my belongings lining the living room. I had plans to organize and label everything.

It was extremely unlike me to just throw shit in a box and call it done. Jackson would've never allowed us to pack our own stuff to begin with—it was beneath him. And my parents, well, they would be appalled at my 'careless' way of living right now, too.

But there wasn't a roadmap for this period in my life. I've never had to start over, and I'm beginning to think maybe this is how it always feels. Like you're flying and drowning all at once. Like you don't even know who you are.

"Alright then, I'll just start here." He smiles, grabbing a few boxes, stacking them on the dolly, and I hand him my car keys.

"Thank you." I smile as he finally leaves, and the front door clicks behind him.

I turn slowly toward Penny, unable to meet her gaze. Her eyes, wide with a mix of confusion and amusement, say it all.

"So, that's a turn of events." I shrug, pushing past her into the living room to assess what's what. She is hot on my trail. "Are you going to tell me why Red has suddenly shown up to play hero, because I am not fooled and neither should you be. Oh, my god, Aud...is he stalking you?"

I laugh and sit down on the couch, desperately needing to take a load off. "He was picking up a check from my neighbor, saw me struggling outside with the boxes and offered to help. As much as I want to hate him, no one else is coming to help us, Pen. He kind of saved the day. Like seriously, this would be too much for us and you know it." We glance around in unison at the overpacked boxes.

She rolls her eyes. "What about the girlfriend?"

"Okay, so embarrassing story. Mabel is not his girlfriend. She's his dog."

We both go quiet for a moment before bursting into laughter, Penny's cackling echoing through the apartment.

"I'm mortified for you. But it's not like you're dating the man, so it's fine." Penny justifies in between bouts of laughter.

"Exactly, I'm not dating him." I stand and pick up a photo of Jackson and I from a ski trip last winter, examining it. It feels like a lifetime ago. I set it back down on the fireplace mantel, in its rightful place because it's just baggage from another life. One I want to shed.

"Exactly," she replies slowly. "It would be *scandalous* to even *kiss* him." A smile creeps up on her face, but I quickly peel my gaze away and walk to the window that overlooks the street. Gazing out, I have a clear view of Rhett effortlessly loading boxes into my vehicle. A three-row SUV was completely impractical for just one person, but right now, I'm grateful Jackson convinced me to get it a few months ago.

Penny and I keep moving the last few things into the hallway. I avoid her eyes, and she pinches her lips together tightly.

"Alright, what's next?" Rhett strides back into the hall a few minutes later, a grin on his face, not even the slightest sign he's out of breath.

I haven't been around a lot of men who would happily give up their time to help a stranger. Certainly not my ex, and my father would rather throw money at a problem than solve it in any form himself.

Just another sign that Rhett and I were from different worlds.

"Do you want these?" Penny's voice pulls me from my trance, and I swallow hard, feeling Rhett's gaze on me.

Penny balances a box on her hip, pulling out mementos from Jackson and I's relationship that I kept on a shelf in my closet. A ticket to the theater from our first date, a photo of us in Jamaica on spring break. She narrows her eyes, examining something close.

"Leave it. The whole box." I glance back into the apartment through the open door.

"We are done here. If we could just grab the last few bags of clothing, that's it."

Rhett nods, squatting down to load up the final dolly. Penny doesn't move, holding my gaze as I fling a dry cleaning bag over my shoulder and smile at her. A reassuring smile. It was as much for her as it was for me.

"You really are leaving everything else?" she asks. I know it's preposterous to her, even if she won't flat out say that. I packed all my clothes and the few things I wanted. Most of my cherished items from childhood and college are in storage, and I hadn't been planning on getting them out until we moved into the big house.

In truth, I was leaving 75 percent of my stuff behind. I had the money to replace it all if I wanted, but that wasn't the point. I didn't want to replace it. I didn't want any of it. I wanted to shed the weight of my past. I didn't want anything that reminded me of Jackson.

"I'm good. I have what's important to me," I shrug.

"It's your call, babe."

Rhett was waiting at the elevator, holding the door open as Penny stepped in. Before locking up, I peered into the apartment one more time.

This is the only goodbye I get to control—because Jackson was never going to give me the closure I deserved. But as I walk away, I'm struck by how good it feels, how freeing. Stepping into the elevator isn't hard like I imagined it would be.

After all, I'm saying goodbye to an illusion.

Outside, Penny and Rhett load the last of the boxes into the SUV, and I shut the doors behind them.

"Would you like me to follow y'all to your place and help you unload?" Rhett asks, his crystal blue eyes shining under the rim of his old baseball cap. A sudden knot of fear tightens in my stomach. What if saying no means this is the end? Rhett feels like a stranger who's somehow seen too much, and the thought of cutting him loose now feels more uncomfortable than continuing this...friendship?

"Actually, I roped my neighbors into helping, so you're off the hook, Red," Penny chimes in before walking around to the passenger door.

Rhett's face falls slightly, but he readjusts his baseball cap to hide it.

"You are now free of me." I slightly bow, awkwardly laughing. "Thank you for everything. I owe you."

He pauses, his tongue poking out to lick his lip and leans on the car as his eyes bore into me.

"Let me take you to dinner tonight." His voice is low and husky, and I thought I heard him wrong.

"Oh..." I start, my mind racing to find a reason to say no, but I can't find one. There is no logical reason to decline the invitation, even if his question made butterflies storm my stomach. In a few hours, Penny is going to the airport to fly out for a destination elopement she's shooting tomorrow, leaving me alone on a Friday night to unpack. Which just sounds sad and lonely.

But dinner with Rhett. That feels like a choice.

Like a major choice.

"It's only dinner, I promise," he interjects, like he can read my racing thoughts. So, I nod with an expressionless face.

"Yeah. Okay. Let's do dinner. A thank you dinner."

Rhett smirks, chuckling as he pulls out his phone.

"I guess that means I need your number." He winks at me, and I put my info into his phone, parting ways as quickly as I can. Which also means glancing back to see him strut away to his truck.

And look way too good doing it.

"Say nothing," I blurt out, sliding into the driver's seat as Penny swivels dramatically towards me, her mouth wide open.

"Audrey Elson, did you just agree to a date with Red?"

"It's dinner. It's simply a 'thank you' dinner." I calmly pull out of the parking spot with my fingers tightly gripped around the leather steering wheel.

Penny taps her nails on the dashboard. "So, let me get this straight. He is taking *you* out to dinner…to thank you…for…"

I grow flustered, my words jumbling in my mouth. "I don't know…he…we…it's just dinner and…"

"You like him."

The words hang in the air between us as we wait at the red light. Rolling my eyes, I try to settle the butterflies in my stomach.

"He probably pities me. I'm sure dinner is a formality. It probably feels like the proper thing to do for him."

Penny snorts. "Yeah, okay. Honey, I don't think that man cares about formalities. I think he sees a gorgeous single woman who he keeps running into and he wants to see where this goes."

"Well, joke's on him then, because I am not ready for a boyfriend. My life is a freaking mess right now. I barely know right from left."

"Who said anything about a boyfriend? It could just be a casual fling. A summer fling!" My best friend claps like she just thought of the cleverest idea.

Chewing my lip, we turn down the next street, and it occurs to me I still need to tell Penny about the job offer and transfer to New York.

Now isn't the right time though.

"That's it. I'm canceling it. I don't know what I was thinking. I cannot go on a date with *him!*" My palms grow sweaty on the steering wheel, and I want someone to shake some sense into me.

"Aud, listen to me." I park the car into front of Penny's apartment and put on the hazards, leaning my forehead on the steering wheel, overwhelm sinking into me with its deep talons.

"Don't overthink this. You like him, yeah?"

The car feels like it's spinning.

"He is a nice guy, I guess," I mumble into the steering wheel.

"Then go to dinner. The worst that can happen is you have a really good meal and don't spend tonight alone."

"And the worst is..."

"The worst is you end up making out with him."

I peek out from under my hands at Pen and we both laugh.

It's only dinner. And Penny's right. It beats being alone tonight.

Chapter Fifteen

Rhett

Shaking out my arms to rid myself of nerves, I take two steps at a time up to the third floor, adrenaline coursing through my veins. This building is much different than Audrey's old apartment, with its sleek and modern large glass windows.

Her door came into view. Apartment sixty-four. Suddenly my lace-up leather boots sound loud and squeaky on these shiny concrete floors. I put on clean jeans and a short sleeve button down shirt. *Shit, is this the same thing I wore to Bourbon Barrel?*

It's too late now, if it is. I pause in the hallway and pull out my phone to triple check the reservations for the sushi restaurant. It's only two blocks away and we have fifteen minutes to spare, so at least I have that going for me. Women like men who are punctual, right?

I wasn't the planning type— hell—I wasn't the dating type. I couldn't remember the last time I took a woman out to dinner. My dates in the past started at a bar and usually ended in my date's bed. But that's the old me. The new me is shaking in his boots at the idea of eating dinner with someone other than Ky.

Her apartment door opens before my knuckles have the chance to even make contact, and my words are stolen right from my damn tongue.

Audrey has on a long navy skirt that ties around her waist and a top that falls off her shoulders. She said she was exhausted, but it doesn't show. Her idea of exhaustion must be different from mine because she looks like she just stepped out of the salon.

As her hazel eyes reach mine, she quietly pulls the door shut behind her, stepping into the hallway. She smells sweet, like the star jasmine flowers lining my mom's garden. At that thought, my stomach does an unexpected routine of somersaults.

"Hey." I remember how to speak as she flashes me a smirk. "You look beautiful, Audrey."

Audrey was *beautiful*. But she pauses in her step when I say it, pink spreading across her lightly freckled cheeks.

"Oh, thank you." She quickly pinches her brows together, like she doesn't believe I really mean it. I guess I'll have to work on showing her how beautiful she is to me. "Shall we?" she asks, but before I can even answer, she waltzes past me, leading the way to the stairwell I just came up from, her hand on the door as I take wide strides to catch up to her. "Hopefully parking wasn't a pain." She flashes me a polite smile before taking off down the steps, her skirt balled up in her fist as I try to keep up with her fast pace.

"It was fine," I reply, feeling like I'm chasing her through the stairwell. Maybe she's nervous, too. Or she wants to get this over with as fast as she can.

As we approach the lobby, I practically have to jump ahead of her to catch the door and hold it open to the sidewalk.

"If you move any quicker, I won't be able to get the doors for you," I half-joke and she scans me up and down quizzically.

"Well, Rhett, I guess you better learn to walk faster then." She pauses to flip me a real smile this time. One that reaches her eyes, and everything stills for a moment.

Every time she shows me a little piece of what I can only assume is the real Audrey, not the persona she wears like a shield, I have the same feeling I did on the rooftop.

I might be in trouble.

The kind of trouble that makes me feel alive, that makes me want more.

Though inside I might be a fucking mess, I would not let her see anything but a cool, calm and collected man. That's what she deserved after her fucking mess of an ex.

Gently placing my hand on the small of her back, I guided her to the left, towards the restaurant. I pull my hand away as we start down the sidewalk, not wanting to make her feel uncomfortable.

I get the feeling she is the kind of woman who would want to take things slow. So, I remind myself again—this is a first date. Even if I can't take my eyes off her.

The city buzzes with its usual noise, but the space between us grows still as we fall into step, side by side, on the sidewalk. Small talk was never my strong suit. I've always been the type to cut straight to the point. Not that it's always worked in my favor.

Maybe that's why I never could keep someone around long. Certainly not long enough to put a ring on a finger, which is what my mom gets on my case about every Sunday evening.

But right now, I only have one goal in mind. Make sure Audrey smiles tonight more than anything.

"Have you ever been to Sushi Blue?" I asked as we approached a crosswalk.

Audrey glances up at me. "Once, a while ago. How about you?"

I look both ways, nearly holding her back until it's safe to cross. I can't help my overprotective nature.

"Me? Oh no, I don't eat down here often."

Or ever.

"More of a cook at home type guy?" she asks, and I nod.

"Something like that."

Homebody would be more accurate.

I hold the door open to the restaurant and as soon as we walk inside, I feel wildly out of place. I notice eyes glancing our way. Probably just because Audrey is stunning and who wouldn't look her way. But my nerves say they are also probably wondering what a guy like me was doing with a woman like her. I was wondering the same thing. But I let on to none of that, as we're led to our table. Audrey sits down when I pull out her chair, keeping her eyes down.

I sit down, too, but feel fidgety as hell. This place is quiet and dim, and I feel like everyone is talking in whispers, and I don't know what half the menu is. I should've thought this through better.

Audrey picks up the menu, her eyes gliding down it like this was an everyday thing.

Good, at least she'll be comfortable.

I settle on the first thing I spot on the menu, knowing it doesn't really matter; I'll eat just about anything. When Audrey sets her menu down, her attention shifts back to me.

"You know what you're getting?" she asks, and I nod.

"Yeah, I think so."

She smiles politely and I lean my elbows on the table, closer to her. I know that's probably not proper etiquette but as she sits stiffly in her chair, I'm desperate to make her relax.

"Alright, so besides being a great line dancer, tell me something about yourself."

Her head rolls slightly with her eyes but she cracks a tiny smile.

"You making fun of me?"

I laugh, throwing my hands up. "Hell no, never. You really weren't bad."

"Well, thanks. And I hate this question, my brain goes completely blank whenever I have to talk about myself." She stirs the straw in her water.

"Fair enough." I drag my palm down my jaw. "Alright, tell me your favorite movie. Or favorite flower. Something ridiculously stupid."

Her shoulders relax a tiny bit, and the air feels less heavy as she chews her lip in a way that makes me wild.

"Blue hydrangeas."

I tilt my head, not sure I heard her right.

"I know it's not really a flower, but hydrangeas are my favorite. The blue ones specifically." Her lips pull up in a grin and I nod, happy with the answer. Another tidbit about Audrey Elson.

"Any reason why?" I ask, seeing how much she'll let on, how many things I can learn about her.

"I grew up in New England and in the summer when the hydrangeas in everyone's yard were in full bloom, it was really pretty. They always made me happy."

"I'm guessing you miss it then?"

A fleeting shadow crosses her face, and she tilts her head ever so slightly.

"No, I don't actually."

My lips part, about to change the subject, seeing this may be a point of pain, but she interjects, her golden flecked eyes back on me as she perks up in her seat.

"My turn." Audrey leans forward. "Why do you hate the city so much?"

"Oh, coming in for the kill, I see," I joke, rolling the paper from my straw in between my fingers. "I grew up in the country, on a farm. I guess I don't see the appeal of the city. It's loud, and crowded, everyone's rushing around. People are kind of assholes."

Audrey's gaze drifts, unfocused, as if her thoughts have carried her somewhere far away.

"I can't say you're entirely wrong. But do you like living out there alone?"

I shrug. "I have Mabel. And my mom, sister and nieces live all within a few minutes. I never feel alone."

"It must be nice to have family nearby." Audrey smiles, lips closed, but it doesn't reach her eyes. Hair falls over part of her face, and she pushes it back behind her ear as the waitress comes over to take our order.

Once she leaves, I continue, hoping it doesn't feel like I'm interrogating her.

"What about your family?"

"I have one older brother, Andrew. We don't see each other often. He's a surgeon." She pauses, her mouth still open, like she is unsure how much more she wants to say. "My Dad owns an investment banking firm in Manhattan, and my mom is...well, she stays quite busy."

Her words are clipped, so I don't push her.

"Alright, I'm done grilling you." I feel like an ass now, but Audrey smiles up at me.

"It's fine. I'd rather be here than spending my night unpacking my clothes."

"So, I'm just a miniscule upgrade from unpacking?" I tease and Audrey laughs.

"Okay, that came out horrible. I *am* glad you invited me for this 'thank you' dinner." She crinkles her nose, and it's so damn adorable, I forget to respond for a moment.

"Well, I'd rather be here than just about anywhere else tonight."

The lighting is dim, but I could've sworn she blushed.

Chapter Sixteen

Audrey

Over Rhett's shoulder, a couple takes their seats directly behind us, and immediately I recognize their faces. The guy is Jackson's best friend, Dale, and his girlfriend, whose name was escaping me in my bout of anxiety. I'd spent so much time with them. They've been to our apartment, we've been on group vacations, and they've been at every company outing the Tippins Group has put on in the last two years. It's been crickets from them since the breakup though, which wasn't surprising.

Jackson Tippins was born with the scale tipped in his favor.

His friends would automatically take his side, supporting him, without so much as a second thought to me. I was just a casualty in the war. It would only be a matter of time before his friend saw me here with Rhett, though. This was a small, intimate setting, after all.

I shouldn't care if they see me out to dinner with a new friend two weeks after my breakup. But that doesn't stop the nerves from bubbling in my stomach.

Just in time, the waitress reappears, blocking their view of me, and sets down our food. When I glance up at Rhett, his blue eyes are studying me.

"You okay? Is the food not what you wanted?" he asks, and I swallow the lump in my throat at his kindness.

I so badly wanted this dinner to be a good idea.

We can't get up and switch tables now. Hell, I can't even go to the bathroom without risking being seen. I hate that it even matters to me, but the thought of Jackson finding out I was already out to dinner with someone new makes my stomach twist. Not because I care what he thinks—I absolutely don't. But I know how quickly things like this make their way back to my parents, and that's the last thing I need. I'm still trying to piece together this new life of mine, and the idea of them weighing in, or shaming me before I've figured it out is something I want to avoid at all costs.

All I know is when I focus on Rhett, I feel calm. And I'm not ready for this night to end.

"This is one of my favorite meals actually," I assure him, but my chopsticks still hover in the air over the sushi roll as Rhett leans on the table and grins that half-smile that makes me blush.

"How can I make this better?" he asks, and it's enough to bring tears to my eyes.

Maybe this was a bad idea, maybe I wasn't emotionally ready to go out to dinner with a new *friend.*

"Everything is fine, seriously. It's not you, I just..." I dial down the volume down of my voice, but it proves too late. Dale's head snaps up at the sound and we catch each other's gaze.

Luckily, Rhett doesn't follow my gaze as he leans back in his chair.

"I want to be with you this evening...I want this...but I don't want to be *here.*" My words fade out and I feel awful, tucking my head down.

I purposefully avoid looking over his shoulder again, keeping my attention on the man at the table with me.

The only one who deserves my attention.

To my surprise, Rhett doesn't look disappointed or anything remotely close. His shoulders relax and he places his napkin next to his untouched entree.

I let out my breath. I was waiting for him to snap at me, to say something to make me feel small or ungrateful, like Jackson would've said. But he's not him.

"You want to get out of here?" A twinkle sets in his blue eyes.

I toss my napkin on the table, too, even though I'm ravenously hungry, and nod my head.

"Yes...would that be okay?"

Before he answers me, Rhett motions for the waitress.

"Could we have some boxes to-go, ma'am? I'm not feeling too well." He puts the charm on and the waitress takes our food away to pack it up.

"I have an idea. It's maybe a bit random, but it doesn't involve other people at all..." He scrubs his jaw with his hand, his knee bouncing up and down. I have to admit, he's kind of enchanting.

"I'm intrigued," I offer, and he chuckles. Honestly, I'd go anywhere to get out of this suffocating restaurant.

Rhett paid the bill quickly, and went to get his truck, telling me he'd be back in a moment to pick me up. I insisted I could walk, but he was even more insistent on being a gentleman.

As I rise and smooth my skirt, deliberately turning away from Dale, a spark of excitement flutters through me. I don't know what the night holds, but anything is better than going back to an empty apartment. With anticipation bubbling in my chest, I stride toward the door—only to feel the thrill evaporate, replaced by a sinking dread, when Dale calls out my name.

I close my eyes and spin slowly on my heel, plastering a fake smile on my lips.

"See babe, I told you it was her." His girlfriend turns in her chair, looking up at me with a smug smirk.

"What a coincidence!" I offer politely, gripping my purse tightly at my side.

"How are you?" Dale asks, a wicked gaze in his eyes, and my mouth hangs open for longer than intended.

"I'm good, thanks."

"I'm so sorry to hear about *everything*," his perky girlfriend chimes in, not sounding apologetic at all. I'm sure my breakup to *the* Jackson Tippins provided all the gossip she needed for a year.

An ill-timed laugh, which is way too loud for this restaurant, escapes me as I wave my hand dismissively at them both.

"Please, don't apologize. I'm doing good, but I do need to run, so good to see you both."

They look stunned, as I kiss my fingertips and wave. A rumbling engine draws my attention outside, where Rhett's white truck idles.

I push the awkward interaction from my mind as soon as I step onto the sidewalk, where a man with rough hands and a beautiful smile holds the truck door open for me.

"Darlin'." Rhett's hand stretches out, and my palm fits perfectly in it as he helps me into the passenger side.

We drive out of the city, away from the mess and into the unknown.

CHAPTER SEVENTEEN

Audrey

There was something so heartwarming about the way Rhett spoke about his hometown. Roseville was a rural town twenty-five miles east of the city, one that didn't get much attention. But as we rolled through the two-lane main street under the setting sun, and people waved to us, I couldn't help but smile. It felt like I just entered a Hallmark movie.

"So, this is where you grew up?" I murmured, looking out the window at a lit up gazebo in the middle of the town's park.

"Born and raised. It's simple here, but it's home." I nod in response, though I don't know how it feels to be sentimental about home. I left at eighteen and never looked back.

"It's really charming. I've never spent any time out here. Other than the Bourbon Barrel, I guess," I admit sheepishly.

"Well, I'm honored to be your guide. I actually live just a mile down this road." He points ahead as we turn down a narrow road, lined with tall vegetation on one side. A farm of sorts.

"Here we are..." Rhett announces as the truck slows its roll. We turn left into a long, winding gravel driveway, lined with oak trees that spread their roots far into the green grass. Rhett cranks the window down, and I glance over at him, noticing his other arm draped lazily over the steering wheel. As the tree line ends, a small, white two-story house comes into view.

"Home, sweet home," Rhett says wistfully, and I smile because it's exactly as I pictured it when he said he lived in a farmhouse. The house was complete with a wraparound porch and aged tin roof. The expansive porch was full of mismatched items; a dining table with chippy blue paint and different sized chairs around it, and a rocking chair sat next to an antique looking bookcase with potted plants and herbs. I didn't take him for a gardener. Though, he does keep surprising me. Then there was a collection of rocks piled on the steps, and a few tennis balls scattered. Probably Mabel's.

We parked next to an enormous oak tree with a wooden swing hanging from it.

"We definitely aren't in the city anymore," I said, feeling like Dorothy in *The Wizard of Oz*.

Rhett lets out a hearty laugh, shaking his head in a way that makes my cheeks warm. "It needs a lot of work. The steps are loose, so be careful when you walk up. The second floor is completely gutted, but I bought it for the land, really. It's peaceful out here. A man can think."

When my shoes hit the grass, I draw in a deep breath, and it smells like I'm a million miles from home. A million miles from that restaurant. It feels like I stepped into someone else's life. And I like it.

'Someone else's life' was good to me.

"Okay, so chill right here. It'll just be a few minutes, and I'll be right back to show you the plan." Rhett rubs his hands together, a coy grin on his face. Hesitation pulls at my stomach, as he gently takes the take-out bag of sushi from my hands.

"Show me what, exactly?"

"Don't you worry about it. You're gonna like it." His self-assurance was both infuriating and appealing.

"And if I don't?" I muse, hands on my hips.

"Then I'll drive you home and you'll never see me again."

My body stiffens at that suggestion.

"I'll be back in a few minutes, Audrey." He winks and leaves me standing in his front yard as he walks around the corner of the house.

I don't know what to do as I stand there in between the truck and the oak tree, so I walk to the tree swing and sit down gingerly, pushing my feet in the grass, swinging back and forth.

How did I get here?

The sky has turned a dark pink, with wispy clouds of purple woven through, and it looks like they sit right on the house's tin roof. It's breathtaking really, so I pull out my phone to snap a picture and send it to Penny. She replies immediately.

Penny: So pretty! But where are you? I need proof of life.

Audrey: I'm at Rhett's house, dinner was a bust, but I'll fill you in later. He is setting up a 'surprise' for me right now in the backyard.

Penny: Okay, so you're either about to get fucked or murdered.

Audrey: Penny! You're honestly the worst.

Penny: I know.

Audrey: Also, I'm not getting murdered OR going to sleep with him. This is just dinner that turned into something different. It's a 'friend date'.

Penny: Have you checked out his ass or pictured his lips on you? Because if you say yes, sorry to break it to you, it's not a 'friend date'. Whatever the hell that even is.

Instantly, my throat grows tight, and my patience wears thin. I hear movement from the backyard but can't see a damn thing. I have no more time to contemplate what to do next, though, because a blur of reddish-brown fur comes barreling around the corner of the house straight towards me.

The dog matches the photo Rhett showed me earlier today, when I thought Mabel was his girlfriend. As I stand from the swing to greet the infamous Miss Mabel, Rhett's husky voice sounds from the side of the house.

"Dammit, Mabel!"

"Hi there, pretty girl," I cooed, squatting down to pet the bloodhound who was demanding my full attention. She is big but was still a puppy with giant paws, and even larger ears.

Rhett comes jogging towards me with his shirt unbuttoned down to the middle of his chest. *Oh, my god,* Penny is right. This is a booty call and I'm just so damn naive. I wrap my arms around me, even though Mabel is still nudging my legs with her wet nose.

"Sorry 'bout that. Like I said, she's got no manners. Or knows how to sit and stay." Rhett whistles for Mabel, who pays him no mind.

"Who needs manners when you're this cute?" Mabel leans on me, her droopy eyes making it impossible not to pet her more. I have a particular weakness for wrinkly dogs. Growing up, I begged my parents for an English bulldog, but that proved to be fruitless. Then I met Jackson, who disliked dogs, claiming it was because he was allergic. But there had never been proof of that, either.

"Everything's set up, you ready?" Rhett gestures toward the backyard, pausing to let me catch up before falling into step beside me. Parts of his property *were* in rough shape, but there was a rustic beauty to it. The house was small, the white paint peeling in some spots, and the bare garden beds desperately needed some love, but I loved the honesty of it all. Unlike my polished apartment, this place felt like a *home*.

The wind blew my navy skirt up around my knees and Mabel trotted noisily beside me, claiming me as her new best friend, with Rhett on the other side of me. I glanced at his biceps, straining against his shirt, and thought about what Penny said.

I couldn't be sure anymore if this was a 'friend date'.

Maybe it wouldn't be so bad if it wasn't.

But as fast as the thought came into my head, it left.

Because I couldn't belong here. In four months, I'd be leaving this state for good.

My mouth parts with pure surprise as we round the corner, and the backyard comes into view. We walk right into what looks like an outdoor theater, complete with twinkle lights and dinner. Our food was arranged on a coffee table in front of a U-shaped outdoor sofa. It was nicer than I was expecting, and I didn't know what to say.

"Welcome to my backwoods movie theater." Rhett winks, dropping onto the outdoor sofa, his arms stretched over the back. I sat down next to him, my ankles neatly crossed and tucked close. "Thanks for suggesting we leave the restaurant." I puff out my cheeks and release a quiet chuckle. "I think I like this better."

In all my time with Jackson, he'd never set up anything like this. He bought me expensive gifts and took me on vacations his assistant planned. He didn't think on the spot or *do* romantic dates.

This was different.

Mabel's nose twitches in the air as she squeezes between Rhett and my legs. I pop a piece of sushi in my mouth, moaning at how good it tastes right now.

"I get one more question, then we can discuss what we'll watch," he says, and I laugh, averting my eyes away from him. Something about the way he looks at me makes me feel like I'm wearing my heart on the outside of my skin. Like I can't hide anything.

"Okay, but I'm not very interesting. You're going to be disappointed," I said but he just shrugged a bit.

"I don't believe that one bit." Rhett leans in, his elbows on his knees, flexing his muscular arms.

"Okay...ask away."

"Tell me something about yourself that might surprise me."

I ponder it for a minute, scratching Mabel's ears as I do.

"Okay, fine...but you can't make fun of me."

"Promise." He smirked.

"One of my absolute favorite things to do is bake." I pause, waiting for backlash but it doesn't come. "I used to bake when I was stressed. I am actually really good."

"Wait, I'm confused." He scrubs his jaw. "Who the hell would make fun of something like that?"

"Because it's cliche, it's pedestrian."

Rhett shakes his head vigorously. "Well, you're wrong. Baking takes skill, and it makes you happy. Ain't nothing cliche or dumb about that."

"Thanks." I bite my lip as the butterflies swarm my stomach.

"So, why don't you bake anymore? You said you used to."

"Oh. Well, I got busy with my job, with life..." *With wedding planning, with pleasing a man who I was never good enough for.* "And Jackson used to hate it when I baked. He thought it was a waste of time, so I sort of just stopped."

I knew it sounded weak. And I hated myself for bringing up Jackson in front of Rhett.

"Okay, well, that's the dumbest shit I ever heard," Rhett retorted, and when our gaze meets, I crack a smile, making him smile, too. "Hell, if someone wanted to bake for me, I'd be bowing down at their feet."

Just like that, I swear a piece of my heart clicked back into place.

"Not everyone is as appreciative as you," I muse, gently tapping his knee with my fingertips.

"So, tell me about Rhett," I say, quickly pulling my hand back to my lap.

"First, I don't bake." We both laugh. "I'm a carpenter; learned the trade from my mom's father. I was born and raised down the street in the house my mom still lives in. I spend most of my time here, with Mabel. And I'm a homebody who has an unhealthy obsession with old movies and old music."

"You forgot that you save people who find themselves crying on rooftops, and you help move strangers when their moving company ghosts them...and you have the world's cutest dog. Anything else I'm missing?" I tease.

"You forgot to add I have incredible taste in women." He leans forward and my breath hitches.

"Oh..." I pop another piece of sushi into my mouth, leaning back against the cushions of the sofa, my heart dropping into my stomach. "So, what are we watching?"

But the movie didn't really matter. Rhett puts on a classic I've seen a million times, but even if it was something new, I wouldn't have been able to follow the storyline. The words wouldn't have made sense. Just like the feelings stirring inside of me as I sit here next to Rhett with string lights above me, a dog at my feet, and the peace of the country around me.

I don't know how I ended up here, and part of me wants to run; far, far away.

But the other part of me never wants to leave.

Halfway through the movie, I have to use the bathroom. Rhett leads me inside, holding the old screen door open, as I walk into the kitchen. The white cabinets and butcher block countertops are charming, and the original pine floors creak as I walk across them. The kitchen was definitely renovated, but there's also a mixture of bachelor pad items, like the folding chairs at the beautiful farmhouse dining table. I think back to the showroom-esque home I shared with Jackson, and overwhelming warmth fills my chest.

This is what a home is supposed to be, for most people, I think.

Rhett taps his knuckles on the bathroom door. "I'll wait for you outside. But would you like anything to drink?" He points over his shoulder at a vintage style refrigerator.

"Do you have Diet Coke by chance?" I asked, crinkling my nose.

"Of course, I have Diet Coke." Rhett smirks. "But the question is, do you want whiskey in it?"

"Of course."

"That's my girl," Rhett said, turning on his heels back into the kitchen.

Thank god, because my face turned bright red as I ducked into the bathroom. I grip the pedestal sink and attempt to clear my head.

Rhett was back outside by the time I came out, so I took a moment to linger inside. It's not polite to snoop, but I can't help but look at the gallery wall of family photos in the hallway.

There were photos of what I could only assume was a young Rhett. They were adorable. One was him standing next to a river with an older man's arm around him. Another was a photo of a pretty woman with the same blue eyes hugging what I'd assume was Rhett a few years back. And the most precious of all was a picture of Mabel under a Christmas tree with a red bow around her neck.

I'd wager that under the tough exterior of the rugged man sitting outside waiting for me, was a soft heart.

I could only hope.

Because for most of my life, I was surrounded by cold exteriors and colder hearts disguised as love.

CHAPTER EIGHTEEN

Rhett

I thought because I hadn't been on a real date for years, that tonight would be awkward.

What I never imagined, or rather wouldn't let myself imagine, was her laughing in my backyard, her arms wrapped around my dog like they're best friends, her voice carrying through these old oaks like she'd always been here, always belonged out here.

But it happened and I'm glad I followed her into her apartment, not taking 'no' for an answer. But as my knee bounces, my hands fidgety as the night continues on, knowing I have to take her back at some point, all I can selfishly think of is how to see this girl again. I don't think my dog would ever forgive me if I didn't bring her back.

She keeps taking sips of the cheap whiskey and Coke I made her, commenting on the movie, and I'm barely keeping up, my thoughts on everything but the movie.

"So, you have any fun plans this summer?" I ask, hoping she doesn't have a million dates lined up.

But I'd be a fool to believe Audrey will stay single for long. There's probably a stadium full of guys who've been waiting for their chance with her.

She sets her drink down, shaking her head as she swirls a gold bracelet around her small wrist.

"Not anymore." She shrugs and I curse myself, wishing I could eat my question. I hate that I made her think of *him*. "But over Labor Day weekend, I usually go back to New England. My parents throw an end of summer soiree at their beach home in the Hamptons, and my brother and I would most likely be dismembered if we didn't show up. They like to act like it's a casual barbeque, but hiring a private chef to cook lobster table side doesn't exactly scream 'casual', you know?" She rolls her eyes, sucking in a breath.

"Can't say I do." I chuckle but she scrunches her nose and shakes her head.

"What about you?"

"You're pretty much looking at it. I have a full calendar of jobs and most Friday nights you can find me right here in this yard. I'm not much of a planner."

"That sounds amazing, actually." Audrey's face lights up, and her hair falls over her bare shoulders as she stares off into the meadow behind my house. "I never thought I'd be moving in with my friend, Penny, this summer. That was definitely not in the plans." Her face falls and I get the urge to throttle a man's neck who I never met.

At the same time, I should be thanking him for freeing Audrey from a lifetime of whatever shit he was going to throw her way.

"Plans are overrated. All my favorite memories happened spontaneously," I reply, chuckling but Audrey doesn't match my sentiment. She stares at me for a moment, and I can't decipher what she's thinking. Which drives me wild. "If you ever want to get out of the city and blow off some steam, you can come on by. There's about ten acres beyond this yard, and the only one who ever explores it is Mabel. She'd probably like some company."

She narrows her eyes and for a moment, I wonder if I went too far. The truth was, I wouldn't care if Audrey showed up and kicked back in the glider on my front porch whenever she pleased. She wouldn't even have to talk to me, though I couldn't promise I'd be able to keep my eyes off her for long.

I wasn't always a nice guy. Lord knows I've been an ass more often than not. I've broken a few hearts. But I was trying to leave that in the past, carve out a life I could be proud of. I had no idea what it was supposed to look like yet, but I liked the idea of it involving Audrey Elson.

"You're just extending an open invitation to a person you barely know…to what, sit on your porch?" Her eyes were still narrowed at me.

"Okay, when you put it that way, you make me sound like a crazy person. But yeah, that's pretty much what I'm doing."

She nods slowly. "Hmm…"

"You're not going to suddenly pepper spray me, are you?" I joke, and see a glint in her eye, followed by a tiny smile.

"No, Rhett, I'm not going to pepper spray you. I'm just wondering how the hell we crossed paths."

"You regretting it already?" I down the last bit of my whiskey.

"Actually, I'm not." She smiles, locking eyes with me, and at that moment, I knew one thing about this summer.

I would be doing whatever it takes to see her again.

Chapter Nineteen

Audrey

As the moon illuminates our path and gravel crunches beneath our feet, Rhett walks me to his truck at the end of the night, the air thick with unspoken words between us.

I steal tiny glances of him as we get closer, slowing my pace, willing this night not to end. He didn't try to kiss me tonight. He was respectful, listened more than he talked, and I found myself wondering when I'd see him again.

Rhett stands with me at the passenger side, neither of us reaching for the door handle.

"I—"

"Can I—" We speak at the same time, and both release tiny laughs. I trace his lips to his eyes, unsure where to look, unsure my ribcage can hold my hammering heart much longer.

"What were you going to say? You first." My voice is low, breathy.

His palm brushes the side of my jaw until he's cupping my face gently. I nearly forget the basic functions of my body as he boxes me in against his truck.

"Can I kiss you?" he asks, his parted lips already so close to mine, I can almost feel them, taste them. I nod softly in his grip, my eyes shuttering closed as his blue eyes settle on my lips. Rhett's other hand slides up the small of my back, pulling me into him. I melt in his warm grip, breathe in his woodsy scent, and let out a tiny gasp as his lips brush gently against mine. They are full and soft, and all I can focus on is how I need *more.* Rhett snakes his other hand up, my face cupped between his calloused strong hands, and I grip the front of his shirt, releasing the built-up tension through my parted lips. The warmth of his tongue caresses my lips and I shudder under his grip.

His touch makes me forget where I am. And who I am. A single kiss from this man sends a ripple of electricity through me, but when he pulls away, breathless, all I can do is smile like a fool, lost in the intensity of the moment.

"Thank you," I breathe out, and he cocks his head back slightly.

"You're thanking *me*...for what?"

"For stalking me."

This gets him to laugh, and the sound reaches places of my cold heart I'm not sure have ever been touched.

"I never thought I'd get you to say yes to a date." He cheeses hard, his eyes crinkling as he looks down at me.

Through hazy eyes, I slide my hand down his arm, feeling his corded muscles, and grab his hand. I squeeze it before dropping it, even though I feel unsteady in my footing.

Because as I turn towards the trunk and murmur, "I should be getting back," the only thing running through my head is that I've never been kissed like that.

Rhett starts up the engine, and I sit closer to him this time on the bench seat of his old pickup truck. We make small talk as we drive through the night, and his hand finds mine in the dark, holding it gently.

I answer his questions while struggling to silence the thoughts swirling in my mind about what this meant.

Because that kiss felt like the first one that made time stop, like they talk about in books and movies. It was the kind that made me forget everything except the other person connected to me. Everything I thought I knew about love, about relationships, I'm beginning to question. I'm beginning to wonder if I know anything at all. Other than the fact that I'll never forget about tonight. Rhett rescued me again.

That's more than any other man ever has. Even the ones who claimed to love to.

If tonight was a onetime thing, I'm grateful, because for one night I got to be a different Audrey. I got to be carefree, away from the people and things that weigh me down.

And the man next to me is responsible for that.

Chapter Twenty

Audrey

I check my phone three times before I accept the fact I won't be getting any more sleep. Nothing new there.

The apartment is silent at 5 a.m., but I'm itching to get busy, so I shuffle into the kitchen and switch on the under-cabinet lights. They cast enough light to see what I'm doing without breaking the peaceful magic of the early morning. Early mornings before anyone else is stirring are my favorite. Usually, I can think the clearest at that time, too...*usually*. But this morning my mind can't process anything besides a man with rough hands, and blue eyes, and soft lips. So, I do what I haven't been able to do in a very long time.

Like muscle memory, it begins. The clinking of metal bowls, a bag of flour thudding on the countertop, the oven beeping as it heats up. I fasten my hair back in a clip, roll up the sleeves of my sweatshirt, and pull up a recipe on my phone.

White chocolate macadamia nut cookies with cranberries; one of my favorites. If I ever opened a bakery, I'd have a variety of unique cookies. Opening a bakery is just a daydream of mine, like when people daydream about becoming a popstar or something crazy like that. Maybe in another life.

I beat the sugar and eggs together while fighting off thoughts of his mouth hovering inches from mine. I find myself subconsciously running my fingers along my lips, as if I could still feel him there. Last night, when I said goodbye outside Penny's apartment building, he kissed me again; long and hard, hungry, and wanting.

The kind of kiss I could easily become addicted to.

Shaking my head, I scoop the cookie dough onto the sheets, and quickly the apartment smells sweet and sugary.

Baking eases my mind—or it used to. But after finishing the cookies and packaging them up neatly in containers, I am still restless.

So, I gather more ingredients and make something I've never made before. For a dog who isn't mine. And for reasons I was not ready to dissect.

It would be ridiculous to show up at Rhett's house with cookies and dog treats a day after our first date...right?

That was borderline stalkerish and downright weird. He didn't even live nearby, so I couldn't pretend I was 'in the neighborhood'.

As I press the bone-shaped cutter into the blueberry dog dough, I decide it was absolutely an unhinged idea.

I attempted to unpack, but the tiny walk-in closet in Penny's guest room is barely a fraction of what I'm used to. While I'm grateful, it makes unpacking feel pointless. Even my favorite trashy reality shows can't distract me from my unfolding life.

Right at noon, as if he somehow knows I'm spiraling, my phone lights up with a text from Jackson.

> **Jackson:** Did you see my email yesterday? The attorney drew up all the paperwork for the house, you just need to sign it. By the end of the week, it'll be in your name.

> **Audrey:** What? I never saw an email. I never asked for the house, Jackson, why would you think I wanted it?

> **Jackson:** You're welcome? It's paid for, so you're coming out on top here, Audrey. I get the apartment; you get the house. I could've left you with nothing, remember that.

I have to fight the urge to chuck my phone at the ground as I read the texts, imagining his degrading tone. It makes me nauseous.

> **Audrey:** Just tell me where and when to sign the paperwork.

The little black cloud which was Jackson Tippins was always showing up at the worst moments. The thing was, I didn't really want the house a year ago when we bought it. I thought it was too much, and I still do. But Jackson always gets his way, and frankly I didn't have it in me to fight this. It didn't fully make sense to me why he insisted I take the house, though nothing he has done lately made sense.

I sit down to open my email after we stop talking, and indeed see a glaring email from him, the attorney cc'd. It's a multi-million dollar home that's now mine. He'd expect me to move into it, and so would my parents. But what if I sold it? What if I sold it and moved to New York, as a big *fuck you* to Jackson?

It could be my small act of rebellion.

But my bigger act of rebellion was the other man blowing up my phone.

> **Rhett:** Hey, I really enjoyed last night. Hope you finally got some sleep.

Instantly, my shoulders relax from where Jackson's words tensed them.

> **Audrey:** I did, thanks. It was great. Tell Mabel I said hi

> **Rhett:** Maybe you can tell her yourself sometime. I'd love to see you again.

> **Audrey:** Yeah, I'd like that. Let me check my calendar and get back to you.

Wow, could I sound any lamer?

> **Rhett:** Sure thing. Just text me!

> **Audrey:** I actually baked a bunch of cookies. Penny and I won't eat them. I'll be in the area. I could drop some off?

Immediately I regret it, but before I can redeem myself, three dots appear.

> **Rhett:** Are you kidding? You've made my day. I'll

He sends me his address and before I know it, I'm getting ready, and loading up three dozen cookies, and dog biscuits into my car.

First though, I made a pit stop in Forest Hills to check on the progress of the house Jackson insisted be mine. Walking through the front door, I stopped to talk to the contractor, and as he filled me in on an update, I glazed over; thinking about the months spent picking out finishes and floors, wall colors, and landscaping plans. It all seems like a blur now, and I can't believe Jackson and I had spent a week deciding between two shades of beige for a bedroom we'd never even sleep in.

The contractor told me I could take a walk through to see the finished second floor, but I politely declined and walked as fast as I could back to my car. Pushing the thoughts of that foreign life from my head, I drove straight to Roseville.

I keep wondering how truly unhinged this is. I mean, maybe a neighbor would do it, right? But I'm not a neighbor. And I lied when I said I'd be in the area. Forest Hills is nowhere near Roseville.

But before I can convince myself to turn around, I find myself turning down the narrow street that leads to his winding driveway, my stomach turning abruptly with it.

The plan was simple: drop the cookies on the doorstep and go straight back home. It's nearly dinner time anyway, and I had a bubble bath, and a new bottle of red wine waiting for me. It would be fine.

Carefully walking up the loose front steps, I placed the containers on his worn out door mat and texted him quickly.

I think part of me would have made any excuse to see this house again. If only to make sure last night wasn't an apparition—considering everything about my life the last few weeks has felt surreal.

But it was real, and every warm familiar feeling came rushing back to me as I stood on the porch. Peering into the front window, the house was dark.

"If you're looking for something to steal, you came to the wrong house!" Rhett's sudden voice sends me flying back, hand clutching my chest as I snap my eyes shut and take a deep breath.

"Holy shit. I didn't know you were home." I latch onto the porch railing, as my face grows hot.

Thank god for the porch railing, because I also wasn't ready to be greeted by a glistening, shirtless man with a toolbelt low on his hips. Rhett squints at me as I frantically search for something to say.

He slowly and painfully drags his eyes over me. I swallow, fanning myself for a moment.

"I've been working all day in my shop." He nods towards the two-story garage behind the house.

It never occurred to me he could be working from home. Rhett proceeds to reach into his back pocket, pulling his buzzing phone out. "Just got your text." He smiles, reading it quickly as I bite my lip, trying not to stare at the artistic ink splattered across his chest.

"You made my dog treats?" His brows knit together.

"Yeah, I had leftover ingredients, so it was simple." I shrug, running my palms down the sides of my hips, as Rhett steps closer, closing the distance between us on the porch.

"You are the most interesting person I've ever met," he says slowly, wiping a bead of sweat off his brow.

"Oh, certainly not." I choke, taking a step back. I've been called smart, demure, composed, and pretty, but never interesting. It throws me for a loop. "Well, I know you're busy, so I won't keep you!" I hike my thumb over my shoulder towards my car.

"I'm actually just finishing up in the workshop." He pauses, placing his left arm on the railing, boxing me in. For the second time in twenty-four hours. "Would you like to stay for dinner?"

My brain goes blank because nothing about being in this man's presence makes me act normal. I was fine yesterday until the kiss. Until I fully accepted that it had not been a 'friend date'.

There's no simple explanation. Rhett simply unravels me.

"Full disclosure...I didn't cook it." Rhett bites his lip, shifting his feet. "My mom dropped it off this morning and I'm only a tiny bit ashamed to admit that."

"That's so nice of you, but I don't want to impose."

"Darlin', it's me and the dog...it would be nice to have a person to talk to over dinner."

I couldn't find a reason to say no. It was dinner with Rhett or returning to an unpacked apartment bedroom. He wins again.

"Okay, thank you. I'd love to stay."

Rhett leans forward, kissing me on the temple, which is somehow even more intimate than a kiss on the lips. "I have to clean up in the shop and rinse really quick, but I won't be long. Make yourself at home. Cups are above the microwave, and the fridge is full of...well, beer and sweet tea."

"Go, I'll be fine. Seriously. I'm a big girl, I can take care of myself." I attempt a joke, my stomach still fluttering.

His lips twitch like he's going to say something, but he obliges and skips down the steps towards his garage. I walk through the front door into the quiet house and go straight to the kitchen. Looking around, I try to distract myself, but as I glance out the kitchen window, I see Rhett carrying a large stack of lumber over his shoulder, making it look easy, and my core clenches in unspeakable ways. My god, was that all it took for me to turn into a horny puddle? A man doing manual labor?

Quickly, I peel myself away.

Rhett told me to make myself at home, so I do just that. Well, to the best of my abilities. Because usually when people say that they mean have a seat, take your coat off, have a glass of water. But I had a feeling Rhett actually meant it. I didn't know him very well—*yet*—but he'd struck me as a person who'd give you the shirt off their back. I hadn't known many people like him. Or maybe, none at all.

I peek in the fridge and chuckled because he wasn't lying. There's a twelve-pack of beer, a pitcher of tea, the makings for a sandwich, and some questionable containers. Plus, one large casserole dish with a smiley face note stuck to it; from his mom, I'm sure. No wonder his eyes lit up when I brought him cookies.

I pour myself a tall glass of water and head back outside, settling onto the wooden porch swing with my legs tucked beneath me. The yard is cast with a warm orange glow, the beginning of the summer evening. Sounds of frogs and buzzing cicadas welcome me, and of course, the panting of a dog whose loyalty I won over without even trying.

"Come here, girl," I whisper to her.

Mabel slowly gets herself up, trudging over to me with those dopey eyes and ears that flop in the breeze. While I scratch her ears, my phone dings and I pull it out to see a new email. I open it to be greeted by a picture of a new apartment available in NYC in my neighborhood of choice. I scroll through the photos. It's not bad; it has the pre-war architectural details I love, but the view is gray buildings and city lights.

Mabel nudges my hand, insisting I keep petting her. Sliding my phone back into my pocket, I scratch her neck, my eyes drifting across the sprawling front yard.

I wish the city had views like this.

"Want a treat?" I tease, remembering I had one of the homemade biscuits in my pocket, hoping maybe she'd be around when I got here.

Mabel lets out a howl, startling me. "Shh! You're going to get me in trouble!" I hiss at her through a smile. I pull a treat from my pocket and break it in half, holding it up to see if she knows 'sit' and 'paw'. She slaps her big paw hard in my palm, demanding I give her the homemade treat. I drop it in her mouth, and she swallows it whole, staring at me expectantly for another one.

"Good girl!" I coo, cupping her face in my hands.

"You know you're creating a monster. She's going to fall in love with you, might even try to follow you home," Rhett teases from the ajar front door, where he stands with a beer loosely dangling from his fingers. I hadn't even heard him come out.

I was still leaning down towards his dog when I glanced up. His hair is wet and messy, his skin bronzed and glowing under a white t-shirt, which makes his blue eyes shine.

"I can think of worse things," I add, forgetting what we were even talking about. All I see is him.

"Ready to eat? I have it heating up in the oven now."

"Yes!" I push myself off the porch swing, taking one more glance at the beautiful front yard. "It's so peaceful out here. It reminds me of the summer camp my parents would ship me off to in upstate New York. Minus the drama that only teenage girls can manifest."

Rhett chuckles, holding the door open for me.

"I think that's a compliment." I walk past him, smelling his pine body soap. "I can't relate, though. I spent my summers collecting eggs from the coop on my Pawpaw's farm and sneaking cigarettes behind the barn with my cousins. My summer smelled like barn animals." He laughs, following me down the short hallway into the kitchen.

"Oh, we snuck our fair share of cigarettes. I was a very wild teenager," I reply, turning over my shoulder to raise my eyebrows at him. "Hence the mandatory summer camps, so my mother didn't have to track me down."

"So, you have a wild streak in you?" Rhett rakes his eyes down my body, making me blush.

"I *used* to."

Rhett brings the bottle of the beer up to his lips, pausing as his eyes hold mine. "You sure about that? I bet there's still something wild in there."

He tips the bottle back, and I watch the column of his throat shift as he swallows the amber liquid. Sucking my bottom lip in, I'm grateful for Mabel who pushes herself between Rhett and I.

But the little distraction doesn't eradicate the way it feels to have Rhett's eyes on me.

With one glance, he lights me on fire, making me feel more alive, and more aware of the air around me than I'd felt in a lifetime.

CHAPTER TWENTY-ONE

Rhett

I guess I could've been embarrassed I was sitting at my kitchen table, serving homemade barbecue my mom dropped off in a casserole dish to Audrey. I loved my mom; that wasn't the issue.

But after Dad died, she started needing *me* more. She found so much joy in cooking, and with my work schedule, most days I forget to even eat, so she made it her mission to bring meals to me. I knew it was good for her to stay busy, so I relented. I also never intended to share a meal my mom made for me with a beautiful woman.

But hey, it's better to just lay it all out as it is, right? No hiding shit.

And seeing Audrey sit across from me in my kitchen was stirring up things in me I dismissed years ago. She brought a lightness to this house I never thought I'd find.

But maybe I was getting ahead of myself.

"Please tell your mom this the best cornbread I've ever had." Audrey's eyes rolled back in her head as she took another bite of the homemade meal, and I let out a breathy chuckle.

"I will." I took another bite myself. "If I tell her I shared dinner with someone though, I highly doubt she'll care about the taste of the food."

"Oh, yeah? Why's that?" Audrey sets down her fork, her hazel eyes locking in on me.

"I think she's beginning to worry that my only remaining friends are

Mabel and Ky—who I'll never be introducing you to, by the way. He knows too much about me and has no filter, which makes him a wild card," I half joked.

"I like wild cards," Audrey said, and I shook my head.

"Exactly why you won't be meeting him for a while."

"Well, I'd have to keep seeing you for that to happen," she adds dryly as she tucks her hair behind her ear, her eyes cast down.

"Is this your way of telling me it's over?" I tease but my heart races in a way it has no business doing.

"I'd have to know what *this* is to decide if it was over."

I sit up straighter, leaning back in my chair so I can get a better gauge on Audrey, though it's nearly useless. She is unreadable at times. But my god, do I want to crack her code.

"This is *dinner*," I start and as she rolls her eyes, her lips curling up in an annoyed smirk, I continue. "Just dinner for two people who can't seem to stay apart from each other for whatever reason. This is me, trying to figure out how to stretch this meal out as long as I can because the moment your car pulls out of my driveway, I'll be left wondering how the hell I can convince you to see me again. That's what this is."

A tiny smile creeps up on her face, and her eyes soften.

"Can I be painfully honest with you?" Audrey asks, and I hold my breath, eagerly leaning towards her. Hoping this means she is learning to trust me. I want to be a safe space for her to land.

"Of course."

"I don't know what I'm doing..." She lets out a humorless laugh. "Like in every aspect of my life. I feel like I've lost control of everything lately. And I'm only telling you this because I don't want you to have too many expectations."

It's not what I expected to hear, but I place my hand on her knee, scooting my chair closer so my legs are barricading hers. She was honest with me, and now it's my turn.

"That makes two of us. I have been drifting through life, one day at a time, just getting by. But I know ever since I saw you on that rooftop, I haven't been able to stop thinking about you."

She smiles shyly, tilting her head towards me, getting closer and closer. It's just us in this kitchen, but when I look into her eyes, it's like we are the only two people in this world.

"Maybe...maybe we can be lost together?" she offers, reaching right into my chest and grabbing the fragments of my beating heart.

My heart is hers. Even if I tried to stop it, it's already hers.

Our foreheads touch gently before Audrey speaks the words I'd been waiting to hear since she got here.

"Will you kiss me now?"

Chapter Twenty-Two

Audrey

Rhett pulls me from the chair I sat in, lifting me to my feet. Our foreheads rest against each other before his lips touch mine, my breath caught in my throat. My palms find his sturdy chest, and I steady myself against him, needing him closer.

The kitchen walls fade away, along with time, as he walks us backwards into a door. Reaching behind him, Rhett turns the doorknob, pulling me with him as I laugh against his delicious mouth. A bedroom opens before us. His bedroom.

This is where old Audrey would've freaked out. Maybe she was still here, in me, worrying about moving too fast. Worrying about how different Rhett and I were, about how our worlds didn't align. Worrying about how Jackson had been the only man to see me naked. But as Rhett's eyes ask for permission, and I nod, clinging to him, I silence the *old* me.

We fall clumsily inside the small room, and Rhett backs me up until my legs hit the edge of the mattress. My hands grip the bedspread behind me as a soft moan slips out, Rhett's lip tracing a path down my neck to my collarbone, igniting a spark that lights up my entire body.

His fingers slip under my shirt, my skin igniting with the gentle yet needy touch. He pulls my shirt over my head, and cups my face, kissing me softly again. I find his belt buckle, undressing him slowly, taking in the ripple and strength...and kindness of the man before me. In a few slow motions, our remaining clothes are puddled on the floor.

Rhett backs me up onto the white duvet, until my back hits the rustic wooden headboard. The evening light shines through the window, casting shadows across his face, and it's quiet besides the hammering in my chest. As Rhett kneels over me, boxing me in, he pauses, and I trace the shape of his lips with my fingertip, moving down to the tattoo spanning his chest.

His skin is warm under my touch, his eyes ocean blue as they grow lustful, looking at me.

He hasn't even touched me yet, and already this is the most intimate I've ever felt with anyone.

My heart was raw, but with him it felt safe.

"You're so beautiful, Audrey," he murmurs, dropping down to his elbows so his chest is hovering over mine. "All of you," he adds, before my mind melts and his lips find mine again. He kisses me gently, then with more vigor, his mouth moving down my neck. My chest rises with each breath, as he lavishes my hardened nipples, and I inhale sharply.

I feel everything...his rough palm cupping my jaw, his soft lips on the most sensitive parts of me. I wonder if he can feel my heart racing beneath his head.

I wonder if he can feel the shock radiating from my heart—the disbelief at how natural it feels to be here with him. To trust him with the most vulnerable pieces of me. To let him see the tangled mess of my soul, and a body no one else has touched since the man who shattered it.

Rhett's hardened length presses against my thigh, but he pauses, pulling his mouth away from my chest where he'd been kissing me, sucking until I was breathless.

"Tell me to stop, and I will," he says with a strained voice. I glance down at his powerful body over mine, and I shake my head. I want to come undone.

I want to feel what it's like to be with Rhett.

Hanging onto the back of his neck, I guide my hips up, needing to feel him inside of me, to finally lose *complete* control.

To prove to myself I am in control—that every decision in this new life, whatever it may become, is mine and mine alone. No one else gets to decide for me.

Without breaking the spell that we find ourselves in, he reaches over to the nightstand, grabbing protection and rolling it on quickly. Rhett swallows my moans as he enters me, supporting my arched back when he thrusts in slow, methodical motions. We never broke again from each other, my eyes never leaving his, his mouth never leaving my body for more than a second.

Rhett takes his time, his fingers finding my sensitive spot, focusing solely on my pleasure while I drag my nails down his back, unable to contain the ecstasy as I writhe in his arms.

And as we both lay still, breathless on the bed inside his farmhouse bedroom, the setting sun casts a pink glow through the windows.

From now on, there is a distinct before and after in my life.

Before I met Rhett on the rooftop. Before I accepted the promotion. *Before, before, before.*

I was now in the after. The complicated but blissful after.

"I wish I had something else, you sure this will do?" Rhett hands me a long t-shirt and I happily slip it on, breathing in the scent of him. Cedar and musk. Rhett smooths out his wild hair in the mirror over his dresser and catches me watching. I blush, but his lips pull to the side. I'm not used to being noticed after sex. Jackson would either pass out or start scrolling through emails, but Rhett...he doesn't give me a chance to recover before filling me with more butterflies.

"Join me outside?" he asks, and I follow him onto the screened in porch off his bedroom. The porch is like the rest of the house, quirky but charming with its slightly tilted floor. Wind chimes hang over a set of wicker furniture, complete with pink and white floral cushions. I sit down on the sofa, sinking into the cushion, and watch Rhett light a citronella candle.

"I didn't take you as a cottagecore man," I tease, as he sits down next to me, reaching an arm around my shoulder.

"A what?" he asks, cocking his head to the side.

"Oh, it's just the aesthetic of this porch is very quaint and pastel...and you're very...not?" I cringe, frustrated by how easily Rhett flusters me, leaving me unable to string together a simple sentence.

But his hearty laugh eases my worry, and he smiles at me. "I built a sunporch for an older couple last summer and they insisted I take their old outdoor set and all the decor. They were so sweet; I didn't want to hurt their feelings. So, I guess that makes me cottagecore." He winks and I just shake my head, heart warmed by how considerate of a guy he is.

I also didn't want him to think I cared about material things like the furniture in his house. Sure, his home was patched up in most places, but I felt something here I'd never felt anywhere else.

I felt accepted. There were no pretentious precursors to being here. It almost felt unfair.

Like, what did I do to deserve being here, with him?

"All I get at my job is dry eyes from the computer screen and permanent knots in my neck from stress."

"If only you knew someone with large hands willing to massage you,"

Rhett adds, winking at me, and this time I knowingly blush. I wouldn't say no to a massage from this man. Ever.

We fall into a comfortable silence, letting the heat wrap around us as the meadow just beyond the house begins to come to life. The meadow makes me think of the books I read as kids. I didn't grow up in a yard that was meant to play in, or a house that garnered imagination. Certainly nothing *charming*. The Elson homes were built and furnished for impressions, not comfort.

"What made you buy this place?"

I glanced up at Rhett, whose arms dangled around the back of the sofa as he gazed over his property.

"I bought it because of my dad, actually." He clears his throat. "He died twelve years ago." My hand finds his and my heart aches.

"I'm so sorry, Rhett." He smiles weakly and continues, his eyes tracing the old porches' wood beams.

"Thank you. We had to pass this house to get to my grandparents, and every time we did, my dad would always comment about what a shame it was that they let it go. The family moved to the city and let it fall apart. No one wanted to buy it. It needed so much structural work done. About five years ago, my lease was up with Ky. I was coming out of a rough spot, but I had money saved, and I found myself driving out this way, saw the house, and knew I had to have it." Rhett licked his lips, his blue eyes now on me, talking directly into my heart.

"Wow, so it was meant to be."

"Guess you could say that. Everyone thought I was crazy. You should've seen this place; it was a damn mess. I shared the kitchen with a family of racoons for a month." He laughs, reminiscing. There's a heaviness in the air and I stay silent, giving him the space to talk. "In a way, this house saved me."

Somehow, I understand. This place heals, I can feel it.

But I also know how it feels to need a distraction, to need to be busy enough that you can escape reality.

Like this relationship.

My stomach plummets but I squeezed Rhett's hand.

"I feel honored to know." I grin at him, lightening the mood.

"Something about you city girls, you could get a dog to confess he stole a bone."

I shove him playfully, but Rhett pulls me into his arms, kissing my temple.

It doesn't seem right that only twenty-four hours ago was our first date. But if we are being honest, I started baring my soul to Rhett the night on the rooftop and never really stopped.

CHAPTER TWENTY-THREE

Audrey

The purring and sputtering of a coffee maker woke me from my slumber Sunday morning. As I peel my eyes open and see the shiplap walls around me, it takes a moment to register where I am. And that I shared the bed last night with a blonde-haired man who held me all night. It was never in the plan, but somewhere between playing cards on the screened in porch and laughing my head off as Mabel body slammed the bedroom door, trying to get in to sleep on the bed, I grew tired. And as naturally as Rhett and I found each other, I found myself sleeping in his arms.

Rolling out of bed, I'm grateful to have a moment to pull myself together. I scurry into the bathroom after grabbing my clothes from yesterday and freshen up the best I can. Luckily, I never go anywhere without an obscene number of toiletries and cosmetics. Though this morning I forgo the blush, as my cheeks seem to have a permanent rosiness, and my skin a new glow that I'm not angry about.

Ten minutes later, I mosey out into the kitchen with my hair in a braid, wearing jean shorts, and a button-down linen top. And maybe a few spritz of perfume.

With his back to me, Rhett stands in front of the coffee pot, filling two mugs. The clock on the stove reads 9 a.m., and a bout of panic rises in my chest.

I haven't slept past 5 a.m. since the day Jackson left me. I guess it was long overdue, but I also still have an apartment— or room—to unpack.

"I was just about to get out of your hair," I pipe up.

Rhett turns around slowly, his blue eyes raking me over and crosses his arms. "Good morning to you, too." His gray sweatpants lay low on his hips, leaving little to the imagination and an Atlanta Braves baseball cap hides his messy mop of dirty blond hair.

Embarrassed, I slap my hand to my eyes. I should've left last night. My god, what was I thinking? "Good morning, I'm sorry. I just...I don't want to overstay my welcome and I'm sure you have stuff to do."

Rhett offers me the coffee mug. "I'm in no rush, seriously. At least have coffee with me?"

I hesitate but I crumble quickly because I can't deny coffee, and I can't deny him.

"Okay." I take it from him, and grin over the hot steam. "Thank you."

He bobs his head, and I try my best to keep my eyes off his bare chest and V-shaped muscles.

"I'll walk you out soon." He sets his mug down. "I just need to get clothes on, so you can stop eye fucking me." He winks and my jaw drops. I scoff as he walks into his bedroom.

I don't recall banter ever being this easy with anyone but Penny. But before I can analyze more about what that means, Mabel wobbles up next to me, stretching her long legs, her nose in the air towards the countertop.

"What is it, sweet girl?"

Mabel lets out a low grumble in response. I crouch down to pet her, but she protests, nudging my hand toward the counter.

"You want more treats?" I whisper, chuckling as I snatch a treat from the counter. "I'll meet you out on the porch, Rhett," I called out, just loud enough so he could hear me through the slightly open bedroom door.

Mabel follows me to the front porch. As soon as I sit on the swing, she sits, too, trying to give me her paw before I even ask. I break a piece of the treat off, shake her paw, and give her the treat I made.

I can't believe I was going to let Jackson deprive me of a life without a dog.

Mabel begins showing off her other tricks, offering me alternating paws without even being prompted, when the sudden crunch of tires on gravel startles me. I turn, squinting against the bright morning sun as a car drives down the driveway towards the house. My body freezes as my stomach drops—a sense of urgency to get out of here takes over me. I take a few sips of coffee, torn between going inside to hide or being a darn adult, and staying put.

Before I reach a decision, the car stops and out steps a woman with grayish blonde hair knotted on top of her head. Mabel ends her pony show, galloping down the steps towards the stranger.

"How's my grandbaby! Your papa sure is feeding you well, Miss Mabel!" I can't help but smile at this woman's sweet demeanor, but then that smile turns to dread.

Grandbaby...holy shit, this is Rhett's mom.

Smoothing my braid, and rubbing my tired eyes, I pray I don't look like I just rolled out of her son's bed.

A box of leafy greens rests on his mom's hips as she walks toward the porch, a curious smile on her lips. Her blue sundress hangs over yellow rain boots, and as she gets closer, I can see her and Rhett have the same eyes.

"Well, you are certainly not my son," she chuckles, and I stand, taking a few steps to close the gap between us on the porch.

"Hi there, I'm Audrey. Rhett's inside. I was actually on my way out." I nod towards my SUV, even though all my stuff was inside. Including my shoes.

"Nice to meet you, hon. I'm Renee, Rhett's mom, obviously. And please, don't leave because of me! I was just dropping off some stuff from my garden." She offloads the overflowing box onto the table by the front door.

"Wow, did you grow all of that?" I can't hide the awe in my voice and notice a twinkle in Renee's eyes as she admires all the produce.

"I did!" She nods proudly. "Rhett surely told you that he grew up on a farm. When he was little, we grew strawberries, corn, beans...you name it. If I wanted to try growing it, my husband would find a new patch of dirt to make it happen." Her eyes glazed over in a sad but lovely way. "I'm retired now, but I still hobby farm a bit, and sell produce at the farmer's market. Nothing big like it used to be."

"That's really admirable, though. A lot of people can't say they grow their own food."

"You have a garden?" his mom asks, and I shake my head sheepishly. I've never even attempted to plant anything. Jackson said when we finally had our house, we'd hire a gardener to put in a rose garden in the backyard, like it was some grand gesture. He thought they were my favorite flower, no matter how many times I reminded him it was blue hydrangeas.

"Oh no, I can't even keep a mint plant alive on my window seal."

"Hmm. Just keep trying, you'll get it. Gardening truly is the best free therapy." She laughs and I smile because it's contagious. Must run in the family. A family I have no business meeting. This is just a summer fling, and flings are meant to be quick, and dirty, and secret in my case.

Relief floods me as Rhett appears in the doorway.

"Mom! What are you doing here?" Rhett's voice rises an octave, but he pulled her into a hug regardless. Behind her back he mouths *I'm sorry* and I wave my hand, dismissing it.

"Oh, you know, just dropping off a few things. And meeting your lovely *friend*, Audrey." Her eyebrows shoot up and my cheeks grow hot.

"I'll let you two chat, I really should be going."

"You sure?" Rhett says at the same time his mom interjects.

"Where did you say you're from?"

The question catches me off guard, but I hold my coffee mug to my chest and answer politely. "I'm from Connecticut originally, but I live in the city now." I smile tightly, unsure what she'll make of that.

"Oh, how lovely, and how did you two meet?"

"Mom, I think Audrey is trying to get out of here," Rhett adds, leaning against the house. The cheerfulness was gone from his demeanor.

She slaps his chest with the back of her hand.

Rhett answers for me though. "I was doing work in her building. We met a few weeks ago."

"You know that's how your father and I met." Her expression is dreamy again and Rhett fidgets, but his small smile for his mom doesn't falter. It's clear he loves her, and it's endearing to see a parent and adult child relationship that doesn't look like ulterior motives and control.

"Oh, really?" I ask, curiosity piqued.

Renee's hands come together as excitement blooms in her blue eyes.

"We met in California. He came out to see a Giants baseball game with a few of his buddies. I was a cocktail waitress at one of the bars near the stadium. He wandered in, bright eyed and bushy tailed. A tall, lanky North Carolina boy fresh out of college who kept calling me ma'am. He asked if he could take me out for dinner the next day, and well, the rest is history."

"You don't hear many love stories as classic as that anymore," I add, meaning it. "And Rhett didn't mention you weren't from here."

Renee waves her hand. "Oh honey, I'm a California girl. I thought my father was going to kill Nick when he convinced me to move to the East Coast to take over his family's farm. But the truth is, I would've gone anywhere for him. He was my best friend."

It grows quiet and Rhett shifts again behind her, pain crossing his features before it disappears, his eyes finding mine. "Audrey, don't get her started on stories or you won't be home until Monday morning."

"Okay, okay, I'm done! I'm out of here!" Renee laughs, hugging her son goodbye, and waves at me as she makes her way back to her car.

Rhett and I stand there, side by side on the wooden porch.

"Sorry about that." He closes his eyes, pinching the bridge of his nose.

"Don't apologize, your mom is so sweet." I meant it, even if this threw me off. I don't think I ever left a conversation with Jackson's mother Vivianne without feeling like I needed a drink and an anxiety pill. But talking to Renee felt like a warm hug.

"You know how moms are."

I laughed at Rhett's sentiment because if my parents saw me and the way I'm derailing everything right now, I doubt Rhett would describe their response as *sweet*.

"Trust me, there's not a single similarity between your mom and mine. Consider yourself lucky for that."

"How do you mean?" Rhett's brow furrowed, and a lump rose in my throat as I crossed my arms over my chest.

"Oh, nothing. Your mom just seems like a very warm and genuine person." I quickly divert the conversation away from something I'm not ready to divulge right now, or maybe ever. "Anyway, thanks for accommodating me...I know it was unexpected yesterday."

Rhett closes the gap between us, sliding his hand up my neck to my jawline, sending shivers down my spine. I wanted to lean all of myself into him and disappear back into the little cloud we exist on where it's just us two.

"Thanks for the cookies," he says so seriously that we both crack a smile before he kisses me.

"Anytime," I whisper through puckered lips.

I savor the kiss, unable to shake the unexpected fear gripping me that at any moment, reality will hit me, and it could be our last.

CHAPTER TWENTY-FOUR

Audrey

s soon as my tires hit the highway, I make a mental list. Lists make me calm, lists have orders, lists tell me what to do next in life.

I swing by the dry cleaners on the way back to the apartment, and the moment my feet enter Penny's place, I go into full swing. Hair up, headphones in, playlist blasting, unpacking. Not thinking about Rhett.

Definitely not thinking about his mouth all over me or the way our breathing was in sync.

I managed to unpack the rest of my stuff in just under two hours, stuffing the clothes that didn't fit into the dresser and closet under the bed in suitcases. It would have to do for now. This was all temporary, I reminded myself.

I sat on the queen bed, leaning against the moss green, velvet headboard, and took a deep breath. The room was furnished already, it was very Penny. Glamorous, jewel-toned and overly girly. It made me miss her, and even though I'd been to her place a hundred times before, and I technically live here, it still felt weird to be here alone.

Penny wouldn't be back until tomorrow afternoon, and we'd only have half a day to catch up before work began again on Monday, so I decided to see what else I could do. Her pantry was pretty bare and so was the refrigerator. I guess that's the life of a jet-setter, but either way, I decided the least I could do was go to the store and stock up for the upcoming week.

Something told me we'd be having a lot of late-night snacks and TV chat sessions. I quickly jot down a grocery list, grab my reusable bags, and slip on my tennis shoes, deciding to walk the few blocks to the local market.

As I'm checking out, my bags full of charcuterie board essentials and champagne, of course, my phone buzzes in my pocket.

> **Rhett:** I know I'm supposed to wait three days, or some stupid rule, but I'm not really a rules guy so I'm taking my chance. Do you have plans next weekend?

I read the text with a fluttering in my stomach. I thank the cashier, grab my bags and walk home with a phone in my face.

> **Audrey:** A rule breaker, huh? I might have plans…it depends…

> **Rhett:** Well, if you find yourself without them, I'd like to take you somewhere special Friday night.

Somersaults in my stomach again. Why do I feel like a hormonal teenager right now?

> **Audrey:** Only if you promise to make me coffee the next morning.

> **Rhett:** As you wish.

I can't believe he just used *The Princess Bride* on me. Or that I implied I wanted to spend the night again. If I'm being honest with myself, I do. Maybe that means I'm using him to escape my own loneliness, knowing

Penny will be busy again next weekend.

Or maybe I just like this guy.

"Is this what you did all day?" Penny's eyes are saucers as I walk carefully with a charcuterie board resting on my arms into the living room. She's sprawled out on her pink velvet sectional but sits up abruptly when I set it down before her. Penny may be a health freak, but I know a snack board is the quickest way to her heart.

"No! I did laundry, too," I snap back. Maybe tonight I will tell her about the move to New York, but Penny doesn't give me the chance. As soon as I sit down, she is all over me about my date with Rhett. And my impromptu cookie-turned-sex delivery.

"I was gone for two days and you literally boned Red, spent the night on a farm, and met his mom." Penny's lips pull into a smirk, and I roll my eyes but can't help smiling a little, too.

"Penny! First, he grew up on a farm. He doesn't own a farm. Were you listening? And his mom is really sweet. This is all just moving so fast."

She leans forward, squeezing my arm. "I know, I'm just kidding you, babe. This sounds good. This is the rebound you need."

I know whatever Rhett and I have is casual, and that's all it could ever be, but rebound leaves a bad taste in my mouth.

"Don't judge me, because I don't think I've fully processed this all, and I don't know how to explain it, but I really enjoy being around him. He brings out a peace in me, a side of me I haven't experienced, maybe…ever?"

Penny's quiet for a moment. "Maybe he brings out a side of yourself you never got to show around Jackson. It's okay to be confused. You just got out of a long-term relationship. This is new territory. Don't overthink it."

Well, that's impossible. Overthinking it was a personality trait of mine.

"I'll try. I really will," I promise, more to myself than to her.

"I've never heard you so undone. You like this guy, don't you?"

I grow flustered, my face reddening as I turn to my best friend. "Yeah, I do. But it could never work. I mean, look at him. And look at me. We don't belong together. That much is clear."

Penny sighs loudly. "So, let's say, hypothetically, this is more than a rebound. In that case, I'm having a hard time seeing why it can't work. You were never happy with Jackson; let's be real. And Rhett seems to be everything he wasn't. That's a start."

Sometimes I seriously hated Penny for being so blunt.

"Relationships are too complicated. I'm so afraid of making the wrong choice again."

"If Rhett feels right to you…that's okay. Only you know what's right for you. Trust yourself, Aud."

I groan, leaning back on the sofa, looking up at Penny's navy blue ceiling. "I think this calls for champagne."

"I thought you'd never say so." She hops off the sofa to grab the bottle from the refrigerator.

I'd tell Penny about the job and the move another night.

Tonight, I just wanted to be with my best friend. One day at a time.

CHAPTER TWENTY-FIVE

Rhett

The kitchen gleamed—well, as much as an old kitchen like this could. In two days, Audrey was coming to spend the weekend here, and I've been trying to pick up my mess, so my house doesn't look like a construction zone.

Tomorrow is the opening night for the county fair in Roseville. For the past six years, I've been going with Desi and the twins, Jessie and Jenna, but this year, they were dancing in the show or something like that.

And I was taking Audrey.

I still can't believe I convinced her to stay for the whole weekend. I swear, I temporarily blacked out when I texted her that idea midweek. We barely know each other, but for some reason, time doesn't seem to exist with her.

When I'm with her, it goes too fast, and when we are apart the days drag. I don't know whether I should be embarrassed to be thirty years old and never have felt this way, but I try not to dwell on the past. Not much good has ever come from that.

I can't fix the guy I was before, but I can be the guy Audrey deserves.

I'm just not sure if taking her to the fair was the right call. But we are about to find out.

As I pushed the rarely used vacuum back into the cupboard under the stairs, three knocks sounded from the front door, followed by howls from Mabel.

I opened the door, stepping out onto the porch, where my mom was standing in overalls covered in dirt. A covered casserole dish was balanced in her arms.

"I know, I know, I'm sorry," she protested, shoving the glass pan towards me before I could even get a word out. "I had so much summer squash and broccoli that I made three vegetable lasagnas this afternoon. I just dropped one off at Desi's, so here's yours."

"You know you don't have to apologize for food, Ma," I laughed.

"Yeah, but if I keep making you meals, you'll never learn to cook for yourself." She leans back on the railing, crossing her arms over her chest.

"I'm doing just fine. I can make the basics." Which wasn't a lie, even if I rarely cooked. "Stop worrying about me."

She clucked her tongue, but then a sly grin took over her face. "So, you're bringing Audrey to family dinner on Sunday? You must really like her."

There it was. I knew the food was an excuse to pry just like I swear front porches were just gossip vessels in this town.

"Mmhmm," was all I said, and all I intended to say.

"Rhett Anderson, you're as stubborn as your father was."

I shrugged. "I don't want everyone making a big deal out of this. Or scaring her away, okay?"

"I promise. I will behave." She scratched Mabel's ears as the dog wandered on by, down into the garden beds to roll around.

"Is Kylan coming over tonight?" she asked, and I shook my head.

"I'm taking Audrey to the fair, actually." My mom's cheek twitches like she wants to say something that she shouldn't. I know the look.

"Oh, well that's something."

Great, even my sixty-year-old mother thought my date idea was shit.

"Thanks Mom, I'll see you this weekend." I smile, hugging her, and she gets the idea that I don't want to discuss it further. But she stops at the bottom of my porch steps, eyeing the dirt Mabel just rolled in.

"I still don't understand why you won't let me fix these garden beds." She was exhausting a subject that was a losing battle.

"You know the last thing I care about is putting flowers in front of my house."

"Honestly, a few shrubs and some milkweed would do wonders for your curb appeal."

I smiled tightly, running my hand through my already messy hair. "Okay Ma, maybe next summer I'll let you have at it."

She rolled her eyes, but patted me on the chest and waved goodbye, making her way to her car. I whistle for Mabel, who trots behind me into the kitchen as I place the lasagna in the fridge. Then I promptly go back outside, grabbing my ax and a stack of logs.

I'd already chopped enough wood for a summertime of bonfires today but if I stayed still for another minute, I'd lose my mind.

Mabel plops herself in the grass under the magnolia tree, watching me closely.

I'm usually a pretty chill guy; nothing really makes me nervous.

Not until I met a brunette woman with hazel eyes who has permanently taken up residency in every part of my damn mind.

CHAPTER TWENTY-SIX

Audrey

"**P**lease let Ed know I'll be back for the two o'clock client briefing." I smile down at Ed's assistant sitting at her desk before gathering my belongings and making my way to the lobby.

My legs don't feel very steady as my heels click on the stone floor, and my heart races as I exit the building, walking to my car. But as I start the engine and begin my drive towards the stone house in Forest Hills, I've never felt so sure this is the right choice.

I punch in the code and the large iron gate, situated before two stone pillars, opens and I drive forward onto the semi-circle driveway.

Think of all the parties we can have here, Drey. Jackson's voice rang in my head as I rested back in my seat, checking my phone to see if the Realtor had texted me.

It's no longer your decision, Jackson.

A red sedan slowly pulled in behind me and out popped a smiley, auburn haired woman possibly a few years younger than myself.

"Hi, you must be Elena!" I smile, extending a hand as she strides over to me in the middle of the driveway. It's an overcast day, a rarity for June in North Carolina, but the gray clouds are painted like backgrounds against this ostentatious house that was now in my name.

"I am, it's so nice to meet you, Audrey. What a beautiful street and home!" She smiles, staring up at the house, unable to hide her awe. She wasn't listed as a luxury realtor; in fact, she was relatively new to the game. Her social media page was overly joyful, optimistic, and friendly; and I could see she was eager to make a name for herself.

Jackson would've scoffed at the idea, calling up one of his broker friends who would get top dollar and only show this house to the most exclusive circle. But as of yesterday at 2 p.m., after the notary witnessed our signatures, the house was gifted to me. How Jackson got that to happen in less than three days was beyond me, but then again, maybe this has been in motion for a while.

The idea that I was probably the last to know about *everything* only makes hiring Elena that much sweeter.

And anyway, I like to give people a chance. God knows this property could use a good spark of joy.

"Thank you for meeting me on such short notice. I want to get the ball rolling and get this place listed as soon as I can."

Elena snaps her face back to me, her eyes wide as she grins a little too big.

"We will do everything we can to get this place listed as soon as possible. Want to show me around?"

I nod, and walk her around the property, giving her the grand tour. In the backyard, I noticed a line of rose bushes that weren't there a few days ago. Prickly thorns and bold red petals contrast against the brown and gray stone of the south facing wall.

"Wow, what beautiful landscaping! You and your husband must have an incredible team of landscapers."

I hold back a scoff that would be entirely inappropriate, given she knows nothing about me other than the quick contact form I filled out on her website, asking her to meet me here today to sell a house. She couldn't possibly know the last final dig from Jackson would be to fill the backyard with the flowers I hated.

"This landscaping could sell the home alone," she says reassuringly, and this time I do smile big.

Jokes on you, Jackson Tippins.

"That's wonderful. And you should know, I'm the sole owner of the home. No Mr.— just me." I pause and she winces apologetically.

"I'm so sorry, I didn't—"

"Please, don't apologize. If you get this house sold for me, you're doing me a great service." I nod toward the house. "Let's move inside, there's a lot to see." She follows me into the finished walk-out basement; complete with a sauna, home theater, gym, and two guest suites. You know, for all the family that would happily visit me. "My contractor assured me all the finishing touches would be done in a week or two. It's just a few paint touch-ups, but that won't be a problem, right? We can list it before it's complete?"

Elena nods vigorously, punching something into her phone. "Absolutely, that is not a problem. Not a problem at all."

"Excellent. Thank you."

I continue showing her around upstairs and by the end of the hour, we are back out front, standing under the portico.

"Thank you again for the opportunity to list your home. I'm confident this place won't be on the market long, especially not in a sought-after neighborhood like this."

Music to my ears.

I wave at Elena as she drives away and cross my arms over my chest, tipping my head back to the sky.

It feels foreign; yet deeply, undeniably right. Saying goodbye to this house will be a weight lifted off my shoulders. Taking agency isn't merely a step forward; it's a reclamation.

As I open my eyes, the sun begins to peak from behind the clouds.

I could hear my phone ringing while I was in the shower, instantly irritating me. If it wasn't Rhett, Penny, or my new listing agent, there was a short list of other people who could be calling me, none of which I wanted to talk to. Nonetheless, I hopped out, threw on my silk robe and snatched my phone from my dresser. Five missed calls from my mother. I had only been in the shower for ten minutes. Sitting pensively on the bed, squeezing my dripping hair with a towel, I dial her number.

"Is your phone broken?" Her voice greets me, angry and shrill.

"Hi, Mom."

"Do you know how to pick up a phone? If you're going to live so far from your family, we at least need to know you're alive." I put the phone on speaker, wrap the towel around my head, and inhale three deep breaths before responding.

"I'm alive and well."

Since the breakup with Jackson, my mother and father have barely checked in at all. They have been quiet on the matter, making me wonder if they are truly okay with it. Perhaps the needle is finally shifting, and they are learning to accept their only daughter doesn't align with their values perfectly; but that she is still a worthy member of the family. Or maybe that's just wishful thinking.

"I'm calling to talk about your house." She sounds unreasonably annoyed, like my house is somehow a burden to *her*. Her and my father were there when we bought it. Jackson, of course, buttered them up by inviting them to visit the day we closed, surprising them with our new purchase. It only solidified their love of him.

"What? Why?" I sat up straight, my stomach twisting in knots.

"We are redecorating the first floor of our house, and I know how long it takes for furniture, so I thought I'd ship our old furniture to you. You can use what you want out of it."

I crease my brows so much it hurts my head because Evelyn Elson didn't just *give* things away. Not without strings attached.

"That's very *generous* Mom, but not necessary."

"Audrey, you can't live in an empty house. You'll be moving in when the renovations are done, which I believed to be any week now."

Exhaling a sharp breath, and willing myself not to feel so small, not to revert to old *Audrey the people pleaser*, I steady myself against my headboard.

"I've been thinking about it all, and realistically the house is too big for me. It would be lonely to live there by myself, and it's not even my taste." *It's not a farmhouse.* "So, I've been considering selling it."

Actually, the I's are dotted and T's crossed, and a 'For Sale' sign will be in the yard by the end of next week.

"You can't be serious? After all the money Jack—" She paused, correcting herself. "All the work *you* put into it, making it your own. He gifted you this house and you're going to react ungratefully. This home is in the best zip code. You never know what your future holds, Audrey. Don't be rash and ignorant about this."

Her words cut but I can only focus on one aspect. I never told her Jackson gifted me the house.

"How do you know about the deed transfer?"

I could feel the tension through the phone, her pause, before she casually spurts out, "Jackson told your father, obviously. It's a big deal."

Of course.

"Living in that house says a lot about you as well. It has a certain appeal; it will attract the right person into your life."

"What if I meet someone who doesn't want to live there?"

That certainly shouldn't have slipped out of my mouth.

"What kind of man wouldn't want to live there?" She laughed a bit too manically into the phone, like the idea was simply implausible. "You really don't know what's best for you, do you?"

I ignore her condescending remarks as my thoughts flash to Rhett, and I pinch my lips together, determined to never let a word of him slip to her.

Because he was mine, and I was his. And in the little world we had together, I was safe. I didn't have to be an Elson, or an ex-almost-Tippins.

I could simply be Audrey.

Whatever *it* was, I needed to keep it safe.

I needed Rhett to be a secret, my secret. Until I figured this all out.

Chapter Twenty-Seven

Audrey

I f you'd asked me what I'd be doing the last week of June, I would've
said I'd be lost in wedding planning bliss. Instead, I was planning my
outfit for the county fair.

This was decidedly better.

Rhett and I agreed to not see each other during the week—not
because we didn't want to, though. I found myself counting down the
days, tortuously sitting in my windowless office on Friday afternoon,
daydreaming about his smile, his eyes, the way he says my name.

He was my refuge from the life I wanted to run away from, but his job
kept him busy during the week, and I tried my best to focus on mine.

Not that you could say I was focusing well...or being a good employee,
either. It was obvious Ed noticed, too. The way he paced in front of my
office all week, asking me time and time again about unread emails, and
meetings I pretended to remember. I knew he was saving face, worried
about looking like a fool for bolstering my promotion to New York.
This morning, the internal team had been notified I would be leaving in
September, just over three months from now. A handful of my coworkers
stopped by my office, tight smiles on their faces as they congratulated me for
a promotion they clearly coveted. I wouldn't receive the finalized offer until
later this summer when they secured the details and finances, so I didn't see
the purpose of celebrating now. Not that it wasn't a big deal for someone at

my age to get this offer. It just didn't feel as good as I imagined it would've. Old Audrey would've been over the moon, shamefully using it as another reason to gain approval from Samuel and Evelyn Elson.

But now, every congratulation coming my way feels like an added tension in my already buzzing body.

Because time was a thief, and I knew I only had a few months to see how things panned out between Rhett and I. The last thing I wanted was to string him along. My heart is fragile, my wounds fresh. And though being with him makes me momentarily forget the chaos of this last month, I need time to understand what it is I really want.

Plus, it was only practical to keep my options open. Rhett could break my heart and leave me stranded, the same way Jackson did. He wasn't Jackson, of course, but that didn't mean I was ready to fully commit to something unfamiliar. Protecting myself was the smart choice. The responsible thing to do.

Right?

The stir outside my office door jolts me out of deep thought, lifting my head to my computer screen. A burst of fluttering energy tickles my stomach. It's 5 p.m., and in a few hours I'll be with Rhett and Mabel. I unceremoniously slam my laptop shut without even sending my last email and shuffle out of my office, faking pleasantries as I wave at coworkers, and briskly walk home.

"So, explain to me what you're doing again this weekend?" Penny lays on my bed with her head in her hands, eyeing me as I pack my weekend bag.

"He is taking me to the county fair." I shrug, unable to contain my smirk. "And then Sunday, he invited me to a dinner party at his mom's house."

"This is so *Sweet Home Alabama* of you, and I'm here for it."

I throw a pair of shorts at her as she laughs, twisting her long hair around her fingers.

"While you're stuffing your face with fried food, I'll be editing photos tonight." She groans, rolling onto her stomach.

"You could take a break, you know," I suggest, scrunching my nose at her, already knowing her answer.

"I don't mind it. You know that."

I've stopped hounding her for working day and night; it was just who she was. She doesn't talk much about life before college, but I get the gist she grew up with very little. Penny is completely self-made, something I can't say for myself, and it only makes me respect her even more.

"I hear you," I sigh, tossing down an outfit on the bed. "This is so out of my comfort zone."

Penny makes a funny face at me. "Listen to me, this is what you need to do. Get yourself something horribly unhealthy to eat. Ride the Ferris wheel, play one of those rigged games. Stare into those baby blues and leave early enough to fuck under the stars. You'll be fine."

"Penny!" I scream, falling onto the bed next to her, laughing.

"When am I going to start feeling like an adult who is capable of managing my life?" I roll on my side to look at her.

"No one knows what they are doing in their twenties, and anyone who says they do is lying. That's what makes it so exciting. It's not supposed to be predictable. It's supposed to feel like magic. Scary. But magic," Penny adds. "But hey, if nothing works out for either of us, let's just live in your love-shack mansion, throw outrageous theme parties, and never have to worry about men ruining our plans."

I laugh, but then get quiet, casting my eyes away from her curious gaze. "You know I'm selling it."

"I know, but I still think it's a shame we didn't get to throw an outrageous party in it."

I bite my lip, hesitating, but I owe it to her.

"Pen, I need to tell you something." Anxiety grips my throat.

"What?" She props herself up on her elbows, and I take a deep breath because nothing about this is easy.

"Okay, so I was waiting to tell you until it was announced at work, but that happened today so…" *Deep breath*. "A few weeks ago, Ed told me about a new position they are opening up at the headquarters in New York City. And they offered it to me." I pause as her eyes go wide, understanding sinking in. "It'd be a big step up, with a huge pay increase. It would be idiotic to say no. This is the next natural step in my career. So, I told him yes."

My best friend sucks her lips in, her eyes leaving mine, and goes silent. Then she taps my knee with her manicured fingers.

"Wow…Aud, I don't know what to say." She clears her throat and a heaviness blankets me. "You're right, you worked hard for this, and you do deserve it." Her tone was undeniably melancholy, but she offered me a tiny smile.

"I know this is life altering news. But after everything, I feel like I've outgrown this place. I came here for school and only stayed for Jackson." She nods but I continue to justify this choice. Like maybe if I said it enough out loud, I'd believe it. "I don't want to leave you, but you know no matter where in the world I live, you'll always be my best friend." I tried to smile back at her, but my throat constricts with every passing second of this conversation.

"What about Rhett?" Penny whispers.

"What about him?"

"Does he know?"

"What we have is still so new, and technically, I made this decision before we ever got together. Who knows how long this will even last. It's a summer fling, remember?" I joke, but as the words lace my tongue, they feel like acid.

"If this is truly what you want, I support you. You know what's best for you better than anyone else," she replies dryly.

Biting my cheek to prevent the tears from falling, I walk into the bathroom to grab my makeup bag.

"I'll miss you like crazy," Penny calls out and our eyes meet in the bathroom mirror as she sits on my bed.

"We have the summer, Pen. And it's not totally set in stone until I get the final offer, okay?"

She nods but I can tell she doesn't fully believe me.

CHAPTER TWENTY-EIGHT

Rhett

I'm unloading the last crate of tools from my truck when I hear the familiar crunch of tires on gravel. It's funny how something I've heard a million times can suddenly be my new favorite sound. The way it makes my heart hitch would be medically alarming if it wasn't followed by a smile that instantly calms my tormented heart. The smile of a brilliant, brunette woman who was too smart, too pretty, too *good* for me.

But today, it's not me causing that big smile; it's my dog racing toward her.

"Did you just get home from a job?" Audrey greets me, and though she doesn't understand much about my line of work, she is always sweet; asking about it, wanting to know more about something that seems so boring to me.

Today she was like a walking sunflower, her hair in a loose braid that laid over her shoulder. A yellow and white sundress clinging to her frame. Every set of eyes would be glued to her tonight, but that didn't matter; she was coming home with me.

"I did. I'm just cleaning out the truck. I don't normally have someone riding shotgun." I wink at her, and she blushes. It happens every time I give her my full attention and it's made me wonder if no one has ever taken the time to get to really know her.

It blows my mind, but I try not to dwell on it, because it only hurts to think about. All I can focus on is making sure she never feels that way with me.

"What, little ol' me?" Audrey attempts a very adorable imitation of my southern accent and I pause, licking my lips and gazing at her. She squirms a bit, and I love it.

Dropping my tool bags, I hop down from the truck bed, take two strides towards her, and wrap my arms around her waist, pulling her in. Her laughter fills the air as I kiss her softly, tickling her sides.

"Rhett! I'm going to kill you!" She pushes against my chest as I clutch her harder. I stop tickling her, but keep my hands wrapped around her small waist.

"I'd happily die by your hands."

Audrey tilts her head. "What has gotten into you today? You seem extra...happy?"

I throw my hands up in playful defense. "I get to spend the whole weekend with my girl. What's better than that?"

Audrey's smile remains steady, but she stops moving, watching me closely.

"Your girl?" she asks calmly. "I didn't think we were doing labels."

"Well..." Pulling my baseball cap off to run my hand through my hair, I swallow against my throat but remain strong in how I feel. Because I've never been so sure. "You're right. We said no to labels. And I'll honor that if you still feel that way. But Audrey...I'd be lying if I told you I was okay with you being anyone else's. You make me a selfish man...I want you for me."

Her chest rose and fell as her wild eyes steadied on mine. She's always analyzing, flipping things in her mind, assessing the risk. Surely, I'm a risk. A country boy from Roseville who hasn't been to half the places she has, who doesn't have a fancy degree, or house. No trust fund to keep her secure, just these two hands that would fight off anything that threatened her or her happiness. Just a tin roof on an old farmhouse that I'd work endlessly to make sure she felt at home at. But I'm getting ahead of myself. A woman like Audrey has a world of options, and I'm a drop of water in the tank of her life.

"There's no one else but you." Her response is slow and deliberate.

"So, I can introduce you to my family as my sexy, sweet, incredibly brilliant girlfriend?"

Audrey hesitates, but then nods, "That's overkill, but girlfriend...sure."

"Oh honey, I don't think it's enough," I say, my voice rumbling in my chest as I step forward and push a loose piece of hair behind her ears, noticing her breathing quicken as I lightly run my hand down her jaw, cupping her neck, and pulling her close to me.

Our lips mere inches from each other; close enough I can see all the gold flecks in those hazel eyes.

"And so, this means I can introduce you as my rowdy, rough, handsome boyfriend?" she asks, her voice raspy. Her eyes go wide though, like she can't believe she just said that aloud.

"You can tell people I'm whoever you want, as long as you know I'm yours." I don't let her get another word in, unable to hold back from kissing that perfect mouth.

Chapter Twenty-Nine

Audrey

Rhett's hand never left mine as we drove to the fair. He cranked country music and sang along to every word, putting on a show for me as I laughed, watching him with a goofy smile plastered to my face. Rhett was so unapologetically himself. I was almost jealous.

Even after all his loss, he was still able to be a person that exuded sunshine, and it made falling for him that much easier. All my doubts, all my questions, all the sadness from my talk with Penny...they all disappeared when I showed up here today.

All I can think about now is that I get a whole weekend with him. And as his old truck rumbles to a stop in the field we are parking in, I gaze out the window, taking in the fair. The dusky sky is the backdrop to a Ferris wheel with twinkling lights, tall striped tents, and an array of people; both young and old, with smiles on their faces.

"You ready?" He smiles at me, and I nod, unbuckling myself. The last *special date* I was on was months ago, when Jackson chartered his father's private jet to take us to his family's mountain lodge. He worked the entire time on the airplane and didn't even notice I had drastically changed my hair.

I still wonder what I saw in that.

Rhett jumps out of the truck, a sexy grin on his lips as he all but runs to open my door. We walked hand in hand towards the entrance. "I know you're probably used to much nicer things, but I hope you at least have a little fun tonight." He squeezes my hand.

"I wouldn't want to be anywhere else, Rhett. I mean it."

He nods at me, and I hope I can show him how true it is.

"It's kind of a Roseville tradition to come to this fair. It doesn't matter if you're young, old, rich, poor, a farmer or an attorney, everyone shows up for this. That's why I love it."

Rhett's eyes lit up, his lips pulling into a smirk, and I can't contain my smile either.

"Well then, you're taking my virginity. I've never been to a fair."

Rhett's boots stopped in his tracks, and he squares off with me. "You're screwing with me. Never?"

Biting my lip, I shake my head.

"My parents would've never taken us. I spent every summer at camp or with an au pair."

Rhett rubs his chest, his thoughts stirring in that clever head of his.

"Well, I'm honored to be your first." He pulls me into his side.

Once inside the fairgrounds, the rest of the world was shut out. It was silly. I mean, I had traveled to some of the most exotic, beautiful places in the world with Jackson and with my parents. And even though I might've felt alone, or the trip wasn't exactly how I wished it would go, I could appreciate it and be grateful for the experiences.

But something about being here tonight ignites a magic in me. As we walk through the crowds of people, kids in awe of everything around them, the aroma of carnival food, a tightness forms in my chest. I'm struck with a nostalgia for a memory I never had.

I've spent so many years clinging on to things I thought would make me happy. Or at the least, things I thought I should want to cling on to, like expensive weddings, and big houses, and jobs with impressive titles. But now, on this simple date, with a guy who looks at me like the stars that shine above, I wonder what it would be like to let go of all those things. The things I once thought made me *me*.

It's scary, maybe the scariest thing I ever asked myself.

Rhett tugs on my hand, turning us down another row of games, and I let myself return to him.

"That looks like Mabel!" I call out with my arm draped around Rhett's as we lazily meander towards a game tent. There's a bloodhound stuffed animal prize hanging at the water gun game.

"She would lose her mind if she saw that."

"Let me get it for her!" I take a step toward the booth, which is already filling up with teenagers and kids.

"You know these games are all rigged, baby," Rhett teases and I scoff, sitting down on the red stool anyway.

"All games are rigged if you don't know what you're doing," I snap back, slapping a few dollars on the counter. All the years of watching Jackson gamble has given me a false sense of assurance—if you're just confident enough, usually you win.

"You played this before?" Rhett bends over, his lips near my ear, sending shivers down my sides as his husky voice fills my ears.

"Well, no, I've never played *this* one, but I was on my high school's archery team. This can't be harder than that."

The game bell rang, and I'd never pushed my thumbs so hard before. I didn't flinch, didn't take my eyes off the stream of water until the buzzer rang again, and number four lit up.

"I won! I won!" I jump up, the teenager running the game looking less than impressed. Leaping up, I wrap my legs around Rhett's waist, as he cups my ass and kisses me.

"Take your pick from the middle row," the game attendant mumbles unenthusiastically, and Rhett drops me to my feet. Without hesitation, I pointed at the bloodhound.

"So, the lesson is, never tell Audrey Elson she *can't* do something," Rhett whispers in my ear, one arm around my shoulder as we walk away, victorious.

"Damn straight," I nod, clutching the cheap stuffed animal.

"Rhett Anderson!"

He stops in his tracks, and we both turn to look over our shoulders. A woman his mother's age walks towards us, a funnel cake in one hand.

"Mrs. Little, how are you?" Rhett lets go of me, pulling the older woman into a hug. She beams up at him, a glint in her eyes, admiring him like a mother would.

"I'm doing great, my grandkids are around here somewhere. They go nuts here." He chuckles kindly.

"Mrs. Little, this is Audrey. My girlfriend."

Her smile changed to something more polite, as she held out her hand, shaking mine.

"It's so nice to meet you," I reply, noticing her glance at the stuffed animal in my arms.

"Kylan mentioned you were seeing someone." She winks at Rhett like it's an inside secret.

"Of course, he did." He cocks his head back. "Mrs. Little is Ky's mom. She was also my third grade teacher."

"I sure was and let me tell you something...Rhett was a good student but boy was he mischievous. I never thought you and Kylan would graduate high school!"

"Ahh, Mrs. Little. I turned out okay, I'd say."

She touches his arm fondly and looks pointedly at me. "He's like my second son. He's a special one. This man rebuilt my entire porch after the hurricane last year and didn't even charge me."

"That's what you do for family," Rhett replies, and an unwelcome tightness returns to my chest.

What would Rhett think of me once he knew my family dynamic or the lack of one?

That's why he will never meet them. That's why he will remain my little secret.

We spent the rest of the night trying copious amounts of food I didn't even know you could deep fry. Rhett said he saved the best for last, twirling me around as he walked backwards, boots stomping, blue eyes shining in the lights, leading me to the Ferris wheel entrance.

I peer up at the large white and red spinning wheel, and bells go off in my head.

"Oh, no thank you. I'm afraid of heights," I admit feeling childish, but Rhett pauses, pulling my hand up to his chest. My palm rests on his thick muscle, the warmth of him radiating down my fingertips.

"I won't let anything happen to you, Audrey. Promise."

I bite my cheek, wanting to fight against it, but his thumb draws faint circles in my palm.

Excitement lingers in his blue eyes, so I nod.

With nervous flutters in my stomach, I let him guide me closer. There's almost no line, and while he gives the attendant our tickets, his hand not leaving mine, I smile, pushing my fear deep down. Rhett lets me scoot onto the red bench before getting in beside me. He drapes his arm over my shoulders, and instantly I feel a little safer.

As the views of all the lights and people beneath us get smaller and smaller, my knuckles get tighter on the bar over my lap. This is ridiculous. I'm nearly twenty-seven years old and about to have a panic attack on a Ferris wheel at the county fair in front of an impossibly kind and handsome man. This cannot be happening.

Rhett must sense my unease because he softly tilts my face towards his with his fingertips on my chin.

"Hey, hey." Rhett softly smiles, all ruggedness gone. "Keep your eyes on me. I've got you."

Squeezing my eyes shut, I exhale deeply, then open them, focusing on Rhett. Scooting my body closer, until I was nearly on his lap, I let him continue talking.

"Okay, on a scale of one to ten, tell me how your first county fair experience is going?"

I laugh, taking a moment to ponder it.

"Other than feeling like I might fall to my death at any moment, it's a ten." I bite my lip, glancing sideways at him. He smirks.

"A ten? Wow, I really set the bar high here."

"I'm serious! Truthfully, tonight is the most fun I've had in a long time," I admit sheepishly.

Rhett's brows twitch. "Really?"

"Is that embarrassing? That probably makes me sound like I don't have a very fun life."

Jackson would've never taken me here. His idea of a fun date was a day at the golf course, finished with two many scotches at the club his father owned. Something that entirely didn't involve my preferences.

Rhett shakes his head. "Nothing embarrassing about that. You know what's sad? The way society acts like we have to have less fun as we get older. It's a scam. We need more fun as we age." His voice is filled with conviction, and I study him closely.

"I've never met anyone like you, Rhett Anderson." I rest my head on his shoulder. We ride like this for a moment until he clears his throat.

"My dad used to take me and my sister to this fair every summer. He'd give us twenty dollars each, which was a lot of money for us back then." Rhett's fingers trace the bar across our laps as he talks. "We never went hungry, but to say we grew up frugally would be an understatement." He glances up at all the stars starting to peek out above us.

"You were eighteen when your dad passed, right?" I ask, piecing together conversations we've had.

"Right before I turned eighteen, yeah. I had plans to go to college before he died. But my mom couldn't run the farm by herself, so I stayed home to help."

"I'm so sorry Rhett...that must've been so hard." My throat was tight, watching this incredibly strong man open up to me. Rhett shakes his head, a humorless chuckle escaping his lips. "It's ironic, just as I was starting to get my freedom, about to have a summer of fun before leaving for school, everything fell apart. But that was so long ago. It's another lifetime, really."

I could never put myself in his shoes; to know what it was like losing a parent or having to pick up the pieces for your family. I had spent my life scrambling for my family's approval, only to be shoved to the side, feeling unwanted and yet on the hook, unable to free myself.

"Well, I hope you eventually had that fun and free summer."

His heavy blue eyes lift to meet mine as we start to descend from the top of the Ferris wheel.

"I think I'm having it with you."

If I wasn't held in by a metal bar across my lap, I think I would float away into the night. I blink away tears I refuse to let him see, and lean into him, resting my head in the crook of his neck. I hold his hand in mine, choked by the words racing through my mind.

The Ferris wheel starts rising again and as the ground grows smaller, the tight pinch in my core never comes. I expel a breath, letting myself feel the truth. Right here, right now, with Rhett is the safest I've felt in a long time.

"What about your family?" he asks, breaking my trance.

"My family...you already know enough about them," I chuckle dryly. "They are not like your family."

Rhett pauses, a flash of confusion crossing his face. "Oh, how so?"

If he knew how my family looked at me, if he knew the expectations they held for me or anyone involved with me, I wonder what he'd think. Or what he'd think of me if he knew how hard it was to shake the need to gain their approval. Maybe he'd feel inadequate or want to run away because the pressure is too much.

"They are all busy with their careers. We don't do a lot as a family, not back then and not now. My parents like to pretend we are a tight family unit. The all-American picturesque family. It's all a lie." I bite my lip, hoping I didn't say too much again.

"I'm sure they love you in their own way," he says, and I didn't disagree.

"I hope," I add. They love me in a conditional way. How could I possibly explain they give or withhold their love depending on how successful I am, or by how much I've screwed up.

Rhett turns my face toward him again, his finger hooked under my chin. I peered into what I was beginning to see were oceans of depth, of love, of understanding. Underneath the rough exterior, the rowdy behavior, and the carefree attitude was a man who cared very much. A man who barred his heart to me in the most unexpected ways.

"You know you deserve better than that, right?"

"How can you say that? You don't know me very well."

"You're right, I don't. But I do like to believe I'm a pretty good judge of character."

I pause, as Rhett's blue eyes lazily trace my lips, as I silently will him to kiss me. Lacing his fingers around the back of my neck, he kisses me deeply.

"You're okay yourself, cowboy."

I step off the ride minutes later, with a new energy buzzing through my veins.

The truth is, I have no idea what life will be like for me in a few months, but I know this summer, I'm going to embrace the carefree girl inside me—the one who longs to be loved, seen, and heard. I'll let her have her moment.

And I'll help Rhett have his, too. Because he deserves it, because *we* deserve it.

Maybe we can be each other's lifelines. Just for a while, until we find the shore.

Back at the farmhouse, the sky is black, but under the porch lights, Mabel greets us, tail wagging fiercely.

"Look what we got you, girl!" I pull the stuffed animal out from behind my back, and she stares at it, then me, her mouth opening and closing, unsure what to do. Rhett and I glance at each other laughing.

"She is cute as hell, but I never said she was smart," Rhett fires off, kneeling down to ruffle her long, floppy ears.

"Don't you listen to him, Mabel. You can be both smart and pretty. Here, take the toy." I gently nudge it towards her, and Mabel cautiously grabs it with her front teeth before galloping inside towards the living room. We follow her in, watching her drop the toy in her bed, sniffing it feverishly like a true bloodhound.

"Did I ever tell you how I got Mabel?" Rhett asks, flipping on the small lamp on the kitchen counter as I trail behind him. We stand in dim lighting, heat lightning sparkling the sky outside the kitchen window.

"No, I don't think so, actually."

"She was being trained for the county as a search dog. But at around nine months, she didn't pass her tests. Guess she couldn't stay focused on a scent long enough and just wanted to play. Anyway, Desi is the secretary at the sheriff's office, so she found out about Mabel failing her tests. Next thing you know, Desi shows up at my house with this clumsy ass dog. I had no choice but to take her in."

"Why didn't she keep her for herself? I can't imagine her little girls wouldn't want a dog." I try to imagine my own brother, Andrew, doing anything remotely thoughtful for me.

His fingers drummed the countertop in the dimly lit kitchen. "I love my sister, but she likes to fix things. Things she has no business fixing..." Rhett pauses, puffing out his cheeks as he runs a hand through his hair. "Her and my mom thought I would end up a lonely old man in this house. I kept refusing all the dates my sister was trying to set me up on, so I guess she thought the next best thing was to dump a dog on my doorstep."

I scoff, running my fingers down the front of Rhett's chest, watching his pupils dilate. "I'm so glad she did. But also, I'd like to hear about all these dates you refused," I muse but Rhett stands still with a dreamy smile on his lips, a depth in those icy eyes that makes the breath hitch in my chest.

"That's the past."

"So, you just decided you wanted to start dating when you met me?"

Rhett nods. "Pretty much." He smirks. "And now I'm afraid you're going to be the ruin of me."

My lips twitch in a half smile, unsure how to respond to the twinge of sadness in his voice. Like he believes I will break his heart, like he expects it. But those thoughts dissipate quickly as he scoops me up by the waist, placing me on the island.

I gasp playfully as Rhett holds me tight, planting kisses down my neck in a way that tickles. Our chaos causes Mabel to fill the house with her howls.

The heat between us switches quickly, as I greedily unbutton Rhett's shirt, needing him closer to me. My heartbeat intensifies, desire building with every touch.

"I need you," I whisper into his ear, his eyes grow hooded, and the world around us disappears.

Wanting fingers work at buttons and belts, the thud of jeans hitting the ground around Rhett's ankles.

Rhett takes the hint, his soft lips nibbling little bites down my collar bone, pulling my yellow sundress over my head. I remembered to wear my matching black lacy set, and I mentally thank Penny for insisting I did.

I pause as the light ping of dropping rain starts above us, tilting my head back to look at the ceiling.

"It's the tin roof. It's loud when it rains," Rhett says almost apologetically but I shake my head.

"I love it."

And I do. And I love the way the dim lighting makes his eyes appear bluer, the way it feels like we are tucked away from the world; safe in this little kitchen, safe with each other.

"Where have you been all my life?" Rhett's question catches me off guard, but I don't have an answer. I've been chasing a lie, an illusion that would've never included him.

I tighten my legs around his waist and lean in to kiss his neck. He smells like the cedar wood filling his workshop and feels as unswayable as the old oaks in the front yard. Nudging my mouth back to his, I kiss him with a new lust, tasting the sweetness of him.

Rhett growls into my neck, his fingers circling my sensitive chest. When it's clear neither of us can take another moment of torment, he lifts me off the kitchen island, and we move as one, inseparable, but we don't make it to the bedroom. Rhett pushes my back into the kitchen wall, and I smile as he bites my lip, feeling my walls come down even more. All I can think about is getting closer, feeling him fill me, take me.

"Right here…I can't wait any longer…"

Rhett does as I ask, setting me on my feet. The roughness of his hands pulling my panties down gingerly makes my skin tingle, and when he parts my legs with his, you can barely hear my gasp above the sound of the rain on the roof.

I try to stay upright, lacing my fingers through his messy, blonde hair.

"Harder…please…" The words shock me, even if they come naturally with Rhett. I didn't know you could feel so seen and so safe at the same time. But with him, I do. He invites me to be uninhibited. So, I dig my fingers into his biceps, and he wraps his large hands around my waist, intensifying his thrusts, supporting my weight against him.

He's rough when needed and soft when I least expect it, a respite of warm water dripping onto the cold stone that my heart has become over the years.

"I could worship your body all night…" His voice is hoarse, and enough to push me over the edge.

A raspy gasp escapes me, pushing me to my limit until there's nothing left to hold back. Throwing back my head, my eyes shut, I shudder around his length as he simultaneously comes into me. Rhett bites my bottom lip, returning me to him.

I feel Rhett everywhere. Every inch of my skin buzzes with him, with the warm embrace of his arms, the gentle but strong grasp of his hands on me. Reminding me he is here, holding me together, holding us together.

Us.

There's that word again. There is no denying anymore there is an *us*.

Rhett's blue eyes shine at me like he's looking at the most beautiful thing he's ever seen.

And in his eyes, I see a world I'd like to stay in just a little longer.

CHAPTER THIRTY

Rhett

"Good morning." Audrey's voice sounds like honey, and I spin to see her enter the kitchen wearing my blue Atlanta Braves shirt. She has her own pajamas but seems to prefer my worn-out cotton shirts—and I'll never deny her. Seeing her barefoot in my kitchen with my shirt on awakens something primal in me.

I pull two mismatched mugs from the cabinet, placing them on the counter as the coffee maker sputters behind me, probably on its last leg.

"Sleep well?" I offer her a lazy smile, pouring black coffee into a mug.

"I was pretty exhausted." She smirks suggestively, and I raise my eyebrows in pride.

"I'm actually not sorry for that." I wink, handing her the mug as she blushes.

"Good." She takes a sip, closing her eyes as she does. Glad I'm not the only caffeine addict. "I have a real question, though. Do you always wake up at the crack of dawn to play Martha Stewart?"

Turning my attention to the bacon on the stovetop, I shrug, tossing a kitchen towel over my shoulder. "Comes with the territory. Farmer's son. I try sleeping in, but my body won't let me."

The toaster pops up with two bagels and I snatch them, throwing them on a plate. "And don't be too impressed." I point at the meat sizzling in the pan. "You're looking at the extent of my cooking skills. I can use a toaster and make bacon."

The kitchen does smell pretty good though if I do say so myself. It doesn't suck making breakfast when you have someone to share it with.

"I don't know the last time someone made me breakfast who wasn't hired to do it. So, thank you." Audrey chuckles, smiling at me over the cup of coffee, her hazel eyes sincere but I peel mine away as tightness forms in my chest.

Clearing my throat, I shrug, flipping the bacon. "It's no big deal. I like taking care of people."

Correction: I like taking care of you.

"I can see that," she adds, and moments later I plate up our food, handing Audrey hers.

"Want to eat on the front porch?" I ask, and she looks down at her bare legs, but I read her mind before she can object. "We're out in the country, baby. No one's gonna see you but me and Mabel."

"Alright, if you're sure." She hesitates, but I rub the small of her back, leading the way down the hall with creaking pine floorboards, towards the screen door that's bent out of shape from the hound dog leaning on the other side. Mabel's already out there waiting for us on the sun-drenched porch.

I sit at the table, pulling out a chair for Audrey.

"It looks like it's going to be a beautiful day. It looks impossibly green, too," she says before a bite of bacon. In a million years, I never thought Audrey would be the kind of person who was easy to please, but it seems the smaller acts are what make her smile.

"It's the rain. It makes everything come alive."

She considers it, nodding as she scans my yard. It does need mowing, but I don't think I'll ever get sick of this view.

"Do you ever see yourself leaving this town?" she asks, sounding almost cautious. I don't have to think about the answer, though, because I don't.

"To be honest, I never really thought about leaving. I have everything I love here."

She nods, holding the chipped mug to her chest.

"What about you? Are you a lifetime North Carolina girl now?" I lay on the accent thick, knowing it makes her smile and it does for a moment, but then her eyes leave mine, searching her plate. Audrey shrugs ever so slightly.

"You know, I'm not sure. I don't hate it here, I'm just not sure what my future really holds." She tried to keep her voice chipper, but it didn't mask the way sadness etched on her face.

"You leaving me already, darlin'?" I ask, my pulse skyrocketing, ready for my heart to be stomped on before this thing even had a chance to bloom.

"I didn't say that." She sits up. "I'm simply taking things day by day. This is all new, you know?"

I nod because I truly do understand. But what she doesn't know is that I'd do anything to convince her there's no better place than here.

"So, what's the plan for the day?" Audrey asks, changing the subject abruptly.

"If you're okay with it, I thought we could chill here. I need to finish up about an hour or two of projects in the workshop...but the hammock is all set up for you."

She swallows, clutching her mug to her chest again, her bare feet running back and forth on Mabel's belly splayed beneath us.

"I didn't know you had a hammock?"

"I set it up yesterday before you got here." I roll my shoulders in a shrug.

Audrey sits up taller in the chair, a skeptical look crossing her face.

"Why did you do that?"

"Last week, you said that all you dreamed about was having time to lay in a hammock all day, reading a book." My brows crease together. "You did say that, right?"

Audrey shakes her head, pulling herself out of a daze. "Yeah, I did say that..." She reaches up, tightening her messy bun. "I guess I didn't realize you were listening to me."

"I listen to everything you say." Scoffing at her, I reach down to pet Mabel. "So, how does that sound?"

She bit her lip, her eyes lighting up. "It sounds freaking incredible. I do have a new book on my Kindle, actually..."

"Good. The afternoon is yours." I smile, happy if she is.

"Perfect," she mimics, standing up to refill our coffees; but not before I pull her into my lap, breathing in her sweet jasmine smell, kissing her soft lips deeply, running my palm across the top of her soft leg, trying to keep thoughts of last night out of my head. It's going to be near impossible but I'm trying to be well behaved.

Audrey laughs, swatting my hand away, and winks at me from the doorway as she struts back into the house, leaving me wondering how the hell I got so lucky, and wondering when I'll wake up from this dream.

CHAPTER THIRTY-ONE

Audrey

R elationships aren't supposed to be this easy, right?

Maybe it's just my innate cynicism, always waiting for the other shoe to drop. Or maybe Jackson left me more jaded than I care to acknowledge, but I find myself staring into space, counting all of Rhett's green flags.

"You're awfully quiet, darlin'. What're you thinking about?" Rhett dries his hands on a dish towel, before settling back into the counter, looking at me.

I decided to say exactly what I'm thinking. "Just wondering why you're so nice to me." I say it like a joke, but I don't think it lands like one.

"You act like it's a bad thing or it's hard. I don't know who in your life ever told you that you weren't easy to fall for. I'll never tell you what to do, but I'd suggest you stop listening to that voice."

Rhett's words sink in sharply, and I know he's right, even if it's hard to stomach. I just spent the last few hours baking in the sun with a tall glass of iced tea next to me, reading in the hammock he positioned perfectly between two oak trees. All because of him and how he listens to me, takes my tiny little daydreams seriously. No one has ever done that for me.

"Well, thank you. I appreciate you, Rhett," I reply, and he nods, his baseball cap not hiding the small smirk on his lips. "What?" I ask, wondering if there's something on my face. Instinctually I wipe at my mouth.

"Did you enjoy the show this afternoon, ma'am?" I feel myself turn red, because without further explanation, I know what he's referring to. The hammock gave me a straight view into the workshop, where I stole glimpses of him doing his woodworking all afternoon. I had to reread chapter five three times, and it's all his fault.

"You know, I'm not an expert at what you were doing, but I don't believe woodworking without a shirt on is advisable."

"Would you like to file a formal complaint?" he teases, inching forward, and I tap my lips with my finger.

"Absolutely not." Rhett closes the gap, kissing me. He's messy with saw dust but I don't mind. After watching him in his shop, I'm pretty sure I'll never look at carpentry the same.

"Oh, by the way, my mom and sister are *very* excited to meet you tomorrow."

My dirty thoughts drop quicker than a fly as a new bout of nerves have me in a chokehold. I've been trying not to think about tomorrow, thinking I would be fine. I've been to countless dinner parties where the pressure to impress the hosts was at the forefront of my mind. Where *very important* guests of my parents' or Jackson's coworkers surrounded me, and I had to keep my conversation polite, and reserved. But being invited to the Anderson weekly family dinner tomorrow was in an entirely new class.

"Oh, wow."

Rhett's brows furrow slightly, and he pinches the back of his neck.

"Please don't worry or overthink it. It's no big deal, really."

I scoff, tapping my nails on the kitchen counter. "A dinner party with your family *is* a big deal. I just want them to like me. I know our relationship kind of came out of left field and—" I stopped, flustered and fidgeting in my bare feet.

Rhett lets out a low chuckle, stepping up to me. My stomach flips as he tucks my hair behind my ear, an amused smirk on his lips. If only we could all be as cool and casual as Rhett Anderson. Add effortlessly beautiful to that mix, too.

"If by *dinner party,* you mean a potluck with two kids and three dogs running around, then honey, it's a dinner party."

I let out a loud huff, but Rhett continues, his amused smirk persistent.

"And they will love you. Seriously, don't worry about it. If anything, I should be worried they'll scare you off."

I cross my arms across my chest, chewing my lip, and Rhett drapes his arms around my neck, stooping down to meet my darting gaze.

"Don't get me wrong, the food will be good. My mom puts farm to table restaurants to shame. But please, don't stress it. Okay?" I love the way his accent grows thick when he talks about his mom, and I lean back to get a better look at him. "We can stop at the store and grab something to bring."

"We can't just buy something from the grocery store, Rhett!" I gasp, truly appalled at the suggestion.

"It's fine, I assure you." He waves, clearly having fun with my dramatics.

"You just told me your mom is an amazing cook. Let me at least bake something to bring."

"No one is expecting that."

"I don't care, I refuse to show up with store-bought potato salad like a bachelor." I pause, glancing at Rhett who feigns offense. He puts a hand to his chest, and I shake my head, pulling up a recipe on my phone and continue, "No offense, but you have me now. Things are changing, *darlin'.*" I mock him and Rhett secedes. "Mind going to the store with me? I need to get a few things. Unless you have lavender essence and fine almond flour?"

"I'll grab my keys." Rhett reaches for them and hooks me in to kiss my temple.

"Thought so," I reply quietly, silently going over the recipe in my head. I need these cookies to come out perfect. Nothing less will do.

The timer for the macaron's beeps, and I have to side-step over Mabel, who's inconveniently planted herself under my feet in this little kitchen.

Two dozen lavender macaron shells come out perfectly, and as I pipe the zesty lemon filling, a lightness fills my bones. A slight breeze fills the kitchen from the open window over the sink, and I finish the last cookie.

"I'm seriously impressed with myself right now." I step back admiring my work, talking to Mabel, my only audience. The last time I made these was two years ago when Jackson was in his last year of grad school. He was always busy, leaving me to be by myself after work, so I started baking more and more. One particular night, the last time I ever attempted to make this complicated French cookie, everything figuratively crumbled. He was stressed because of finals but unfortunately, I caught the brunt of that stress. Jackson came home late from studying at the library, and I was really excited to see him, thinking this would be a sweet gesture. Our apartment smelled like a bakery, with plated cookies and tea. I set up the little dining space, inviting him to unwind with me, to merely take ten minutes and catch up; a rarity in our relationship.

He barely had made eye contact with me as he came in, agitation coating his features as he threw his backpack onto the sofa without a care.

"I can't Audrey, I have class in the morning." He didn't even look at me, but I bit back my tears, and cleared my throat, attempting again; thinking maybe he simply needed me to show him it was okay to take a break, but I was wrong. So, so wrong.

"Babe, please sit with me for a few minutes, it won't kill you," I encouraged, kissing his cheek, searching his face until his tired red eyes met mine.

"Audrey, when will you grow up? You have work in the morning, I have school, and now the kitchen is a fucking mess. This little hobby of yours is getting out of control." Hostility laced every word.

Everything went silent between us and a cloud settled around me as he pushed past, straight into our bedroom, closing the door with force. That night I ended up throwing the entire batch away, put my favorite new cookbook back on the shelf and cleaned up the kitchen in complete silence, not making a sound as tears spilled down my cheeks.

He broke my heart that night, and I think a little part of me knew then he'd never understand me, never see me for me. But I took his words to heart and didn't bake again for a very long time.

My throat is tight, thinking about that night, until Mabel paws my foot, begging me for a cookie. I toss her one of her homemade treats instead and gently stack the cookies in a container, and place them in the refrigerator. The front of my new apron— the one I bought at the store today— is dirty with powdered sugar and butter, but it brings a smile to my face. I start to unlace the tie as the back door opens. In steps Rhett, sweat glistening on his face as he wiped a fine film of saw dust off his hands onto his jeans.

"Holy shit, I feel like I just walked into *The Great British Baking Show* tent."

My mouth falls open at the mention of my favorite show. "You know that show?"

"I was forced to watch it against my will. My nieces love it."

I laugh, picturing him watching it with his nieces.

"Hey, you have a little flour in your hair." Rhett motions, and I touch my head, as if I could feel flour.

"No, I don—"

But he doesn't let me finish before taking a pinch of flour from the open bag and flicking it onto my head. My mouth falls open, a dramatic gasp leaving my mouth.

"Rhett, you did not!"

He winks cockily at me, and this time, I grab the leftover lemon filling, squeezing it onto his head before he can dodge me. We both stand in shock as it drips onto his shoulder. He doesn't flinch, which only makes my heart race fast. My eyes darted between his face and his hand creeping towards the open egg carton on the counter.

"You...wouldn't...dare..."

But he does, grabbing the egg as I leap over Mabel, running out the backdoor of the house with Rhett chasing me.

"Sweetie pie, you forgot the eggs!" he yells, and I laugh so hard, I nearly trip, running through the grassy backyard. Mabel bounds out after us, galloping with a toy in her mouth like it's some kind of new game. I circle the garage, pausing to catch my breath, but Rhett rounds the corner, and we stare in a standoff, the egg still in his grip.

"Truce?" I ask, breathily, my hands on my hips and Rhett nods.

"Truce," he replies, relaxing his shoulder. I take my chance, snatching the egg from his palm and smashing it on his chest. A wild look crosses his blue eyes and as I turn, he grabs my apron strings, pulling me into him. Egg smears all over the front of me, too.

"You're awful!" I holler, joking as I laugh from the depths of my core.

He shook his head, feigning disappointment. "And now look at us." He clucks his tongue.

"I guess you're going to have to help clean me up..." I bite my lip seductively, knowing what it does to him and watch Rhett's eyes grow wide in response.

I didn't have a chance to finish my sentence before Rhett bent down, threw me over his shoulder and hauled me into the house like he was running for a Super Bowl touchdown.

CHAPTER THIRTY-TWO

Rhett

Audrey's gaze meets mine in the mirror above the bathroom sink, her pink lips breaking into a smile as her laughter fills the small space, prompting me to join in as I take in the mess we made.

"Here, let me help you." She reaches for the towel, carefully dampening it in the sink under the running hot water. I watch as she grows quiet, turning to face me. I tower above her, so she nudges me to sit on the lip of the clawfoot tub. Audrey gently wipes the icing off my shoulders and face, her eyes tracing my features.

"You're going to have to wash this out in the shower. I'm sorry." Her fingertips trail from my hair to my neck, sending chills through me.

She doesn't know how a simple touch sends me into overdrive, unable to think about anything but her skin touching mine.

I slowly lean back, reaching into the antique clawfoot tub, twisting the handle, letting the water get warm. Audrey stays rooted between my legs, clutching the towel in her hands, watching me intently.

Without speaking, I gently remove the towel from her hands and bring it to her cheeks.

"Thank you," she whispers, filling the space between us, thick with tension.

"I'm going to kiss you now," I reply, and she nods, eyes shuddering as I stand in this tiny bathroom.

Kissing Audrey is the drug I never knew I craved.

Her palms find the hem of my shirt, nudging it up, so I take the reins; pulling it over my head, letting it fall on the floor at our feet. My heart is barely contained under the bones in my chest. But I'm beginning to wonder if it doesn't belong there anyway.

Because maybe it was always meant to be Audrey's.

Her eager fingers pull at my jeans, trying to undo them quickly while our lips stay locked together, but I smile against her and shake my head.

"Not so fast. I want to take my time with you."

My cock swells against my denim as her pupils dilate with anticipation, but I'd keep my word. It was time to show her just how good she deserved to be treated.

Switching spots, I set her on the edge of the tub and kneel before her. Bringing my mouth back to her tender neck, I unbutton her shirt, letting it fall off her shoulders as she exhales sharply, her skin exposed to the hot steamy air around us.

Her chest rises and falls with labored breaths, and I grip her waist, keeping her steady on the tub. I would never let her go, never let her fall.

Audrey was mine, all mine, and I needed her to know how seriously I took that.

With parted lips, I use my teeth to free her breasts from the lacy lavender bra she wore, drawing her nipple into my mouth as she rolled her head back, digging her fingers into my shoulders. I licked and sucked, getting high off hearing her tiny moans and exhales. High off the sweet smell of her, the need in me growing with each passing second.

As steam rose from the shower behind her, I pulled back, unclasping her bra, and hooking my fingers into her shorts.

I knew my palms were rough, my fingers calloused from working with my hands every day. Opposite of her velvet soft skin, unmarred, but she never complained. Her waist was made for my grip, and her thighs divided like they knew what was coming next.

In truth, I'd do anything she asked of me. Anything to hear her rasp out my name, anything to make her feel good, anything to see her come undone in my arms.

It was enough to make my cock stand alert, her eyes and hands finding my length.

"Rhett, I want you," she breathed out, but I shook my head again.

"Not so fast…" I growled, kissing and biting the sensitive skin of her inner thigh while she ran her fingers through my messy hair, gripping me.

She pulls hard on my neck, making me want more, and as I work my way up to her center, she inhales sharply.

"Fuck, Rhett…"

I smile cockily against her core, which is slick just for me. With one hand gripping her thigh, the other cupping her perfect breast, I drag my tongue through her center, getting high on her racing breath.

Holding her steady, I taste her. Audrey's eyes fall shut, her chest rising quickly, my name echoing off the bathroom walls as she presses herself into my face while I continue devouring her.

I would stay here forever just to hear my name, again and again.

"Rhett, I'm… going…. to… come."

Audrey shudders, whimpering in my arms as I pull away, kissing her softly on the chest.

"Now I promised to clean you up…" I graze her arm, quickly shed my pants and pull her into the shower with me, wrapping my arms around her from behind while she lets me explore every inch of her again. We made love until the water grew cold, until our panting turned to laughter, until I couldn't stand any longer. We retired, damp, to the bedroom, to lay the remainder of the evening in bed.

And it didn't matter what was going on around us, what came before or what would be next.

All I saw is the woman I'm falling madly in love with.
All I see is Audrey.

CHAPTER THIRTY-THREE

Audrey

The next evening comes quickly, my stomach bubbling with nerves as I lay my outfit out on Rhett's bed. I don't know how it happened, but I have a few pieces of clothing hanging in his closet. I'm not sure if meeting his family or the fact that I plan on leaving those clothes here frightens me more. Both make this thing between us more real, that's for sure.

Penny texts me a picture of herself on the balcony with a glass of red wine, wishing me luck this evening, leaving me wishful for my own glass of wine to take the edge off. Unfortunately, Rhett's fridge is full of domestic beer and a half full bottle of whiskey.

"Okay, the white dress it is, Mabel." She lifts her eyes to me, laying like a puddle on the floor. I've grown used to her always being near, always listening to my random monologue.

There's no floor length mirror in this house, only one over the antique dresser in the bedroom, so I have to assume this dress still looks good on me. I slip it on, and rip the tags off, throwing them into the trash can. It's a beautiful white eyelet dress that makes my barely sun kissed skin glow. I pair it with leather sandals and gold hoops. I figure it's put together but casual enough for this so-called potluck Sunday dinner. I was taught to always dress like you're about to meet the president, and that type of ideology sticks with you for life.

To combat the summer heat, I clip my hair loosely back, and as I dab a splash of perfume on my neck, the bathroom door cracks open. Rhett enters slowly, our eyes locked in the mirror. A white towel hangs low on his hips, and I hold in the small moan trying to escape my lips.

His stare is too much, so I peel my attention away, adjusting my hair, but Rhett stays standing there, running his hand through his damp locks.

"What?" I ask quietly, turning around and leaning my hips back on the dresser. The room feels smaller than it already is, and my limbs feel buzzy.

He blinks lazily, slightly shaking his head as he moves towards me. "You're stunning, Audrey."

The way my name rolls off his tongue makes my skin tingle.

"Oh, this? It's nothing. But thank you."

He comes over, boxing me in between the bed and the dresser and I'm too aware that all he has on is a towel.

"I could get used to this; you know?" He breathes on my neck, kissing it gently.

I have an almost irresistible urge to run my fingers down his rippled chest and outline his tattoos with my fingertips. I want to learn the story behind each one, learning another piece of this layered man. A feeling I never had with Jackson. He held me at arm's length, but Rhett holds my heart in the palm of his hands.

My breathing quickens as he leans in, placing kisses down my exposed collarbone, his hands roughly tracing the outline of my hips up to my breasts. Shuddering under his touch, I open my eyes, focusing on the man in front of me.

"We better get going," he whispers in my ear before kissing the sensitive skin on my neck.

"You are a tease, has anyone ever told you that?" I playfully shove him, but he barely moves.

"Every day, darlin'."

I leave him in the bedroom, not sure I can handle any more *heat* and exhale my breath in the kitchen, making sure I have everything I need. The macarons are secure in Tupperware. I feel like I should've grabbed Renee flowers. But maybe I'm overthinking it.

Rhett walks out into the kitchen, his cowboy boots tapping on the wood floors, and he lifts my face to his with a single finger under my chin.

"Don't worry, they are going to love you."

I feign a small smile, nodding.

Rhett's childhood home is only a few minutes away, and the car ride goes by in a flash. Breathtaking magnolia trees line the property, and a humble but charming yellow house appears behind beds of wildflowers. The second the truck comes to a stop, Mabel leaps from the open bed, sniffing the other two messy dogs who make up our greeting party.

"I told you we were a rowdy bunch." Rhett winks, stealing a quick kiss before leaping out of the truck. As I open my door, I hear little voices.

"Uncle Rhett! Mom, Uncle Rhett is here!" Two blonde haired girls run barefoot through the front yard towards us. They both have sundresses on, full of grass stains, and one is wearing crooked butterfly wings.

I can't help but smile and Rhett offers me a hand, squeezing it right before I'm bombarded by kids and dogs, all vying for our attention.

"This is quite the hello!" I tease and his nieces giggle, staring at Rhett and I.

"This is Jessie." Rhett ruffles the hair of the little girl with butterfly wings. "And this is Jenna." The other one has on rainbow rainboots. "Girls, this is Audrey. She's going to have dinner with us, and she made cookies for y'all."

Both of their faces light up, and they come closer to look into the container.

"What kind of cookies?" Jenna asks, standing on her tiptoes to get a look into the box I'm holding.

"They are macarons. Have you ever had one?" I ask, unable to remember the last time I talked to kids. I hope I'm doing this right.

They gape at each other.

"My mom said those are fancy cookies and she can't make them!" Jessie announces point blank.

Rhett bends down, tickling Jessie. "You can count on this one to be brutally honest."

Just then, Renee and a spitting image of her round the corner of the yellow house.

"Girls, let them have some air!" The woman next to Renee calls out; must be Desi.

"This is my dog Sammy, and the old yellow dog is my Mimi's dog, Tato," Jenna says, eying me up.

"They are very cute. Did you say Mimi's dog's name is Tato?"

She nods, giggling. "Well, his real name is Potato. But we call him Tato. Because he lays in the sun like a baked potato," she explains, and I smile at her and the dogs. I like this little girl.

"Welcome to the circus." Renee and Rhett's sister greet us. "I'm Desi." His sister extends a hand, her face as welcoming as her mom's.

"It's so nice to meet you...and thank you for inviting me to your family dinner."

Renee dismisses it, "Are you kidding? We are thrilled."

"Uncle Rhett's never brought anyone to dinner before," Jenna adds, wrapping herself around Mabel's neck.

"Okay, Jenna, I think it's time I push you on the swing." Rhett swings towards her and she screams, as he chases her into the backyard.

"Well, that is true." His mom laughs. "But if that's something to eat in there, this will also be the first time Rhett ever showed up with food."

I hand her the cookies, following them to the backyard where Jessie and Jenna hang off Rhett like a tree. His grin is ear-to-ear, and my heart unexpectedly flutters. Not sure what to make of that. Or any of this, really.

"They might be their uncle's biggest fan." Desi saddles up next to me at the long table on the back patio. Renee is at the grill, which is full of vegetables, presumably from her garden.

"As if his ego wasn't already through the roof."

Desi laughs, her smile the same as her brother's. Charming and coy. "Oh, I like you. Let me get you a drink. Red or white wine?"

"Red, please!"

As soon as the glass is in my hand, Desi turns to me again.

"So, tell me about yourself. We only just found out my brother had a girlfriend this week." She creases her eyebrows. "I'm sorry. Is that the label y'all prefer?"

"Oh, it's fine. It's all really new," I reassure her, adjusting my gold necklace. I tell Desi the polite stuff; what I do for work, where I'm from, where I live.

"Dinner is ready! Come on girls!" Renee calls out, and everyone joins Desi and I at the table.

Rhett wasn't kidding. The meal looks incredible, and I have to stop myself from complementing every single dish as it makes its way around the table.

"So, did you finish the bookshelves yet?" Desi asks her brother as everyone dives into the food.

Rhett shakes his head. "I finished cutting the trim today, but I have to put it all together. End of the week it should be done."

"Have you seen Rhett's work? He calls himself a carpenter, but he is really talented with small details and millwork."

"Damn Desi, who paid you to be nice to me?" Rhett taunts and his niece's eyebrows spring up.

"You cussed, Uncle Rhett! You owe us a dollar!" they say in unison.

He narrows his eyes at his sister who shrugs before pulling out his wallet and handing a dollar over to the enamored six-year-olds.

"He did show me the custom front door he was working on this weekend...but I haven't seen his finished work," I added.

"He has a new client in Forest Hills, you know that neighborhood with the multi-million-dollar homes?" his sister adds, and my hands freeze midair, but I nod, heat pooling in my neck. Forest Hills, where I owned a house I hated, one Rhett didn't even know about. "Rhett recently did stunning custom work in one of the luxury apartment buildings downtown, too, the historic one. Uhm...Brecken Building I think it's called...and the owner didn't even thank him, write a review or anything. I know the money is good, but those people suck—"

"Desi." Rhett's deep voice cuts his sister off.

"Sorry. I get carried away." Desi flashes a smile at me, and I swallow a sip of wine, my throat still tight. Rhett's fork hovers over his plate and I press my leg into him by accident.

"You know, you two never said how you met," Renee chimes in.

I open my mouth, but Rhett beats me to the answer.

"Audrey lived in a building I was doing work on. The Brecken Building." He pointedly says to his sister, and now I *do* shove my leg into his on purpose.

Desi stops chewing, looking up at me, her cheeks pink.

"Oh, my god. I am so sorry, Audrey. I didn't mean anything by that. I'm just protective of my brother. Really, I'm sorry."

Rhett clears his throat, and I dramatically shake my head. "Don't even worry about it. The thing is, you're not entirely wrong about the people in that building…" I take another sip of wine, desperately needing a refill. "I actually moved out of there recently."

"Oh!" Renee gestures her fork between Rhett and I. "Are you two moving in together?"

Again, I vigorously shook my head.

"Oh no! No. I moved in with my best friend. I'm still downtown."

"Okay, well this has been a *lovely* family dinner, huh?" Rhett jabs through tight lips to his mom and sister. Though I could already tell this wasn't the type of family to hold grudges.

It was a dynamic I only saw in other families, or TV shows, really. I never got this close of a look at it. I felt like a fly on the wall in a place I desperately wanted to belong but wouldn't even know how to begin.

"I don't care how you met, or where you lived, or where you're from. I'm just really happy you two met when you did." His mom's eyes were full of kindness, her gaze putting me at ease.

"Thank you, Renee."

Those were words I knew would never come out of my own mother's mouth to Rhett. She would absolutely care where he was from, would faint at the idea of eating a potluck style dinner, and would never make him feel welcome.

The girls got up to play, and Desi helped her mom take the dishes inside. As I stood, Rhett turned towards me, wrapping his arms around me, my back pressed into his chest.

"I owe you," he whispers into my ear, kissing my temple, and I close my eyes, squeezing back the tears. Thinking about how he welcomed me into this. This beautiful family, who made meals out of love, who cared about each other's happiness, and at the smallest hint of uncomfortableness accidentally directed towards me, he felt like he *owes* me.

I kept my body facing away from him, so he couldn't see the hurt weighing in my eyes. I could never repay him with the same kindness. All I had to offer was myself and even that came with no promises.

Rhett was right. There was nothing to worry about. His family welcomed me with open arms. His nieces acted like they already knew me, taking me by the hand to show me their hiding spot in the yard. The dogs circled me, bringing me sticks like we were best friends. Renee made me feel like I was a prized guest, and Rhett kept asking me if I needed anything, refilling my drink when it was low, like his sole job this evening was to make sure I was okay.

At the end of the night, I unclasp the gold chain from around my neck and place it on the dresser. As I do, I catch a glimpse of myself in the mirror and gently touch my collarbone.

It was so easy to be *here*. It was frighteningly easy. I never knew anything to be this easy. Being with Jackson wasn't easy, being my parent's daughter wasn't easy. Showing up and doing a job that paid me but didn't bring me joy wasn't easy. I was taught life wasn't supposed to be easy. I was supposed to challenge myself. Push for more, strive for perfection, work for my relationships; like they were businesses, not acts of the heart.

But being here, wearing an oversized shirt of Rhett's, hair up in a messy bun, messy dog at my feet, heart full of honest conversation, family surrounding me...even if it wasn't my family, that felt *easy*.

Tears clouded my eyes as I pulled onto the highway early the next morning on my way to work. It was becoming increasingly hard to live this life where I was two different people who didn't know how to exist in the same world.

Jolting me from the thought, my phone rings and I pick it up, assuming its Ed's assistant calling me at 8 a.m. on a Monday morning. But I should've looked at the name.

"Good morning, Audrey."

"Hey, Dad..." I replied cautiously, glancing in my rearview mirror as if he might pop up behind me.

"Are you on the way to the office?"

"Yes, I am driving in this morning." I omit the part about leaving from my secret boyfriend's house.

"I'm calling to congratulate you on the promotion," he states, my mouth falling open as I rack my brain. I am certain I didn't tell him about the promotion. Outside of work, only Penny knew...I was careful about it.

"I talked to Ed yesterday," he adds and my mouth shuts, my fingers digging into the steering wheel.

Can anything just belong to me?

"I was going to tell you and Mom myself later this week, but I guess he beat me to it," I lied. I wasn't planning on telling them until it actually happened, not needing their opinion on everything, but that little bubble of hope burst.

"Ed figured we knew. Most people would call their parents to let them know good news like that." It wouldn't be polite to point out we aren't *most people*. He clears his throat uncomfortably. "Either way, your mother and I are proud of you. You should've gotten this promotion a year ago, but that's neither here nor there. It's done and that's what's important."

My tires skid as I hit my brakes, swerving around the car in front of me. Did I just black out or did Samuel Elson say he was proud of me? That my mother and him were proud of me? I must still be sleeping. If not, this would be the third time in my life I've heard that from his mouth.

"Oh...thank you," I stutter.

"It's way overdue that you return to New York. It suits you better. You're an Elson after all," he laughs but I can't find the humor in his sentiments.

"You're not still upset I won't be marrying a Tippins?" I bite my tongue as soon as the words come out, wishing I could suck them back in.

"No, I'm not mad. Sometimes space is necessary." He pauses, and I hear a knock at a door, assuming he is in his office. I don't think space is the right phrase because I don't ever plan to see or talk to Jackson again. But my father didn't see it that way. He never burnt bridges, even with people he highly disrespected, because his philosophy was that you never know when you need to *use* someone in the future. I didn't agree. Burn the damn bridge.

"We are excited for this future of yours, Audrey, let me make that clear."

In translation he is saying: *We are happy you'll be back in proximity, back in our control, back where you belong with us, with people like us.* His obsession with Jackson disappeared so quickly it felt like whiplash, but then again, I didn't try to understand the emotional workings of my father. If they did continue their business together, he hasn't indicated it, and I didn't want to open that discussion up. "Okay, I have to run," he added quickly, barely giving me a chance to reply before he hung up.

I drive the rest of the way in utterly confused silence.

They are proud of me for the person I'm not sure I am anymore. Or ever truly was.

CHAPTER THIRTY-FOUR

The numbers blur together on the screen, and I lean back, pushing away from my desk with a sigh. This windowless office feels like it's slowly draining the life out of me, and its only Tuesday. Needing a break, I pull out my phone and dive into recipes, saving nearly a dozen new dishes I can't wait to try.

I promised Penny I'd have dinner with her tonight, and tried to play it cool, like I wasn't dying for the weekend to roll back around so I could escape the city and get back to the little town of Roseville.

My phone buzzes and a smile takes over my face.

Rhett: We miss you.

He sends a selfie of him and Mabel on the front porch, a beer in one hand, a tennis ball in Mabel's mouth.

I sent back a picture of me in my gray office, thumbs down.

Audrey: What's the plan this weekend?

I sent the text before realizing we never exclusively talked about seeing each other again this weekend. All I knew is I found myself automatically wanting to, picturing myself with him, escaping *this* sad reality.

> **Rhett:** So, my sister asked if I could watch the girls Saturday night so she can go to a concert…and they asked me if you'd be there. You don't have to say yes, but I think they'd love it.

In response, I sent a picture of a cake I've been trying to find a reason to make.

> **Audrey:** Only if they will help me make this?

> **Rhett:** First you steal my dog, now my nieces. I can't compete.

Biting my lip, grinning like a fool, I glance at the clock. There's no way I can get myself to write another email or file this report today. At one point I loved showing up here. Problem solving, seeing my reports in comparison to my peers, overperforming, staying late, doing all the things, and more. But everything changed. Slowly, then all at once.

So, I slam my laptop shut, grab my purse, and quickly exit the building that was beginning to feel like my prison. Ten minutes later, I see Penny waving at me from a table in the back of the restaurant.

"I didn't expect you to leave work early." She stirs her pink cocktail, eyes on me as I unload into the chair across from her.

"I didn't exactly ask permission. I couldn't take it anymore. My ability to concentrate these days is gone." I run my palms down my face as Penny cocks an eyebrow.

"Okay, just say it."

"Nope." She picks up the menu, pretending to read it.

"Come on, you can't do this to me!"

"Ever since you met Red, you've…"

Dread coils in my gut. I'm not sure I'm ready to hear this.

"Failed at everything else?" I retort bluntly, but Penny scoffs.

"No, I was going to say you've shifted your priorities. And I don't think that's a bad thing. I'm only wondering what you're going to do about New York."

The waitress came by to take our orders, giving me a moment to gather my thoughts. I hoped an answer would come to me, but I was still drawing a blank as she walked away.

"I have no idea, Pen. My parents are finally proud of me. My brother sent me a congratulatory text, did I tell you that?"

Penny blinks a few times, clearly as confused as I was about hearing from my brother. It was the first text from him since Christmas.

"That's great…I guess? But I didn't know you cared so much about what they thought?"

My breath gets stuck in my chest because the answer wasn't easy. Not easy to explain, and certainly not easy to navigate.

"Lately, I've been feeling like I'm living a double life. One with Rhett that has totally caught me by surprise. Then one where I'm still trying to fit into my family. And for some fucked up reason, I can't let go of either dream." Frustration bubbles at the surface but Penny doesn't shy away, she just looks on like a friend who's seen it all. "Because in my heart I want both to exist. I want them to love me no matter what I chose, or who I chose."

Pen hands me her napkin before I even realize I'm shedding tears.

"Maybe you can have both," she offers up, even if she knows that's naive, and I smile, even if I know it doesn't reach my eyes.

What a nice dream that would be.

CHAPTER THIRTY-FIVE

Rhett

I don't know why I agreed to build a pergola in the middle of July, but I try to focus on my girl next me as I cool down inside her blacked out SUV, the AC blowing straight onto my overheated chest.

We're breaking our rule—*no seeing each other during the work week*—but I was beginning to wonder why the hell we made that rule in the first place.

"You know, Desi said the girls haven't stopped talking about the rainbow cake y'all made last weekend. They want one for their birthday, apparently."

Audrey laughs to herself. "I'd love to make them one, when is their birthday?"

"Not for another ten months," I reply, driving my point home that Audrey has quickly become a star in my family.

She smiles sweetly, but I can tell she is distracted by something. Worry comes in the form of a sudden headache, something I'm not used to. That is...not used to caring if I fucked up with a girl. In the past I'd count my losses and cut ties, but now all I want to do is fix what's wrong, without pushing her further away.

The car idles on the street outside the house I'm working on. The rolling roads of Forest Hills are lined with lush trees and sprawling lawns; the kind that look almost too perfect, like the grass has been spray painted deep green. I prefer a more natural landscape, but Audrey fits right in today. Her hair is sleekly pulled back, and she's wearing a navy skirt with an cream top; jarringly different from the casual, carefree look she has on weekends with me. She's impossibly elegant, polished, and at home here, as if she could effortlessly occupy any one of these houses.

I've never given much thought to the neighborhood she grew up in, because she hasn't opened up about her past much, but I reckon it was probably similar to this one. I know she'll share in her own time when she's ready. I'm not planning on going anywhere.

"There's a park down the street we could eat at, or I'm happy to sit right here with you," I offer, finally cooled down, hoping I can get some clarity on her aloof behavior.

I bought us lunch and she picked it up from a bistro down the street, but we still sat in the idling car with the bag of food resting in between us.

Both her hands stay clutching the steering wheel as she slowly turns away from me.

"I... uhm...I want to show you something if that's okay."

"Sure." The headache pounds away.

She pulls away from the house, but we don't leave the neighborhood. Instead, we drive deeper in, winding down a road where the properties are somehow even more massive.

Audrey doesn't speak as we drive slowly, and neither do I. But it's not a comfortable silence either, like it usually is when I'm driving her around in my truck. There's tension in the air as she slows down at the end of the cul-de-sac, pulling up to a gated driveway of an expansive Tudor style home with a manicured lawn. A 'For Sale' sign is perched just outside the gate, and I watch with bated breath as she types in a code, the gate opening before us. We pull forward slowly.

"What are we doing here?" I ask as she shifts the car into park, unbuckles her seatbelt and leans back, resting her head against the leather headrest, still not making eye contact with me.

"It's a nice house, yeah?" she all but mumbles, and it takes a minute to register she is actually talking to me.

I dip my head to peer out the window at the house stretched before us. It stands tall and studious, its gray stone covered in ivy. It reminds me of a fortress.

"Yeah, it's nice," I say, but it comes out like more of a question. "Are you thinking about buying it?" I tease, studying Audrey, but she is unmoving.

"No." She rubs her palms on her legs, turning to me. "I'm selling it."

"I don't understand."

"Will you come inside with me?" she asks without further explanation, and I step out of the car with her. We approach the enormous mahogany front door, and she pulls out a key, pushing it open. Her shoulders sag, and I'm jittery in my work boots entering the dark foyer behind her. She moves to flip on a light, and I peer up at the massive chandelier twenty feet above us.

My heart stammers wildly as Audrey wrings her hands together, bouncing on the heels of her feet.

"Rhett, this is my house," she lets out with a humorless chuckle.

"I don't understand," I speak slowly, and Audrey bites her lip, nodding in quiet acknowledgment.

"Jackson bought it for me."

Holy shit.

She offers me a small smile and beckons me to follow her down the hallway and into the great room. Huge floor to ceiling windows run the length of the kitchen and living room, flooding it with natural light. A large yard with pruned shrubs and short cut grass sits outside the windows like a picture book. It's beautiful and grand, but seeing Audrey standing here now, I can't say it fits her. At least not the version of her I've gotten to know the past month.

Audrey places a palm cautiously on the enormous marble island.

"We bought this house a year ago, but never moved in. We were renovating it...and all the work was finally completed this week. Jackson signed the house over to me when we split." She lets out a dry laugh, tapping her pink fingernails on the stone. "I think in his own fucked up way, this was supposed to be an apologetic gesture. He really thought I'd want to live *here* after everything." She sucks in her lips, and I want to wrap my arms around her, but Audrey moves to the window, gazing out at the property.

"My parents told me it was foolish to list this place. And for a minute, I let that consume me, wondering if there's something inherently broken in me—like maybe I'm destined to reject everything good, as if I'm wired for ruin, drawn toward my own self-destruction. And—" she was rambling, but I cut her off, wrapping my arms around her waist and spinning her to face me.

"No, you're not," I say firmly, clutching her chin in my hand. "Screw what everyone else thinks. What do you want?" I pause, as Audrey's lips tremble, her eyes misting. I kiss her lightly and pull back so I can look into the hazel eyes that have become permanently etched on my mind. "And no one in their right mind would want to live in a home this large by themselves."

This gets a small chuckle out of her.

"You live all alone," she muses.

"Yeah, and I didn't realize how much I hated it until I met you."

Audrey's eyebrows twitch, her breath pausing. "Oh yeah? Is that so?"

"It is." I pull her into me, kissing her hair, and she rests her head against my chest. "You going to tell me why you brought me here today?"

"I didn't want to hide this anymore. I've been so worried you'd judge me if you knew. Or maybe think I'm ungrateful. I just didn't want you to see me differently."

"Different than what?"

"Than how I feel when I'm with you. Because..." She steps back and gestures around the great room that's the size of my entire house. "This isn't who I am anymore."

"I know that. You don't have to prove anything to me. I'd love you even if you were penniless. Your money has nothing to do with how I feel about you."

Audrey pauses, her eyebrows lowered over eyes that could stop my heart right in its tracks.

"You love me?" Her voice cracks, sharp and raw, and the silence around us feels heavy.

I didn't even realize I'd said it. But if I'm being honest, I think I fell in love with Audrey the moment I met her on the rooftop.

"Yeah, I think I do." My heart pounds in my chest as she stands frozen, worry filling every inch of me, thinking that I just fucked up, that this is it. This is the end, where she high tails my ass out of this house, or tells me this is all too fast, like I can take back words. But she doesn't. Her palm moves to rest on my chest, and surely, she can feel the way it surges at her touch.

"I think I love you, too."

Those words hang in the air, raw and exposed; words I've never spoken to anyone before. Maybe they were always only meant for Audrey.

Tipping her chin up, I plant a soft kiss on her mouth. She pulls back, peering up at me.

"You know, I never actually spent any time in this house, other than with the designer and checking in on the renovations. I want to change the way I remember it, though. I don't want it to be a black mark in my past." She clasps her hands in front of her chest and bats her eyelashes.

"Will you eat lunch with me here?"

She could've asked me anything at that moment and I would've said yes.

So, we eat our sandwiches, sitting on the stone floor, our backs against the kitchen cabinets, laughing about nothing and everything. I make her give me a tour of the house, telling her I'm going to kiss her in every room of the house, so she remembers nothing but the good.

Because damn, all I want is to be good for her. Audrey makes me want to be the best man I can be. She unravels me to my core, piecing me back together each time she shows me another hidden part of herself.

And when we are done, and she locks up the house again, saying goodbye one last time, I have nothing but respect for her.

Most people wouldn't understand why she prefers my farmhouse with its small rooms and creaky floors, or the yard full of wild plants, but I understand it.

CHAPTER THIRTY-SIX

Rhett

Saying I love you didn't change much between Audrey and I, not on the surface at least. We were both still busy with work, and the next weekend her car was parked in my driveway, her lightness filling my house. My kitchen had also been taken over by baking pans, and my freezer was now full of cookies. I could get used to this.

My dad always said love did things to a man, made him do crazy things. I used to roll my eyes, always a teenager who was too tough for feelings. But today, as I finished up a job early, I decided to do something that made no sense.

Being in love with Audrey Elson was the only plausible explanation as to why I slowed my truck down and pulled into the nursery on the corner of my street.

Blackburn Farms was a family run business that ran a U-pick berry operation and sold landscaping plants. I've passed this place every single day, only stopping once or twice over the years, but today, I stopped there with an idea that quickly rooted itself.

"Hi, can I help you find anything in particular?" An older woman beamed up at me with a garden hose in her hand. I knew it being mid-July meant the plant selections would be slim; you either already planted your garden, or you had to wait till fall. But I didn't care. Love didn't make sense, like my old man said.

Squinting against the sun, I chuckle, knowing she is going to think I'm daft. "Yeah, I am actually looking for hydrangea bushes."

The woman's sweet smile falters, but her voice remains chipper. "I think we may have a few left but I have to warn you, this isn't the best time to plant them. You'd be better off to wait until September or October. They will probably die if you attempt to plant them now."

I figured as much, but I shake my head, smiling back. "That's alright, I'd like to give it a shot. Can you point me in the right direction?"

She led me down the aisle lined with greenery, her steps slow, hesitation practically radiating off her small frame. But I was determined to see this through.

Six small bushes with wilted blooms sat in plastic containers at her feet.

"This is what we have left. They are 50 percent off if you really want them."

"I'll take them all." I was about to pull my wallet out when I remembered something essential. "Will these ones produce blue flowers?"

She pulled her lips to the side. "Well yes, they will, but only if your soil is acidic, not alkaline. If you're not sure what type of soil you have, we sell testing kits in the store." She sighed and pivoted to point to flowers on the riser behind her. "Sir, we also have loads of purple coneflowers which would tolerate being planted right now."

"Thank you for the help, but I'll just be taking the hydrangeas. And throw in a soil testing kit."

"Okay. The plants are final sale."

I nod, my lips curling up. "Perfect."

There's no going back now.

CHAPTER THIRTY-SEVEN

Audrey

As I was driving to Roseville, my Friday playlist on repeat, it hit me I hadn't thought about Jackson for a while. Maybe it was the summer heat, the way it wrapped around you in North Carolina, making time still itself. Or perhaps it was all the baking. Every weekend I found myself covered in flour and sugar, dancing barefoot in the tiny farmhouse kitchen I'd inadvertently taken over. That had to be good for the soul. Or maybe it was the way I couldn't keep my hands off Rhett, or my eyes. Maybe it was all of that which slowly erased Jackson from my mind.

Thinking of my past felt like watching a movie through blurry film, and I barely recognized it.

If I were truly honest with myself, I'd admit that each day, New York lingered a little less in my mind. I hadn't opened an apartment listing alert for over two weeks now. And the document outlining the structural changes in my department —thanks to my new position— still sat untouched, unread.

Because somehow that future also felt foreign, a version of life I didn't recognize.

Right here, right now, I didn't have to be anyone but myself. This place and Rhett; it was enough. I knew I couldn't put it off forever, that I had to figure things out soon, but I wasn't ready. I just need a little more time. I need to make the right choice. I couldn't risk making another mistake.

I parked the car, and sent Penny a quick text, telling her to have safe travels this weekend. She had a wedding to shoot in the mountains.

As I gathered my stuff, Mabel galloped toward the car. An instant serotonin boost.

"Hi girl." I smiled down at her, my weekend bag looped in one arm, iced coffee in my other, and Mabel trotting along next to me as I strolled to the front door.

I don't quite make it there before my heart drops in my stomach and time stands still. The screened door opens and Rhett steps out, a curious look on his face. He's still him, faded blue jeans and a white t-shirt spanning his chest. He flashes me a crooked smile, but I can't return it, because something's changed here.

"When did you do this?" My mouth is dry as my eyes flit between him and the flower beds lining the front porch. Where there was once nothing, now sits six hydrangea plants. A few blue flowers hanging on.

Rhett creases his brow, skipping down the steps, stopping at the edge of the new soil. He chews his lips, studying the plants.

"They're a bit ragged right now, but I've been reading all about how to care for them, and by next summer, they'll double in size and be full of flowers. Or blooms. Sorry, this is new to me." He explains, kneeling into the soil, his hand gingerly on the flowers, gaze fixed on me.

"Why?" I whisper. My voice breaks as a warm breeze blows through the yard, pushing loose strands of chocolate hair into my face. I push it back, but my feet remain glued to the earth below me.

Rhett clears his throat and stands. "They are your favorite flowers. Blue hydrangeas. You spend a lot of time on the front porch, and I thought you might enjoy seeing them," he replies so logically, like it just makes sense. Like it's natural to plant someone's favorite flowers in your front yard. I told him my favorite flowers were blue hydrangeas on our first date.

Deep breath.

He didn't buy me roses.

I pinch the bridge of my nose, forcing the tears back.

He planted my favorite flower. In his yard. So, I can see them every day.

Next summer they will be full. I want to run into his arms this very minute and never let go. Yet another part of me wants to run, as far as I can, because what if next summer I'm not here to see them. The thought nearly knocks me off my axis.

"I'm sorry. If this upsets you…"

I drop my items in the grass and reach for Rhett's hand.

"What if there isn't a next summer?" I nearly whisper and Rhett steps closer to me, bringing his arms around my neck, kissing the top of my head.

"I wouldn't have planted these if I didn't see a next summer, darlin'."

He pulls back and I bite my cheek until I taste iron, a hollow ache in my stomach.

I nod, and though he looks confused he doesn't push me to explain, he doesn't make me feel bad for my reaction. He simply leads me into the house, his fingers laced in mine, but before the door closes, I gaze over my shoulder to look at the flowers as tears prick the back of my eyes.

I can't live in this in-between anymore.

Guys who are summer flings don't plant a garden for you.

And you don't fall asleep thinking about how much you love them.

"I know this looks like a hole in the wall, but I promise they have the world's best breakfast."

Rhett has been going on and on about the diner in town all morning. We woke up this Saturday morning to find the kitchen mostly devoid of food, so he suggested we go into town to eat. Walking hand in hand, he guides me down the main street of a town I realized I no longer felt like an outsider in.

"First, I don't judge a book by its cover. Some of the best food I've ever had came from some unassuming street vendors and tiny restaurants."

"After you..." Rhett holds the door open for me as I step inside, the door chime ringing like a call from the past. I'm not exaggerating; this little diner is a genuine time capsule, complete with shiny red booths, a soda counter, checkered floors, and a giant analog clock ticking away on the wall. It's the most charming place I've ever laid eyes on, and the waitress beams at Rhett from behind the counter, her vintage uniform adding to the nostalgic atmosphere.

"Your booth is open, Rhett." She tilts her head to the back. We slid into the booth, facing each other, and before I could ask, the waitress was at the table with two mugs and a pot of steaming coffee.

"I was beginning to worry about you. You haven't been in all summer." She raises her eyebrows at him, glancing my way. Rhett smirks, blue eyes settling on me.

"I've been busy. Rosie, I'd like you to meet my girlfriend, Audrey."

Rosie, who could be my grandmother, instantly changes her demeanor, blushing as she turns to me.

"Well, no wonder you were busy! Nice to meet you, honey."

"I brought her here to try the world's best breakfast." Rhett winks at Rosie as she sets down menus, leaving us be. A warm feeling fills me as I playfully kicked Rhett's foot under the table.

"I think she's sweet on you."

Rhett laughs, bringing his coffee up to his lips. "Rosie's worked here since I was a child. My grandparents used to take me and Desi here on Saturday mornings to give my parents a break. Desi would sit all nice, never making a stir. I, on the other hand...well, my grandpa would have to threaten to whoop my ass because I was always running all around this place."

"So, this is a true hometown staple for you?"

He nods with vigor, resting his elbows on the table.

"I took my first date to this diner when I was fifteen. We sat right there." He points to the two stools at the end of the counter. "And Ky and I carved our names into this table when we were juniors." He rolls his eyes, embarrassed but I chuckle, loving every morsel of Rhett.

"So, which one of you is the bad influence?"

Rhett points at himself. "I *was*. I've grown up though. As you can see." He winks, but I scoff.

"Yeah, right. Okay." I snort and Rhett flashes me a devilish grin.

"Ky is a cool guy. We were neighbors growing up, his mom and dad still live there actually. He's like a brother to me. When my dad died, he spent the summer working with me at the farm so I wouldn't be alone. He was a wild teenager, but he's brilliant, too. He's a tech hot shot now but still lives here in town."

"That's really sweet. Sounds like Ky is your Penny." I smile, thinking about my best friend. "We need to get together, the four of us," I add, and Rhett shakes his head, his eyes twinkling.

"Now you're really trying to start trouble, huh?"

"I don't know what you mean," I add coyly, sipping my coffee. "Well, this place must be special if both you and Ky stayed."

"It is. But enough about me, yeah? You must have stories, too, or a *place* you always went, the hangout spot, as a kid or teen. Tell me about it." He eggs on but I pinch my lips together, pretending to rack my brain for something that's not there.

"Yeah, it's called my bedroom studying, or the tennis court." I shake my head. "I spent a lot of my teenage years doing an insane amount of extracurriculars. Like more than anyone should be required to do. My parents made sure I stayed busy, and if I had a spare moment, it surely wasn't spent hanging out or having fun," I replied, raising my eyebrows. "And as you already know, there were definitely no charming diners. I think I mentioned Andrew and I had nannies until we were teenagers, and there was always a private chef, so going out to eat as a family wasn't a thing. I mean, sure my parents went out on dates, or to events, but Andrew and I were always being chauffeured around, eating on the go or at home alone."

I felt embarrassed for reasons I knew I shouldn't. I grew up never wanting a single item. I had everything and more. But I don't have a single memory of sitting in a diner with my grandparents. It's a foreign daydream that sounds so lovely.

Rhett tries to hide the sadness on his face as Rosie approaches us again.

"What will it be?" she asks, pen on pad.

Realizing I haven't even glanced at the menu, I look frantically at Rhett.

"You like waffles?" He smirks and I nod. "Okay Rosie, two classic waffles with strawberries. Bacon and eggs on the side. Thank you." He slides the menus back to her.

"Trust me, you're going to love them. And if you don't —well shit, I think I'd have to dump you."

"Oh yeah? Who knew so much was riding on breakfast." I kicked him again, but this time he reached under the table, squeezing my leg, making me jolt in my seat, laughing.

"Thanks for bringing me here."

I'm relieved he doesn't ask any more questions about my past. And he isn't wrong. The waffles are better than an orgasm. Well, almost.

"Damn, girl." Rhett enters through the backdoor as I pull the baking sheet from the oven.

I'm a hot mess; my apron shifted sideways on me, three different timers going, and not an inch of countertop is clean, but pride swells in me, because I have done this all myself. Tonight, *we* are hosting Sunday dinner at Rhett's house, and his family will be here any moment now.

"I know, I made a lot. But I never got to cook for anyone really, so this is fun for me."

His eyes roam over everything but he smiles, and relief floods me. I just want to get this right.

"You don't have to buy their love; you know they already like you. Like, so much, and I can't figure out why..."

I snap the kitchen towel at Rhett, but we're interrupted by my ringing phone. I searched around, unable to locate it.

Rhett finds it under the cookbook and tosses the phone at me. I catch it, accidently answering it in the process. Rhett stands there unsure if he should leave, but I hold up my finger, gesturing to him to be quiet. I'm determined to make this conversation short.

Since his existence isn't known to anyone but Penny.

"Hey Mom."

"Audrey, hello, I need to chat, do you have a moment?"

"Uhm, I have a minute. I'm just cooking dinner."

"Oh, how funny," she responds, probably thinking I'm joking, but I stay silent until she continues. I'm not in the mood to entertain her antics. "You haven't RSVP'd and catering needs the final count. I need to know if you're coming to the Labor Day party. You and Jackson never missed this party before and I know you'll be alone this year, but Audrey, it's a big deal for your father. Half the company will be there. I know you'll be in New York—"

I jolt, spinning in my spot, praying Rhett didn't hear a word of that.

"Yes, I am still figuring that all out, Mom. I don't know if I'll be able to make it back this year, due to work."

"Andrew is taking time away from surgery to be with his family."

She had to pull the 'your brother's a surgeon' card.

"Mom—"

"If you're worried about the little upset, I can assure you everyone has moved on. No one is going to say anything about Jackson and you, we are all adults here. The world and this party doesn't revolve around you." Her comment is enough to make me want to hit my phone with the meat cleaver, but I grip it and spin back around, making a silly face at Rhett who is leaning against the wall with his arms crossed over his chest, an unreadable expression on his face.

"Okay, Mom. I will think about it and let you know tomorrow."

"Okay, fine. You should be here, people want to see you, Audrey. Your family misses you."

"Sounds good, good—" But the phone call ended.

Squeezing my eyes shut, I lean against the counter, suddenly drained of the energy I had been brimming with minutes ago.

"Sorry about that," I offer, not meeting Rhett's eyes. He scoffs, and I open my mouth to play off the situation, when a knock sounds from the front door. Mabel stirs, and Rhett turns abruptly, walking away without so much as glancing my way.

"Can I have more please?" Jessie asks, rocking in her chair, pointing at the green beans on the dining table. Desi's eyes grow wide at her daughter.

"You want more vegetables?" She scooped them, peering skeptically at her daughter. "You never eat green beans at home."

"These are better than yours, Mom. No offense." She shrugs, and I mouth *sorry* to Desi who laughs.

"I can't compete with you," she jokes, and I shake my head.

"If it's okay with your mom, and once you're done, I made mini cheesecakes for dessert." I nod towards the kitchen and the girls' eyes light up in awe.

"You know you're going to have to keep this up now," Desi says, and I sip wine, shrugging.

"I love it. Honestly, I'm shocked there's not a good bakery in town. I told Rhett, every town needs a good bakery. It's just a fact."

"I agree," Jenna chimes in and we all laugh.

"Your mom must love having you home for the holidays. I bet you make some incredible dishes!" Renee smiles, and I lower my fork, my chest tightening with emotion. I can't help but let out a soft chuckle as Rhett watches me intently.

"Oh, my mom would never let me cook for a holiday." I rub my hands on the top of my thighs, unsure how to backpedal from here. Renee looks confused as Rhett continues to watch me, making me uneasy. He hasn't been himself since the phone call and it's made my appetite disappear.

"Will you be seeing them at all this summer?" Desi asks innocently. I'm sure it must be weird, since I see her family every week when we share these meals around a table. It's such an intimate thing, a tradition, one I've fallen right in with. But I don't think I've ever talked about my family except for the first time they met me. When it was the polite answer to the polite question.

"I'm not sure yet, I have just been enjoying summer here," I respond, smiling before shoving food in my mouth so they can't ask me more questions.

Here is safe. *Here* is secret. *Here* is where I can escape.

The rest of dinner goes off without a hitch. Desi and Renee keeping the conversation going, the girls playing with Mabel, and when I brought out the dessert tray, everyone crowded around, oohing and aahing. But I didn't grab one, and neither did Rhett. He just stood, leaning against the wall in the dining room, a beer in one hand, the other in his jean pocket.

He was quiet and dread gripped me. I knew when everyone filed out tonight, we'd have to talk. Our eyes met across the room and his mouth stayed in a hard line, like mine.

"You're spoiling Rhett, you know that?" His mom came up behind me as I soak a casserole dish in the sink. The sun outside the window was pink and dusky, and the quietness in the house as everyone ran around outside suddenly felt loud.

I smiled at Renee over my shoulder. "I'm just happy to be able to cook for everyone. It's my pleasure." But she doesn't budge or maybe doesn't buy it.

"Well, we are grateful for you being here. Rhett hasn't been so relaxed...I don't know, in forever."

I think back to the Ferris wheel, the night Rhett got vulnerable, sharing about his father's death and the summer of fun he never got to experience.

It slaps me as I stare down into the sudsy water, yet again a pit forming in my stomach.

"Hey, let him do the dishes, you did enough tonight!" Rhett's mom winks at me, and turns off the water, forcing me to leave the dishes in the sink. I wanted to clean up though, even if Rhett would happily step in to help. I needed something to focus on other than the painful truth of the mess I have created.

CHAPTER THIRTY-EIGHT

Audrey

We both shower, the dishes are cleaned up, and the lights are out except for a few lamps in the living room. I lounge on the opposite end of the sofa from Rhett, while Mabel's familiar snores rumble from the floor in front of me. The baseball game plays on the TV, but I drown out the noise and Rhett's eyes aren't focused on it.

I find myself lost in my Instagram feed, scrolling through photos of my friends and their so-called perfect summer lives. I'm not even sure why I still follow most of them—prep school friends and those who remain stuck in the miserable orbit of Jackson Tippins. It's been ages since I posted anything anyway, not since the breakup with Jackson. There's nothing I'm willing to share with the outside world.

What I have here with Rhett; it's just for us. I glance up at him, sitting stiffly on the couch, my feet near him, but he isn't rubbing them. He is in another world.

"It was really nice to see everyone tonight and be able to host." I add as much pep to my voice as I can manage, tossing my phone aside, as Rhett nods with a tight jaw. His tongue darts out to lick his lips, then he quickly clenches his jaw again.

"Does your family do anything over Labor Day weekend?" I press on. Because I know he heard parts of the conversation with my mother. And I don't know how to address this.

Rhett tips his head back, his blue eyes trained on the living room ceiling, the glow of the TV bouncing off the walls around us. "Audrey." My name comes out like a sigh, and a sense of defensiveness washes over me.

"I mean it's only a few weeks away, it's not preposterous to ask, is it?" I respond with more venom in my tone than intended. His eyes darted my way.

"I don't know if they have plans, but I know yours do." He's monotone in his retort and my heart surges but I try not to show it.

"Well, I'm not going to that. You heard the phone call."

"Yeah, most of it. What I didn't hear was a good reason though," he shot back, and I felt myself flush. I sit upright, my body buzzing with messy energy.

"You have to understand, my family isn't like yours, Rhett. It's not a quaint family dinner party at my parent's vacation home. It's a chance for them to show off their money, for my father's business partners to all kiss each other's asses, for my brother and his friends to act like I don't exist, even in their thirties and—"

"That's a lot of reasons."

"Exactly," I say, turning my attention to the TV, hoping he drops it, hoping he finally understands why I don't want to go back.

"But you used to go with Jackson, correct?"

Hearing my ex's name on Rhett's tongue makes the room spin for a moment. I hate that they ever had to overlap in my life. And there's something else. Hurt. I hear hurt. The one thing I never wanted to inflict on this man who's shown me nothing but love, done nothing but welcomed me into his world, giving me everything, even when he didn't have much to give.

I scoot closer to Rhett, needing to be close, needing to fix this, but his eyes are still icy. I think about touching his arm, but I don't.

"It's different. Him and my father were like this." I hold up my crossed fingers. "And my parents were more tolerable when we were together. It doesn't mean I enjoyed it."

"It's different…got it." He doesn't sound angry, just defeated, which is worse, but I still haven't gotten through to him. "Just answer me this, and I'll drop it." He leans forward on his elbows, and I swallow the lump in my throat. "Are you ashamed of me? Am I not good enough to meet your family, or was introducing me to them never in your plans?"

My heart hammers wildly in my chest as I spring off the sofa, pacing the room. "Rhett, stop. You're being unfair. Of course I was going to introduce you to them."

Is that true? When did I plan to do that?

Rhett stands, too, a humorless chuckle filling the air and disappointment painted on the face I've fallen in love with.

"I'm beginning to doubt that."

"It's only been a few months," I blurt out, and immediately inhale. Because that's not fair and I know it. He introduced me to his family almost immediately.

That stops him in his tracks as he glances at me.

"I see." His voice is somber, matching his walk as he walks out of the living room, leaving me scrambling to regain control of the situation.

But it's pointless; I'm trapped in my own paralyzing silence.

I always knew this day would come, where Rhett would ask about meeting my family. But I had hoped by then, things with my family would be smoothed out, and everything would finally make sense to me.

How horribly, horribly naive of me.

Sleep never comes, no matter how long I spend with my eyes shut in this bedroom. Rhett fell asleep almost instantly, or maybe he is faking it. I think about waking him to talk, my hand hovering over his shoulder, but pull it away for one reason or another, and silently slip out of bed, feeling my way in the dark to the door. I step over Mabel who lifts her tired eyes, but decides she can't miss out, and silently follows me out of the bedroom.

I don't bother flipping on the light in the kitchen. The moonlight is enough to illuminate the space so I can find my shoes. I snatch my sweater off the bench by the back door and wrap it around me, because even though it's still warm outside, I've had an icy shiver since our talk.

"You coming?" My whisper reaches Mabel in the dim kitchen, and she slips around my legs, trotting quietly into the backyard.

At the edge of the grass, I stand, arms tightly across my chest, the dog sniffing the ground not far from me. The worn tree swing becomes my stopping point, and I sit, lazily rocking back and forth, dragging my toes in the sandy soil under me.

The humid air fills my lungs as I tilt my head back, peering up at the stars. I haven't seen the stars this bright since the night on the rooftop. The night that was both a definite end and a definite beginning.

I have no plan. No plan as to what I'm doing out here at midnight. No plan for this future I've been carelessly carving.

A lump forms in my throat, one I can't get rid of by swallowing, so I let the tears fall softly. Tears I've been holding in for weeks, if I'm being honest with myself. Mabel pads over, tired and confused, her nose pushing into my thigh until I pet her.

"You're a good girl, you know that?" I ask her and her tail thumps a few times against the hard ground.

Mabel decided she loved me the first time she met me, and that was that. She didn't falter or stop. She probably always assumed I'd be coming back, never doubting one day I might not come back.

What the hell kind of person does that make me?

She lets out a groan when I stop petting her ears to wipe my misty eyes. "Okay, okay, I'm sorry."

Is this truly impossible or am I just being stubborn? As I ground myself in the moonlight of the backyard, I try to imagine Rhett meeting my family. If not at my parent's Labor Day soiree, perhaps we could go home for Thanksgiving. Though they usually spend it at their mountain home, so it would be a big production of travel. Perhaps Christmas. But I'm sure Rhett wants to spend Christmas here with his nieces and mom, and I would want to help make Christmas dinner...

My breath quickens at the vulnerability of that truth, the truth that slides so simply into my mind. I want to be here for Christmas. With him. With them.

Fuck. Fuck. Fuck.

"I can't go to New York," I whisper to myself, and the words feel so heavy in the air around me. But I repeat it as Mabel slowly slides down to lay at my feet.

"I don't *want* to go. I don't want to work in a high-rise and live in an apartment again and start over. I want to stay here."

There, it's out there.

Those words lift away the dark cloud that's been just a few feet behind me all summer.

With blurry eyes and a heart pounding so hard, it echoes in my ears. I push off the old tree swing. The ground feels uneven beneath me as I make my way back toward the house, my steps hesitant but determined. Through the window, I catch the soft glow of the little lamp by the kitchen sink, its light spilling out like a quiet invitation.

I pause for a moment, taking it in—the warmth of the light, the stillness of the house—and tilt my head down, drawing a shaky breath. The back door creaks as I push it open, my pulse racing as I step inside. I'm ready for this. Ready to let the words out before my mind has a chance to twist them into doubt, before fear takes over, and convinces me yet again that saying it is a mistake.

I'm not doing this for them. I'm doing it for him.

"I didn't mean to wake you," I murmur in the dim light, my eyes meeting Rhett's over the kitchen island. I circle it, coming closer to him. His shirt is too worn and thin. You can see his tattoos through it, but I know how soft it is. I know why he wears it, why he won't throw it out.

I know he can't sleep if he rolls over and finds me not there.

I know he likes his coffee bitter and black, and that when he's restless after dinner he goes to his workshop, working in silence. I know he doesn't talk about his feelings with anyone, except maybe me.

"I want you to come home with me in a few weeks. I want you to meet my family."

It takes a moment, but he shifts against the counter he leans on, taking a step closer to me.

"What? Why?" He narrows his tired eyes at me.

"Because I'm not ashamed of you. I love you. I thought I could protect what we have by keeping it a secret, but if it means losing you..." I can't even finish the sentence.

His lips pull up, a crooked smirk on his tired face. I place my hand on his jaw, his stubble rubs against my palm, and I pull him closer until it's only inches between us.

"I can't promise you it will be perfect, but I'm not going to hide us anymore."

I place my head on his strong chest as he wraps his arms around me.

"So...will you be my date to the most over the top Labor Day party you've ever seen?" I ask as he nuzzles his face into my messy bed head and kisses my temple, his hands winding slowly around me.

"You can count on it, baby."

Relief floods me. There's no hint of anger or hurt in his voice anymore. I could never count on anyone before, not really, besides Penny. But nothing Rhett has done, or failed to do has led me to believe he doesn't mean it with his whole heart. I can count on him.

I kiss him, finding myself desperate for his touch after this sleepless night. Rhett pulls away, but I grab his head, lacing my fingers in his hair and bring him back to me. He doesn't resist, parting my lips with his tongue.

Melting under his touch, my fears get pushed down, just for a moment. Slipping my hands under his shirt, needing to feel his skin, he responds, dipping his hand into the band of my shorts.

"Rhett..." I moaned, having so much more to tell him, so many things I needed to warn him about, but I couldn't think, not while he was stroking me in my most sensitive spot. Not while his lips and tongue kissed, nipped, and swirled around my neck.

Rhett drove his knee between my legs, and when he removed his hand, I instantly felt empty, desperate for him to touch me. The dim light of the kitchen is comforting, the man before me is my safety, and the words are out there.

I don't want to go to New York.

He drops to his knees, his head between my legs as my head lolls back, hands gripping the counter behind me.

He drives me to the point of panting, biting my lip, moaning his name until I shudder on his tongue. Without talking, Rhett carries me to the bedroom, to finish what he started, and when we are both exhausted, satisfied, naked against each other, he falls into a deep, peaceful slumber.

But the relief that flooded me just an hour ago has quickly faded and I find sleep impossible again, no matter how much I beg and trick my body into it. No matter how many times I run through every scenario, telling myself it will all be fine.

I never had to protect anyone but myself against my family, and even then, my only solution was satisfying them in a way that only hurt myself. But I'm not that person anymore, and I don't know what layer of protection I have other than a man who doesn't understand the true weight of the society I was raised in.

I can't shake the feeling that I am leading him into a den of snakes.

CHAPTER THIRTY-NINE

Audrey

Rhett stirs next to me, and a smile pulls on my lips as I watch his long eyelashes flutter awake as we cozy in under the white duvet. Sun shines in, and even though I didn't sleep much, I'm happy to wake up next to this man.

"I can't believe you're up before me," he grumbles, pulling the pillow under his chest to prop himself up. I graze my eyes across his bare torso, back to his eyes that are all on me.

"I woke up and couldn't go back to bed." I shrug.

"Desperate for more of this?" He teases and I roll my eyes hard, even though I wouldn't deny him if he decided to repeat last night's *activities*.

"Actually, I have been busy. I bought our plane tickets and made reservations at a hotel." I pause, tightening the messy bun on top of my head. Rhett's eyes go wide with confusion. "Oh shoot, do you not remember agreeing to come with me?"

He sits up, puffs out his cheeks and runs a hand through his messy hair before speaking. "Of course, I remember...but wouldn't we just stay with your parents? And last minute flights and hotels are usually pretty expensive, I thought? I didn't expect you to buy anything for me, Audrey."

"Please, it's the least I can do. I want us to be comfortable and have enough space for ourselves." I all but laughed at his suggestion of staying with my parents. I was already gambling by bringing a male guest. "Plus, my brother always takes over the guest house with his friends."

He still looks uneasy, but I rest my palm on his bare shoulder, smiling at the warmth beneath it. I love how hot he always runs.

"And please promise me, you won't worry about the money. This is my treat, and I got a deal," I add. A deal only because my last name was Elson and I called in a favor to the resort's manager. I would never tell Rhett how much this trip costs, because I know it would only make him uneasy, and it truly didn't matter to me. His comfort was most important.

"Okay, whatever you say, I trust you." He smiles at me, and I sigh a tiny breath of relief at his change of heart and easy-going attitude that's never far from persuasion.

I highly doubt my parents will be as easygoing when I tell them I will be showing up after all, and I'll have my not-so-secret boyfriend in tow.

"I've seen the guest list, it's enormous, which actually works in our favor. We will arrive make our rounds, you can meet my family, and then we can escape back to the resort."

"Wait, now it's a resort?"

"Technically, I think. I mean it has a spa and a pool, but we can also indulge in room service and body treatments. My treat." I flash an excited smile, knowing I need this little getaway as much as he does.

He hesitates, worry creasing his forehead. I know it's out of his comfort zone, but he'll be with me, and I guarantee when he realizes he can get a top shelf whiskey delivered to him poolside, he will be thanking me for this little idea.

"Listen, you're going to be on my turf, so it's my turn to show you a good time. I don't want you to worry about a thing, I have it all planned. You just have to show up, looking dapper."

"I'm not sure anything in my closet could be considered dapper." Rhett laughs, eyes roaming to his closet.

"Lucky for you, I'm working remotely today and can be done around four...so shopping this evening?"

I clasp my hands together in excitement and Rhett closes his eyes, but he can't help but smile when his gaze meets mine again. He can't resist me when I'm smiling. I know this much.

"You know I hate it...but okay. Let's go shopping tonight. Make me dapper or whatever the hell you said." He pretends to be annoyed but ruffles my hair, kissing me.

This isn't going to be so bad. Maybe this little trip away is exactly what we need together. Maybe it will even be fun.

Rhett meanders into the bathroom, so I glance through my calendar today. I will have to call my mom at some point, sooner than later. Best case scenario is she's pleasantly surprised her daughter is not reeling through a failed engagement but rather flourishing in a new relationship. Worst case scenario, she is rude about it. I can handle that. Plus, they didn't need all the details or the timeline.

I'm just trying to keep the peace between them and myself while showing Rhett I'm proud of what we have. That's what this trip is all about.

Maybe, in the pit of my heart, I hope if they see me, and see the way Rhett looks at me, they will see I'm doing okay. That I'm not a lost cause. That belief keeps me going as I get ready for the day, begin working at Rhett's dining room table, and finally gain the courage to dial my mother's number.

Penny pops another carrot in her mouth, leaning back on her pink sofa, listening to me talk about my weekend as we catch up over our favorite Wednesday night reality show.

"So, walk me through this again. Your mom was totally nonchalant about you bringing a new man?"

"She said, and I quote, 'That's nice, your father will be thrilled you are coming home.' I asked her again if she had me down for two, and she said yes. She was extremely distracted, but she seemed *fine* with it?"

"Wow...even your dad?"

"We didn't talk, but I'm assuming she will tell him. News travels quickly in that household." I smiled tightly. Penny narrowed her eyes at me.

"Okay, and they know he's your boyfriend, right?"

"They know I'm bringing home a guy I'm seeing. I didn't gush about all the details, because there is no point. The party will be huge. I will make my rounds with Rhett to meet them, and my brother if he is around, and then we will disappear. Rhett wants to meet them. He will see how horrible they are, and then I won't be obligated to see them again for another year, and Rhett will get the gist. It's a win-win," I say, self-assured, but Penny remains quiet.

"I hope you're right, babe. Did you tell them about New York?"

I had already told Penny I wouldn't be moving and subsequently will be turning down the promotion offer. As expected, she couldn't contain her excitement. My parents though? I'd been delaying that all week. Rhett and

I flew out at the end of next week, and I knew the closer I told them to our arrival, the better.

"I'm going to call them soon and let them know."

A tightness returns to my chest, but Penny pours me a glass of champagne, and we turn our attention to the TV. It drowns my worries, at least for a little bit.

CHAPTER FORTY

Audrey

Last year, I stepped off the plane for the Elson summer soiree a completely different person than the one I am today. Rhett and I dropped Mabel off at Renee's and drove to the airport this morning. He carried my bags through the airport and waited in line to get me the exact coffee I wanted while I caught up on emails, playing the perfect supportive boyfriend. I knew he was uneasy, and I felt bad, because it was partially my fault. He was about to meet my family who I hadn't put in the best light.

On top of that, it was his first flight. And once we were on the plane, Rhett's unease was more clear, even though he tried to mask it. I'm glad I got first class, so he wasn't crammed in a small seat. I knew if he was nervous about any of it, he'd never admit it. But I knew his tells by now; hands tightly clasped in his lap, foot tapping on the ground.

I was a bit grateful for the chance to take care of him for once, though. It took my mind off the reality of this weekend. And this weekend was about giving him a break, letting him escape the constant grind he was in, and showing him he deserves to be spoiled, too. Just like he shows me.

So, when the flight attendant comes by with the cart, I jump in without hesitation, ordering him a double whiskey before he even has a chance to respond.

"It will help with your nerves," I reassured him, and he went along with it, nodding with a look of amusement.

"I'll be fine the moment I'm out of a metal tube thirty-five thousand feet in the air."

"Okay, well, until then, take this." I pull my weighted silk eye mask from my bag and hand it to him. He holds it like it's a foreign object and I stifle a laugh. "Sip your whiskey, put in your headphones, slip on the mask and lean back. We'll be in the crowded terminal at JFK in no time." I wink, giving him a taste of his coy medicine and Rhett rolls his eyes, but steals a kiss before listening to my instructions. I pat his leg as he leans back, watching his lips twitch in a satisfied smile.

It takes about twenty minutes before Rhett's out cold, giving me a chance to pull out my phone and finally do something I have delayed for too long.

I know the professional and appropriate thing would be to wait until I am back in the office this coming week and talk to Ed directly. He'd no doubt be at his beach house with his wife and kids this weekend, so this wouldn't get addressed until after the holiday weekend. But that doesn't matter; it's the principle of it.

I'm fully aware the repercussions of this email could damage my career, or stall it, but that is beginning to not feel important. Not as important as my relationship with the man in the seat next to me or my relationship with myself.

I type out an email saying what I should've said weeks, or really months ago, copying Ed, his secretary, and the CFO in the New York office. I thank them for all their hard work in arranging the new position but let them know I won't be taking the role.

I hope he takes it as well as my parents seemingly did.

After delaying for way too long, I had finally worked up the courage last night to tell them. After dinner, and after what I knew would be my father's nightcap, I called my parents. I told them I would not be taking the position, and I would be 'pursuing other opportunities in North Carolina.'

I fully expected pushback, or a deep, bone-chilling disappointment. My mother barely reacted, almost as if she expected this of me. My father was more annoyed at how his old friend Ed Pierce would view this. *A flaky, unmotivated Elson.* Family reputation was everything. That's why it was easy to get them to promise to keep this news under wraps, and not to bring it up at the party.

It was in the past. And the moment I hit send on the email, it felt like turning the page in my book. Life was unfolding in North Carolina, and that's where I needed to be.

It's where I wanted to be.

CHAPTER FORTY-ONE

Rhett

At the time most people would be eating dinner, we roll down a seaside street full of expansive homes and lush gardens. With the windows of the rental Jeep down, the verdant smell of cypress, jasmine, and sea salt fill the car. The humidity also feels different from home, the way only the ocean can provide, but it's beautiful here, there's no doubt about that. The glinting sparkle of the early evening sun catches on the ocean that peeks between the stately lots, and I try to relax, even though the shirt Audrey picked out for me is slightly too tight around my biceps. She insisted that a button-down linen shirt under a navy sports jacket would bring out my eyes, complete with dress pants that somehow feel like air. Audrey said it's some new designer fabric and wouldn't let me see the price tag. Either way, I was here, feeling like a fish out of water, but that didn't really matter.

My thoughts—and gaze—tonight are reserved for Audrey. Her chocolate hair is clipped at the nape of her neck with loose strands and curls that fall around her face and make me think of 'sex hair'. When she slipped on the long pink dress, my jaw literally dropped. I joked I was arriving at a Hollywood party with a celebrity, and she just blushed, asking for the third time in a row if she looked okay.

She was the most beautiful woman I'd ever seen. And I still didn't understand how we came together like this, what stars had to align for a match like this, but as I hold her hand in the front seat of this rented Jeep, I decide once and for all to stop questioning it.

As we get closer, the nerves build in my stomach. I consider myself a pretty tough guy, but Audrey hasn't put her family, especially her father, in a shining light. She told me to put on a tough skin because I could be the president, and her father would still find a reason to criticize me. I nodded, going along with it, wondering what the hell her ex did to win him over. Though I already knew it was probably fake or unethical. Either way, as nervous as I feel, it's trumped by the nerves radiating off Audrey.

There are small things I've noticed about the woman I fell in love with this summer. Like the way she sniffs her coffee before the first sip, the way she crinkles her nose when she laughs, and how she starts to play with her hair more than usual when she is tired. But I also know that when Audrey is nervous, she goes inward. And I've been the one talking this entire drive from the resort to the house. My observations have been interrupted by a few words from her, but her hands keep rubbing the tops of her thighs: another nervous tick.

I put on her favorite playlist and let her have quiet time until cars start lining both sides of the street, classic signs of a party, forcing me to slow down.

"We are here..." Her voice trails off, and she pulls her hand from mine, sitting up straight in the passenger seat. I can't imagine arriving at my mom's home riddled with nerves like this.

"You can park here. I don't want to get trapped in the driveway," she instructs abruptly, and I do as she says, parking behind the catering van across the street from a house that looked like it was out of a movie.

"Hey, look at me." I grab Audrey's chin, forcing her to face me. Her hazel eyes focus on me, but I have a feeling she isn't really in the car with me. Her mind is already walking through the door of the home she felt she didn't belong in. "I'm here with you, darlin'. You give me the word, and

I will whisk you away from here. Nothing bad is going to happen to you, not while I'm around." Audrey smiles weakly at me. "I love you."

"Thank you for doing this. I love you, too."

Pulling her close to me, I place my lips gently on hers, she softens under my touch. Selfishly I think about keeping her here, safe, and reminding her how brave, strong, and beautiful she is, but I know we have to face this. And I wasn't going to let her go in there alone.

Audrey walks beside me as our feet crunch on the pebbles beneath us. The driveway, a semi-circle, is meticulously landscaped, featuring the greenest grass and hydrangea bushes so vibrantly blue, they look hand-painted. I wasn't expecting a beach bungalow, but I also didn't anticipate a house with more windows than I can count. Three stories of gray shingles tower over us.

"You grew up spending your summers here?" I ponder aloud, my thumb rubbing her hand as we walk together.

Audrey peers up at the house as we approach the oversized arched front door.

"Kind of. In between different summer camps, this is where I'd be. The property has been in the Elson family for five generations now. It was built in 1905 or something like that. My father inherited it." She exhales a heavy breath, her eyebrows shooting up as she turns to me. "And Andrew will get it next."

"Not you?" My eyebrows crinkle as I look at Audrey. She lets out a small, cynical laugh.

"It's lovely here." She squeezes my hand. "But *this* isn't me. I was more than happy to let Andrew have it. He's the one who wants to carry on the legacy."

"And you want..." I ask, as we are frozen on the front stoop.

"I want to build my own legacy. Whatever that may look like."

Instinctively I put my arm around Audrey, pushing the front door open.

"Let's do it, then." I wink at her, taking a step inside.

Live music fills the entire property, full of people arriving and chatting throughout the backyard, which overlooks the bay. The inside of the house is beautiful, filled with ambient light, but somehow feels cold, too. I couldn't imagine a child running around in here, because even though this is supposed to be a beach home, there is nothing welcoming or casual about it. Even at thirty I barely feel comfortable walking on the floors.

Audrey pulls me through the kitchen, where the catering staff is busy organizing trays of food. She leads me out a side door onto the expansive deck.

"Audrey." I turn towards the deep voice as Audrey slightly tenses beside me before dropping her hand from mine.

"Dad." Her reply is clipped, and they embrace quickly. I don't love the way he is looking at her, like he is evaluating, scrutinizing everything about her. And I don't like how she diminished herself the moment we pulled onto this street.

"Dad, this is Rhett." Audrey gestures, touching my arm lightly.

"Nice to meet you, Mr. Elson." Our hands meet, his grip tight as he peers into my eyes behind the sunglasses that he likely thinks hide the judgment.

"Rhett," is all he says as other people shuffle around us, their eyes on the man shaking my hand.

"Is Mom around?"

Samuel flashes a quick, pearly white smile at his daughter.

"She was talking to the Claremonts' a moment ago, making her rounds, as she does."

We nod in sync, and I plaster on my best smile, waving quickly at her father who dismisses himself.

"I need a drink," she mumbles through a fake smile.

I agreed and we made our way to an outdoor bar set up near the sparkling pool. Audrey decides to not wait for the absent bartender and starts mixing us drinks. She claims homefield advantage and I can't help but watch in awe as she balances two glasses in her hands, pulling the top of a whiskey bottle open with her teeth, her eyes flashing up to me, devilishly. She spits the top onto the ground, wiggling her eyebrows at me. This is the Audrey I know.

"It's not snake eyes. That's what I need right now. But this will do, right?"

I clear my throat and nod because I want nothing more than to wrap my hands around her tiny waist, pull her into my arms, and whisk her away from here, kissing her until she begs me to stop.

"Neat?" She holds the bottle out arm's length showing me the label. "It's the good stuff."

"However you want to make me, baby."

She hands me a glass, slips her hand in mine, and pulls me away from the party.

"I want to show you something." Audrey takes a gulp of whiskey as we walk around the back of the pool house into a garden of blue hydrangeas. Her shoulders finally relax when we are hidden out of sight.

"This is where I would hide during family parties." She plays with the gold necklace around her neck. "I didn't think I'd need to keep running away at this age." She casts her eyes down, but I lift her face back to mine.

"You don't need to protect me; you know that right?" Audrey bites her lip. "There's no more hiding. I can't hide my love for you Audrey, and I have a feeling you can't hide it for me either. Let's go back out there. You might have felt like you needed to hide in the past...but you didn't have me."

She curls herself into me, kissing me. "I probably look pathetic." She huffs, worry still on her face. "It's just I instantly shut down when I'm here.

Or anywhere with *them*. I wanted it to be different this time. So badly."

My heart aches as Audrey downs the rest of the whiskey, and I pull her in for one more kiss, breathing in her sweet jasmine perfume and running my hand along her back, beckoning her back up the path to the party.

CHAPTER FORTY-TWO

Audrey

I spot my parents huddled together on the deck, isolated in the crowd of partygoers. This is my moment. I firmly grip Rhett's arm, ready to introduce him to my mom. To rip the bandage off. To show them Jackson didn't break me.

The live music on the pool deck fades away up near the house, and my mother wears a soft grin as she notices Rhett and I approaching. "Finally, my daughter comes to greet me." She pulls me into a stiff hug, lightly kissing both cheeks. Her blue dress sweeps the top of her sandals, and she smells like the same perfume she's worn since I was a child. Beside her, my dad remains stoic behind his tortoise shell sunglasses. His peppered hair doesn't blow in the breeze, but his lips twitch and I clock the way he covers it with a sip of his drink.

"There's a lot of people here, it was hard to track you down," I reply, holding my Elson smile tightly on my lips. But my mom's attention is already off me, her eyes tracing Rhett's broad frame.

I nearly jolt, smiling up at the man next to me. "Mom, this is Rhett. Rhett Anderson."

He reaches out his hand, and I hold my breath as my mother slips her small, manicured fingers in it, greeting him politely.

"You have a beautiful home, Mr. and Mrs. Elson. Thank you for inviting me." Rhett's smooth southern voice sounded like honey, and I could see the charm work on my mother for a moment. It was hard not to be charmed by him with his baby blues and dirty blonde hair that he let me style today. He looks polished, and the clothes I bought him fit like a glove.

"Thank you, Rhett." She punctuates his name like it's foreign on her tongue, and my neck pricks in response. "I'm glad you were able to get away from work and accompany Audrey. We weren't sure if she'd make the time to see us this summer." One of her eyebrows cock up, a flash of her white teeth, and I know it's a double-edged statement.

Rhett remains in the dark. I've done a good job of shielding him from my parents' unpredictable behavior, but he must sense my unease. He always knows. A warm hand takes residency on the small of my back, steadying me in my spot.

"What is it you do for work? My daughter has told us nothing about you." My father finally speaks, but rocks back on the heels of his leather loafers, shoving a hand into his pocket.

"I'm a carpenter, sir."

My mother nods, murmuring something unintelligible as she sips her cocktail. The metal of my dainty necklace feels like it's burning a line into my collar bone, but it's not. It's just the fierce fire inside me, wanting nothing more than to protect Rhett.

But I remind myself he asked for this. He wanted to meet them.

"Don't let him downplay it," I scoff, placing my hand protectively on his chest. "Rhett owns his own business and is quite talented. You'd be floored by some of the custom work he's done."

"Oh, is that right?" my mom muses and I smile back way too big.

"Yes, it is. You should see the library he is currently building at a home in Forest Hills, it's beautiful." Rhett's hand stills on my back as he clears his throat.

"Oh, is that how you met, was Rhett doing work in your house?" My father smirks, like he dares me to reveal that his daughter fell for hired help.

I grind my jaw before exhaling, refusing to let myself come undone this early in the night.

"No, we didn't meet there." I smooth my already perfect dress and tilt my head at my gawking parents. "Actually, I have good news. My agent, Elena, called me right after we landed at JFK. There's already an offer on the house."

Rhett's fingers strum along my back. Earlier, he kissed me, twirling me around the hotel room when the news came, but that's not the result I expect from my parents.

"Well, isn't that something." My mom swirls her cocktail as she laughs to herself. Probably her fifth cocktail. That's how these parties usually go.

That's my cue to be done with this conversation, so I smile sweetly, and grab Rhett's hand. "We haven't eaten, and the food looks promising, so I'll see you two around, yeah?" I try to diffuse the situation.

"Your father," my mother tapped my dad on the shoulder, her cocktail nearly spilling from her glass. "He spared no expense this year. Andrew is around here somewhere, I'm sure he will be happy to see his reclusive sister," she adds, and I dip my head, pulling Rhett from the carnage. I don't speak while we weave through people, arriving at the spread of food.

"There you go, you met Evelyn and Samuel, so we can eat and head out. Or there's a cute little Italian place not far from here where we could grab a bite." I get too excited at the idea of escaping this hellscape. I notice eyes on me, but I don't acknowledge anyone. I'm already known as Samuel Elson's distant daughter, and I'm not looking to change that title today.

Rhett turns to me, plucking an appetizer from a tray as catering staff walks by. "Everything is okay." His crooked smile melts the piece of me I felt turn to ice the moment I arrived in this damn state. I nod even though I don't buy it.

"Sure, that went better than I was hoping," I admit sadly. "But I know this isn't really your scene, so please, just say the word and we will leave."

"Listen, if you need to leave darlin', we can. I feel ridiculous in these clothes." He laughs, caressing the side of my face, "but you know I can have fun anywhere with you." He pauses, scanning the tables around me. "And say what you will about your parents, but I've never seen a buffet like this. And I haven't eaten a decent meal since yesterday."

"Fair enough." I stand on my tiptoes, kissing him, and pat his chest. "I am going to use the bathroom and I'll be back. Whatever you do, don't get sucked into a conversation with anyone who comes out of the guest house. They are my brother's friends. Grade A assholes and probably high." Rhett grabs a look at the guest house, back to me.

"Got it."

The inside of my parent's house is quieter, and I go through the kitchen to the back half of the house, to the bathroom I know the guests won't be using.

I take a moment to catch my breath and reorient myself. I remind myself of the things I know are true.

I'm at my parent's house at the shore. They met Rhett and it went okay. Just okay, but it could've been worse. They didn't bring up my job or Jackson, and Rhett is being polite. He's being perfect, actually. He is outside looking more handsome than any man I've ever seen. He is okay. I am okay.

Leaning on the sink, I take a deep breath, meet my hazel eyes in the mirror.

You can do this.

Shortly, I'll be back at the resort with Rhett, and everything will be good again. I'll get to show him how much I appreciate him. Warmth spreads through me just thinking about being tangled with him in the king size bed.

"Oh, I'm sorry!" The bathroom door swings open, hitting someone.

"Audrey?" My father stands in the small, dim hallway, but his sunglasses are gone now, and his eyes are in view. It's just us, the murmurs of the party are muffled beyond these walls, and I pause, still on a high imagining my night with Rhett. Letting myself think, for a split second, maybe things could also be okay with my father and I.

He might not accept every part of me or ever stop thinking he knows best. He might be business driven, but maybe, we could come to a mutual understanding. Maybe he could just be happy that Rhett loves me. Maybe it could be enough for him.

"Dad, hi," I breathe out. He looks uncomfortable, and not just because I've boxed him into this corridor.

"Listen, we're all adults here, so I know you'll understand, but I don't want you to be taken off guard. Jackson was invited to the party as well."

It was logical. I know that. Every year, the executives from Elson Enterprises are invited to this party with their spouses and children. It's always been that way. Jackson was the VP of Tippins Group, and the merger was finalized at some point this summer. I'd blocked it all out, unsubscribed from the narrative of that news. But it didn't mean it didn't sting less. It didn't prevent my mouth from growing dry, from my heart cracking open, bleeding onto the tiny bit of joy I manufactured minutes ago.

"I see." But then heat rises in my core thinking about the way my mother begged me to come home, guilted and shamed my long-time absence. All while knowing my cheating ex-fiancé would be in attendance.

My father purses his lips together, clearly done with the conversation, but I'm not. "Did you and Mom not think to give me that important information ahead of time, before you know, I flew up here to introduce you both to my new boyfriend?"

He holds his hands up, like he's exhausted, accompanied by a sigh that fills the space between us.

"Don't be like this, Audrey. We have been more than understanding about the called-off engagement, the house, even the employment news you sprang on us in the last twenty-four hours. I know you're upset things didn't work out how you wanted, but that's the way of the world, honey. Things don't always happen the way you think they should. I thought I taught you to be smarter than this. You know how to deal with this system, how to deal with people." He peers at me, and I pause, not sure I want to believe this conversation is truly happening.

"Excuse me? What are you implying? You really think I should've just laid down and let Jackson treat me like a doormat?" I can barely control my voice and my father glances back, but no one is there.

"We all make mistakes. You of all people should know that." His voice rasps, like this sentiment should be well-known, like it's the hundredth time he's telling me. "But Jackson could give you what you deserve. Together you two would've had it all, don't you see that? You threw that all away, and I think you should reconsider the realities of the world. Where do you want to be in ten years?" I fall silent and my father sighs again. "Listen, I've worked with him all summer, he's very remorseful, you know. He cares about you, Audrey."

I want nothing more than to shove past my father. Fear courses through my veins picturing Rhett out there, a sheep in a lion's den.

"You are no better than him." I shake my head, taking a step in the small space between my father and the wall but he catches my elbow, his mouth close to my ear.

"I'm only trying to look out for you. Can you look me in the eye and honestly tell me your future is with that man out there? Come on now. We are better than *that*." He scoffs and I rip my elbow from his grip, fisting my dress as I rush through the house, searching frantically for Rhett in the crowd of people I never did trust.

Chapter Forty-Three

Rhett

"Are you finished with your drink?" A server nodded towards my empty glass, and I handed it to her.

"I am, thank you." I smile, and a guy next to me, loading a plate with lobster from the grilling station, peers up over his sunglasses. I never understood people who wore sunglasses when it was dusk, but I try not to judge as I nod his way.

"I don't believe I've met you." He wipes a hand on a towel and holds it out. I shake it, noticing instantly the chocolate brown hair and high cheekbones. Must be an Elson.

"Rhett. I'm Audrey's—" but Ray-Ban man cuts me off, a pearly half-smile painted on his face.

"My sister's new boyfriend. Heard a Carolina accent and knew you weren't with the Tippins group." I raise an eyebrow, thinking of everything I knew about Audrey's brother. Which wasn't much; he's a surgeon who she doesn't see often. And she told me not to talk to him until she was back, but other than his annoying habit of wearing sunglasses in the dark, he seemed okay. Nothing I couldn't deal with, at least.

"I'm Andrew, her older brother."

"It's nice to put a name to a face," I add, and he laughs.

"What're you drinking?"

"It was whiskey on the rocks."

Andrew nods towards the pool house, the plate of lobster still balanced on his hand. "Follow me. I have an eighteen-year-old bottle of Glenfiddich we were just about to open. My sister will find you. She always ends up hiding in the pool house anyway," he adds, and I look around, quickly scanning the crowd for a pink dress but decide to follow Andrew anyway.

The pool house is one large open room with a stairwell up to what looks like a lofted bedroom. It's casual but I'm not fooled. I'm sure everything in here costs a small fortune. I enter after Andrew, and three other guys around my age look up from the white sofa they are all sitting on.

"Gentlemen, this is my sister's boyfriend, Rhett," Andrew announces, placing the lobster on the coffee table. I don't sit, just stand, observing, and feeling like I've been transported into the twilight zone.

"How long have you been dating Drew's sister?" one of the guys sitting with his legs kicked back asks. He's also got sunglasses on.

I scrub my jaw. "It's been a few months now."

"Why, Liam, you can't let go of the wet dream you had about Audrey ten years ago?" the other guy asks, quickly clocking my reaction. I give him none.

"Dude, my sister's still off limits. So, fuck you." Andrew pops the top off a brand-new bottle of whiskey. I'm not sure I want to celebrate with them though. "And come on boys, that's no way to welcome our new guest." He smiles at me and finally pulls off his sunglasses. His eyes are bloodshot and glassy. The dime bag of coke on the bar behind him catches my eye and I let out a humorless chuckle.

We might all be the same age, but there's nothing I want to stand here and chat about with these glorified frat boys. I pull out my phone to text Audrey, letting her know where I am.

Andrew holds up the baggie. "You want a hit? I won't tell Audrey. She's a...rule follower? A tight-ass?" he adds, and I resist the urge to dock her brother.

"I'm good, I'll stick to the drink tonight."

Andrew shrugs, pouring amber liquid into a glass, and hands me it. He turns up the music, drowning out the live music outside near the pool.

"You're better than the last asshole. No offense. What was his name, Jackson? Fucker loved his powder," one of the guys on the couch chimes in.

I throw back the whiskey. I know it was meant to be enjoyed slowly, but nothing about being in this dim, loud pool house with these guys was making me feel like savoring something.

Also, Audrey never mentioned her ex having a drug problem? My head begins to pound, wondering if she didn't let on about how much bullshit she truly had to put up with from him.

But then Andrew saddles up next to me, his breath wreaking of cigars and whiskey. I've never wanted to get the fuck out of somewhere so quick. But it's Audrey's brother, and the least I should do is try. For her.

"I had no idea you two had been together for months. Mom and Dad made it sound like it was just a few weeks. You can tell me—did this start during the engagement?" His eyebrows shoot up and mine furrow down.

"No," I reply, my voice gruff, and I'm not sure I care much about being polite anymore.

"Well *bro*, I'm guessing I'll be seeing more of you and my sister, in what, a month from now?"

He sips his drink, but I shake my head.

"I don't know what you're talking about, actually."

"Oh shit, my bad." He places a hand over his chest. "I assumed you were moving with Audrey for her new job. Maybe I got the dates mixed up or something. I just know my parents haven't stopped yapping about finally getting her back home."

As my stomach hollows out and my grip grows numb around the glass in my hand, the sliding door opens, and I turn to see Audrey cautiously step inside.

"There's my baby sis!" Andrew pulls her off her feet into a hug she clearly wants no part of.

"Andrew. You smell like you've been drunk for days." She pinches her nose, shoving him away and throwing me an apologetic wince.

But I'm still stuck thirty seconds in the past.

"You have a new job?"

Shit, I didn't mean to say that out loud.

Audrey steps closer to me, her arms protectively across her chest. "What?"

A loud bout of laughter sounds from the patio outside the door, a toast of sorts starting, but my eyes are locked on hers.

"Are you moving to New York in a few weeks?"

"Rhett, what are you talking about?"

"Audrey, answer me." The room is spinning, and she can't meet my eyes.

"It's complicated. I was, but now I'm not. I officially declined the offer today." Her face falls as she whips her head towards her brother. "What did you say, Andrew?" But her brother just throws his hands up.

"I told him the truth, calm down. Thought you would've told your boyfriend by now." He slinks back into the room, away from us.

"You want to tell me what the hell is going on, Audrey?" I snap out louder than intended and she pulls back.

"I can explain everything, but not here," she pleads with me, but I can't see past this moment. I need the truth, now.

"No, here. Now," I bit out, not caring that four strangers were sitting just feet away.

Audrey bites her lip, her face white as snow, and I know she's fighting back tears. I don't know what I hate more right now, the fact that I'm the last to know I'm being left or that I'm the one out of everyone here who's making her cry tonight.

"I was offered a promotion after Jackson and I split, it's at my company's headquarters in New York City, and I took it."

I tip my head back, closing my eyes, unable to look at her, but she continues. "After the breakup I just wanted to get away. From everything and everyone. You have to understand that North Carolina never felt like my home...until you."

"You need this more than me, man." Andrew tries to pass the bottle my way, but I shake my head. Audrey grabs my hand, sinking her nails into my flesh.

"We aren't doing this here. Please, I can explain everything."

Chapter Forty-Four

Audrey

I hear my heart beating in my ears as I pull Rhett through the sea of smiling faces and past the band.

I glance into the crystal blue water of the pool, the lights from the party reflecting off its stillness, and contemplate making one final cowardly act of diving in, just to create a distraction, to buy myself a few more minutes. Because I have an explanation for what Andrew told Rhett. An explanation for the truth. I just am not sure Rhett's ready to hear it.

The quietness of the house feels assaulting, final, after being outside. I lead Rhett right to the back; through the tight corridor I was in with my father earlier this evening.

The truth hits me in the chest as I keep my eyes on his office doors. This was happening here—in the place I never felt safe in. *Here*, where I was supposed to assert myself, to show my parents their marionette strings were no longer working, that I'd found a man I loved; and more importantly, one who loved me, for me.

Because I was worth being loved for exactly who I was.

That's what I believed up until a moment ago at least.

I don't stop moving until we are inside my father's study, the doors shutting firmly behind us. The room is nearly soundproof.

Rhett walks to the window, gazing out over the gardens, his hands tucked into his khaki pockets.

"Rhett I—"

He turns slowly, his face half in shadow from the setting summer sun.

"You were never planning on staying, were you?"

Tears spring to my eyes but I push them back.

"I wasn't sure in the beginning." My voice is so small, and Rhett shakes his head, betrayal written all over his face. "I was scared, and I didn't want to make the same mistake twice." I try to reason, though I know it's a weak argument.

"So, what was *this?* Was I just something to hold you over, nothing more than a rebound until you figure out what you really want in life?"

I shake my head hard, but it doesn't seem to matter. Rhett's defeated in a way I've never seen.

"We barely knew each other. I didn't know if you'd stay around." The hurt in Rhett's eyes immediately has me regretting my words. It wasn't fair, and it wasn't entirely true.

We fell fast and we fell hard. And I was scared.

So why couldn't I just say that?

Rhett cocks his head back like I punched him square in the jaw.

"When you told me you loved me, were you still planning on leaving?" he asks, his hurt blue eyes cutting me to the core.

"The transfer was still active, yes, but I didn't really want to go. I felt like it was the right thing to do for my career. And I wanted to keep my options open in case..."

"In case what?" Rhett's voice was loud, cutting, and I knew I deserved it, even if it made me flinch.

"I declined the offer, I decided to stay. I chose us! Why aren't you hearing that?" There was an invisible barrier between us, one that wasn't there before.

"Are you hearing yourself? You told me you loved me. My family fell in love with you, I opened my home to you, never judging you for one moment, and this entire time you never planned on staying. In case you didn't notice, I chose you from the moment I met you." He sucks in a breath, his chest growing as I stay silent, truly speechless. "Why didn't you talk to me about it? Honestly, Audrey...do I even know you?"

The ghost of my past grips my throat, and I want to throw myself into the arms of the man I love standing in front of me, but I can't move. My fingers clutch onto the mahogany desk behind me, tears blur his face, and I gasp for air.

"Rhett, you know me, you're the *only* one who knows me. I promise you I meant it when I said I loved you...I *do* love you. You know me. I promise you, please," I plead but his head hangs low.

"Well, darlin'..." He lifts his head, his gaze meeting mine. "I'm beginning to question if you really know yourself."

And just like that, the breath is ripped from my lungs as I stand helplessly, watching the man I love walk away, the door slamming shut behind him with a finality that shatters what's left of my heart.

Going back into the party is not an option. My family should all be up to speed on my life in shambles; I arrived with a doting boyfriend, and a promotion, and will be leaving with neither.

Hastily snatching a drink from the catering tray as staff walks by, I escape through the front door before anyone can apprehend me. My absence is merely a drop in the bucket at an Elson Labor Day soiree. The fruity cocktail is too sweet, but I take a gulp anyway, and as my feet hit the grass in the front lawn, I squint against the darkening sky, my eyes landing on Rhett. He tosses his sports jacket over an arm, and grows smaller, and smaller as he walks down the street, away from the party.

I know better than to call out or chase after him, so I slip off my heeled sandals, clutch them in my hand, and head down the street in the opposite direction of Rhett. The music and chatter of the party fades behind me, and the grittiness of the pavement under my bare feet feels like a harsh but deserved punishment.

Rhett's not entirely wrong in his anger, and that's what makes the ache in my chest deepen with every step I take. I want to believe I can fix this, that I can make him realize when Jackson left me, I was more damaged than I even realized. I have been adrift and lost for longer than I care to admit. And when I met Rhett, when he brought me into his world, when he stopped my tears on that rooftop that night, something in me healed.

Along the way this summer, I found little pieces of myself—not in him—but in how he showed me I could be; what he showed me I could have, the love he showed me that I believed didn't exist.

It took a while for me to accept this love, this change of plans, but I'm all in now. I need him to know that.

After walking past several neighboring lots, their lit driveways and homes concealing secrets of their own, I reach the end of the private street and pause. Turning back, I take in the sea of cars lining the road, a testament to the night's promise. It really is a perfect evening for a party. The air is mild, neither too warm nor too cool, carrying the salty tang of the ocean with each gentle breeze. It's always the most beautiful nights where everything goes horribly wrong.

I sip the rest of the cocktail, tears brimming my eyes, an invisible weight pressing on my sternum. I'd spent so much time on my hair and makeup, so much care picking out this dress. Tilting my head back to the evening sky, I let out a humorless chuckle. Maybe Rhett's right. Maybe I haven't fully let go, maybe I do still care. My chest tightens, the pressure nearly unbearable, and I shake my head, desperate for relief. But there's nowhere to go, no way out, and the need to disappear is strong.

Just as I pull out my phone, hoping to text Penny, a black sports car slows down, passing me, surely gawking at me from behind the tinted windows.

There she is, Audrey Elson. The dramatic, screwed up black sheep, drinking in the street.

But almost immediately the thought is followed by Rhett's voice.

Who cares what they think?

I choke on a sob at the sound of his voice, and glance up, only to see I was alone on the street. He's not here.

My body needs food, and water; not more of this sickly-sweet cocktail my mother would be holding up while my father gave his annual toast tonight. He'd plaster on the Elson smile, thank everyone for coming, and somehow slip in something about the ungodly amount of money he acquired this year. I start walking back toward the house, worry beginning to settle in about Rhett's whereabouts. The glow of my parent's gray and white shingled house comes into view as I hear my name.

"Drey?"

My stomach drops at the sound of that nickname. Only one person in the world has ever called me Drey. I say a silent prayer that I'm mistaken as I spin around at the edge of the driveway.

Jackson Tippins takes a few cocky steps towards me, a lit cigar in hand, his white button down undone around his neck, as he locks a sports car behind him on the street.

I fold my arms across my chest instinctively, hoping the shadowy night disguises the tear streaks down my face. It's been over three months since I've seen his face, and for once I'm flabbergasted at what I could've ever seen in him. He wears arrogance as a proud aura and it's almost too much to handle; so much that it takes a moment to register we are here, standing together on my parent's property.

"You can't be serious," I mumble to myself. "Why the hell did you even show up here?" I jab at Jackson who drags his cigar from his lips. I wave the smoke away from my face.

"I'm actually supposed to be in Vegas this weekend for a bachelor party, but what kind of business partner would I be if I didn't come celebrate?" He shrugs, his eyes narrowed at me. "Plus, your parents nearly begged me to show up after you RSVP'd." He winks, and the streetlights around me start to waver.

Mark this as the second time the blood has drained from my whole body today. Jackson takes a few steps towards me, close enough that I can see his green eyes glistening. They're foreign to me now, cold and sharp, and I can't believe there was a time I could look into them and see my future. Or love.

But right now, all I can do is stand in my bare feet, mouth dry and mind whirling.

"Oh, come on honey, you had to know they wouldn't stop trying to get the pack back together?" As he laughs, bile rises in my throat.

Jackson takes a step closer, close enough I could smell his cologne now, filling me with nausea.

"I'm not too proud to say I screwed up, but come on Drey, you know we belong together. It makes sense." He drops the cigar nub, grinding it into the pavement with his leather loafers. "Don't be mad at your father or me. It's just business, baby. Look on the bright side, in a few weeks, your stocks are going to double." He has the audacity to wink at me. As if money makes this okay. As if cheating on your fiancé, or lying to your daughter, or because it's *just business* made everything okay.

"I need to leave," I mutter, one hand clutching my head, the other pressed against my stomach, as the cocktail glass slips from my grasp. It crashes to the ground, shattering into jagged pieces at my feet, the sound cutting through the air like a scream.

"Holy shit Audrey, try to be an adult and cut the dramatics. I assured your father there was no bad blood between us. Don't make me look like a fool." He held out his hand and it takes everything in me not to scream. Instead, I swat his hand away.

"Fuck off, Jackson. And don't call me Drey." I throw my head back in disbelief. "Need I remind you this mess is *entirely* your fault?"

"This right here, this fit of yours, is exactly why I cheated in the first place. You're a spoiled bitch who—"

Jackson's voice halts mid-sentence, silenced by a deep voice that cuts through the air behind me.

"I don't think you want to finish that sentence."

My body stiffens, and I steal a glance to my left where Rhett stands just a few feet away, his jaw rigid with tension. My gaze snaps back to Jackson as he spits out another insult.

"I don't know who the fuck you are, man, but this doesn't concern you. Step over the glass, Audrey, and come inside. It's time to act like civilized adults instead of this pathetic display. Can you handle that?" Jackson steps forward, grabbing me by the waist and lifting me over the shattered glass.

"Let go of me, Jackson! I'm not going anywhere with you!" He drops my feet to the ground but tightens his grip on my arm.

In a flash, Jackson is yanked off his feet, his fingers tearing away from me as Rhett's fist grips the front of his shirt.

"What the—" is all he manages to spat out before Rhett's free fist makes contact with Jackson's jaw. With my own dress twisted in my hands, I step back, mouth hanging wide open.

Jackson's back hits the grass as Rhett kneels over him, his reddened fist trembling inches from Jackson's bloodied lip.

"Rhett, stop! Get off him!" My limbs shake as I reach for Rhett's shoulder, pulling him back. He stands, shirt askew, and Jackson springs up, hand clutching his jaw. Rhett narrows his eyes, pointing a finger at my ex.

"If you ever so much as look in her direction again, I will snap your fucking neck." His words send chills down my spine, and the tension hangs in the air, heavy and suffocating; as if one single breath could reignite the fight at any moment.

Jackson spits blood into the grass, splatters hitting Rhett's shoes.

"Do you have any idea who I am?" he shouts, palming his own chest.

Rhett laughs, cocking his head back. "I know exactly who you are."

"You'll be hearing from my lawyer!"

"Let's go, Rhett." I turn, grabbing his arm to lead him back to the car. I'm not sticking around to watch this turn into more of a blood bath.

"Should've known." Jackson let out a snarled laugh. "Of course he's with you, Drey."

Rhett flinches, but I tighten my fingers around his bicep. "Ignore him."

"Bet Daddy's real proud of you, bringing home literal trash," Jackson said just loud enough for me to hear, but before Rhett can even respond, I spin around, marching straight up to Jackson. His eyes go wide as my fist makes direct contact with his nose.

I've never hit anyone in my life. But I'd be lying if I said I didn't feel a drop of satisfaction as I pull back my hand and see the shock on his face; even as my hand screamed in pain.

"That's for cheating on me," I screeched, and before he could say anything else, I knee him straight between his legs. As he doubles over, I lean down to whisper in his ear. "He's twice the man you'll ever be."

"What the hell is going on out here?" my mother shrieks, rushing across the front yard in heels. She glances over her shoulder, probably panicking someone will see something.

"You did this. You wanted me to get back with *him*?" I yelled at her, no longer caring who saw or heard me. She clutches her necklace.

"Lower your voice before you cause a scene, Audrey Diane Elson." Her fake smile was long gone as she nearly trembled in her gold heels.

"No." I shake my head, thinking about the reality here. "I will no longer make myself small just so you feel comfortable around me."

Jackson groans, and my mom slaps her hand over her open mouth.

"My god! What the hell happened out here?"

"He got what he deserved," I state clearly.

"You can't go into the party like this," she replied, pulling out her phone, probably to call my father, but I'm not waiting around to find out.

"I'm leaving," I bite out.

"One day you'll understand. This is for you, for the family," my mom replies, eerily calm.

I stop in my tracks, turning around to face her.

"No Mom, see, that's where you're wrong. I will *never* understand. Because I would never choose money over love."

This time, I refuse to wait for a response. Turning on my heel, I walk toward the car, Rhett close behind me. He heard everything, he sees my family for exactly who they are, but it doesn't matter anymore. After tonight, nothing will ever be the same.

It couldn't be.

A wave of dizziness and nausea circles back. It has nothing to do with the drinks on an empty stomach and everything to do with the man who is silently typing the resort address into his phone.

It doesn't matter if I want to reach out and kiss him, thank him for saving me from Jackson, or apologize for the overwhelming regret eating me alive. I should've known better than to bring him here.

I should've continued to protect him.

We ride back to the resort in darkness and silence, giving me the pleasure of reliving the party again and again in my head. When we pull up to the valet, Rhett hands over the keys, and I catch a glimpse of fresh bruises forming on his knuckles. My hand doesn't feel good either, but it's nothing compared to the feeling in my chest, knowing he came back for me even after I hurt him.

I didn't deserve him on the rooftop, and I don't deserve him now.

Rhett

Adrenaline pumps through me as I follow Audrey down the hotel hallway. We were supposed to return to a romantic setting. I even called ahead, asking the staff to bring a bottle of champagne to the room tonight, thinking we'd celebrate our first trip together in the ridiculously luxurious suite she treated us to. It was the least I could do.

I was going to show her just how much I loved her.

Instead, I'm sitting on the edge of the bed, trying not to reach for my cigarettes.

Audrey went straight into the bathroom as soon as we walked in. She looked stunning as we left this room only hours ago, and I had to control myself from pulling her back into the room and stripping that pink dress off one more time before the party. I'd decided it could wait, as she swatted me away with a mischievous grin, promising I'd get *all* of her when we got back tonight.

But now I'm wondering if I ever truly got *any* of her.

How could she think I'd leave her? Had I ever done anything to make her doubt me? Was I a damn fool? Were the signs there all along?

No, I refuse to believe that.

As the shower turns on, I hear her sniffling, surely crying, and a part of my heart cracks open. I hate to see her in pain, but she hid the truth from me for three months.

It took several years to get to where I am; committed and taking a relationship seriously.

Was it in my imagination, all the talk about what we wanted in life? Where we'd be in a few years? The house. The fucking hydrangeas.

I had seen a future with Audrey.

Fuck, I still do.

I can't take it anymore, so I stand up and leave the room, letting the door slam shut behind me. The hallway smells like a candle store, and a couple nearly knocks into me as they pass by, not noticing I'm even there. I start to undo the top few buttons on my shirt and notice it's stained with blood.

Blue brings out your eyes, they are my favorite thing about you. Audrey was so excited to buy me this shirt.

Hightailing it out of the elevator, I beeline for the hotel bar. The entire place is full of fuckers who look like Jackson. Or maybe that's just me seeing red again. *I don't regret knocking that prick out, that's for damn sure.*

"Good evening, sir, what can I get you?" The bartender in a bowtie asked me, eyeing me up and down. I don't bother looking at him, eyeing the shelf behind him.

"Double whiskey, thanks." My voice is gruff, and he mumbles something I don't bother listening to. I scan the bar, feeling out of place—a sensation which never bothered me before. But tonight, it weighs on me heavily.

I always thought it was my superpower to be carefree, but maybe not caring was a mistake. It led me here, fooled by a woman like Audrey.

What the hell was I doing with a woman like Audrey Elson? I could knock out her exes, not giving a shit how barbaric I acted. I could protect her, but clearly, I couldn't give her everything she needed. Or she wouldn't need an escape route from the life I thought we were building together.

My wallet was slim, my house was humble. I didn't have a trust fund to fall back on, or parents' money to bail me out. She claimed she didn't care about those things. But maybe I'm just an ass who was so in love I couldn't see the truth.

I could never give Audrey the lifestyle she was used to, and even if she said otherwise, the approval of her parents meant *something* to her. Something I permanently damaged tonight.

The bartender places the drink on the counter in front of me, and within seconds, it's gone, the burn in my throat providing a welcome distraction from my racing thoughts.

"I'll take another one." I know how it looked, my head hung low, my bruised fingers up to get the bartender's attention. His hesitation was palpable but my craving to numb the pain was bigger.

Feeling a bit numb after four shots of whiskey, I waltz back to the room, my lips in a tight line, knowing saying nothing was better than confusing Audrey with the words of a brokenhearted man.

CHAPTER FORTY-SIX

Audrey

The text asking Rhett where he went remains unread. I'm not entirely surprised, even if it stings. We've traveled here together after all, and I don't want to turn him to the wolves in a place like this. Rhett could hold his own, but I had promised I'd keep him safe here. Whatever that means now.

As I comb my wet hair, going through the motions of my nighttime routine in the bathroom, the hotel room door opens, my heart hammering in my chest.

Meeting my tired gaze in the backlit mirror, I wait in silence as Rhett shuffles around on the other side of the door. There's sounds of luggage opening, the thud of shoes. All of it brings tears to my eyes, but I swallow them back, pull on the weighty robe, like it's an anchor that'll protect me, and slowly pad into the suite.

He didn't turn on the overhead lights, so only a glow from the bedside lamp illuminates him as he stands facing the bed, unbuttoning his shirt. The muscles in his back and neck are tense, and as I stand there awkwardly waiting, I know we aren't going to be talking tonight.

But I can't help but offer my care.

"Can I get you ice for your hand?" My quiet voice cuts through the room like a knife.

Barely turning to look at me, Rhett shakes his head. I nod even though he isn't looking.

"Thank you," he adds but that only makes it worse. Because only Rhett would still be polite to me after tonight.

I want to get him ice, curl up in his lap holding it to his fist, laughing about something odd we saw at the airport together. He'd kiss my neck, and I'd love the smell of whiskey on him. I'd fall asleep tangled in the sheets, my head resting on his tattooed chest, a faint smile on my lips as his heart beats beneath me.

"My father texted me while you were gone. Jackson won't be pressing charges. That's good, right?" I offer, but Rhett barely spares me a glance, so I retreat to the bathroom in defeat, and finish my routine. Twenty minutes later, when I come out, Rhett's on the sofa, his back to me.

I resist shaking him awake to demand we talk. I know better than to force someone to talk before they are ready.

That's what got us into this mess, isn't it?

The sheets are cold against my bare legs as I slide into the king size bed. Down pillows surround me as I breathe in the linen spray.

I lie down, knowing I won't be sleeping any time soon. My eyes are tired, but my stomach hungrily gurgles. The bed is also monstrous; it's meant to be shared. Even my feet feel lonely without a certain hound dog lying on them.

Hours later, as the night outside grows pitch black, and the room is quiet besides the humming AC, I continue to toss and turn.

In my feverish bouts, all I can think about is perhaps our love was destined to exist only in the sweet embrace of summer, like a bittersweet memory. Maybe we were never meant to be anything more than a forbidden secret, a passionate romance flared up only to extinguish as quickly as it ignited.

I finally succumb to sleep, only to wake up in the middle of the night and reach across the bed, searching for him. When my hand finds an empty pillow, the consequences of my actions crash into me.

I had it all planned: breakfast delivered to the room, a day at the pool, relaxing and swimming. We had dinner reservations at a new restaurant on the water. They were supposed to have great seafood, and Rhett rolled his eyes when I told him, saying nothing is better than Carolina fried fish and hush puppies; but then he winked at me and said he couldn't wait for it.

That was the plan, but of course, nothing went as planned. The next morning, I woke to an empty room, Rhett's suitcase still here, but he had made himself sparse. I have one text from him.

Rhett: Went to grab some coffee, be back in 30.

Fisting the thick duvet in my hand, I let out a frustrated groan. Maybe this was good; he was getting some fresh air, with a fresh mind, caffeinating, doing all his favorite things. I could talk to him this morning; we could sit down at breakfast and talk. So, I placed an order for room service, getting all his favorites: thick cut bacon, pancakes, a fruit platter, and eggs benedict for me. Plus, more coffee.

My stomach is in knots, but I hope the smell of food will help. Slipping on a matching set of white linen shorts and a top, I comb my hair and even put on a little makeup.

"Oh, you're back, good," I say as casually as possible as soon as Rhett enters the room. The black baseball cap he wore, which usually makes me weak at the knees, doesn't do anything but draw attention to his tired blue eyes. I suppose he didn't sleep any better than I did.

"Can we talk? Please." Wringing my hands together, I step towards him as he sets a single coffee cup down. Part of me hoped he would come back with coffee for me; it would've been a sign that all hope wasn't lost.

His jaw stiffens.

"Audrey…"

"Rhett." His glassy blue eyes lift slowly to mine. "Please."

He nods, tossing his hat on the bed, fluffing his dark blonde hair back into shape. "I ordered breakfast…in case you were hungry. We can eat and talk on the balcony. Just like home."

Just like home. His eyes darted away.

We don't speak until the food arrives a few minutes later. Rhett and I sit on the secluded patio off the bedroom, overlooking the lush garden. I chose the best suite to give him privacy, not caring if it cost a small fortune. I wanted him to feel comfortable.

"You didn't need to order all this food." He finally speaks as I set the table for us.

"Well, I didn't eat last night…and I thought you'd be hungry, too. This was in the plan all along."

I pop a piece of fruit into my mouth, anxious as he sits there stiffly in the chair, looking out over the garden. He finally sips his coffee, and I let out a tiny breath. Rhett's never silent for long. That's why I loved him. He always knows the right thing to say.

"Who are you hiding from, Audrey?"

"What?" His question catches me off guard, coming out of nowhere. His voice feels distant, even though he's right beside me. Rhett's knee bounces slightly as I lean in closer, hoping it will somehow help me grasp the question.

Then Rhett turns to face me, his full attention now making me pull back. It was always too much in a good way, but now it feels like too much in a way that frightens me. Like he sees right through me.

"I stayed up all night, thinking…wondering…who this girl I fell in love with is." The raspy pain in his voice jolted me, so I reached across the table for his hand, but he didn't reciprocate.

"I'm me…the same person on the rooftop, the one you asked to dance…I'm me. I'm not hiding from you."

A flicker of uncertainty washes across his face as desperation floods me. I never had to fight for a relationship…and now I wish I wouldn't have taken it for granted. He shakes his head, but before he can reply, I rush on.

"I'm not hiding from you…" My voice grows small with the weight of the truth balancing on my tongue. "But I did hide us. I didn't want anyone destroying what we had."

Rhett lets out a humorless laugh.

"All I know is I like who I am when I'm with you. I like who I am when it's just you, me and Mable. When there's no one else and not a care in the world. I like that version of me."

"I like who I am with you, too," he finally says, eyes cast out beyond the balcony before they return to me. And as soon as we lock gazes, I know the next words out of his mouth will hurt.

"But darlin', can't you see? That's not the real world. You have to let people in. We can't exist in a bubble. You can't keep up this facade with them and have me. How can you expect us to build a future like that?"

No, no, no, no. This is not how Rhett Anderson is going to break my heart. Not like this.

"I'm figuring it out." A million words race through my mind, grasping at me, because I can't lose him. "And I do know what I want. I want you!"

He shakes his head, his eyes glossier than ever. "Are you sure? Because for the last three months I've been falling in love with you. For the first time I let myself picture a real future with someone. I let you in all the way. All the way...and you held me at a distance." He taps his fingers on the table. "So don't tell me you know what you want."

Tears stream down my face as Rhett stands, coming around the table. I shut my eyes, but he lifts my chin gingerly with his finger.

"So, this is it, huh? This is how you end it?" I choke out.

"I love you, Audrey." His admission should've filled me with warmth, but those words cut like a self-inflicted wound. "You know I would've done anything for you...but I don't know how to be with you right now."

I nod silently, because no words could ever capture the pain of the bullet that just tore through my bleeding heart.

"You deserve the time to get to know yourself."

"And you deserve someone who doesn't hide you," I reply, looking up at Rhett through tears.

He bites his lips together, remaining silent before walking inside.

That's the cruel truth about life and love, isn't it? You never truly grasp what you have until it's gone. And even though he's in the space next to me, I know he's gone. I know I've done irreversible damage.

And I have no one to blame but myself.

CHAPTER FORTY-SEVEN

Rhett

"Hey man, you gonna drink that? Because if not, I'll take it." Ky's bar stool tips towards me, and I shake my head, sliding the lukewarm beer across the counter. The music in the Bourbon Barrel is way too loud, even the dim lights are pissing me off. I should've just sucked it up and let Ky come over to my house for drinks and food like old times, but I couldn't stomach the idea of sitting in the backyard, shooting the shit.

My entire property is riddled with *her*. It's been one week since we left New York.

One week since I essentially broke it off.

One week of oscillating between anger at Audrey and anger at myself.

One week of wondering if I was overreacting. One week of feeling betrayed as hell.

But the bedroom still smells like her jasmine perfume. The kitchen certainly doesn't smell as good; it's riddled with takeout containers and junk I can't be bothered to put away.

"You look like shit, man." I haven't shaved in a week, and I grabbed this wrinkled shirt out of the dirty laundry bin, no fucks left to give.

"Fuck you, too, Ky." I shove him and he shrugs, polishing off my beer.

"You know you didn't have to come out tonight."

I stand to stretch my legs, looking at my best friend and try to muster up a semblance of joy. I knew I was being an ass. I'd barely said anything in the thirty minutes we've been sitting at this bar, not acknowledging anyone, especially not the bartender who is obnoxiously flirting with me. Part of me wonders if I should fill my bed with a warm body tonight, maybe the bartender, but the other part of me can't fathom letting anyone sleep on the left side.

It was somehow still her spot. *How fucked is that?*

"I know I didn't have to come out." I adjusted my belt, feeling fidgety in this building full of energy when I was devoid. "In my defense, I thought it was a good idea. I can't be in the house, it's depressing me."

"Dude, you're acting like someone died." I narrow my eyes and Ky backs away. "*You* broke up with *her*, unless you're not telling me something."

"I know, I know I broke it off. Remember, she hid something from me for months, something kind of huge. How could I just brush that under the rug?" I asked, but I wasn't looking for an answer.

Ky nods, but I know better than to assume he agrees. He's smart enough not to provoke me right now.

A man with a broken heart is a reckless beast.

"Did I tell you I punched her ex on her parent's front lawn?" As soon as I said it, I didn't know why I did it. Ky lets out a low whistle, his eyebrows shooting up. "What? Say it, Ky." I egged him on, wishing now I had another drink, just so I had something in my fidgeting hands. Instead, I crack my knuckles too aggressively.

"Was this before or after you found out about the *lie?*" I don't like the way he puts the word lie in finger quotes. He doesn't get why I ended shit with Audrey. He's never been in love, so I don't expect him to understand it. And I don't entertain him with an answer either.

"Tell yourself whatever you want man, but this isn't over between y'all."

"What the hell do you know about me and Audrey?" I growled out, feeling bad I was hurling my hurt at my best friend, but I couldn't stop. I need to go home before I do or say something I'll truly regret.

Ky straddles the barstool between us, peering right at me. "You know what, you're right. I don't know much, because you were so wrapped up in her that you never bothered to even introduce us. You were in your own little la la world, but I've never seen you so bent over a girl." He grabs his baseball cap from the counter, fitting it on his head, and waits for a response, but I don't have one.

Because his comment hits me, making me feel like a hypocrite. Maybe Audrey wasn't the only one keeping us in a bubble. But it's too late now.

"I've known you for what... twenty years at this point? I know when you're lying to yourself," he adds solemnly, tapping my shoulder and closes his tab, before I can even uncross my arms and move.

"I'll catch you later man, yeah?" he asks, and I nod.

"Yeah, see you later," I call out after him, my mind spinning and chest tight.

The bartender returns, leaning over the counter, a look in her eyes I don't like.

"Looks like it's just you now, huh?" she muses, blinking slowly at me.

A few years ago, I would've got her name and waited for her shift to be over, driving her home in a lust filled rage, just to forget her name by the next morning. Or I wouldn't have waited and taken her right in the backroom, not a care in the world.

But my chest aches in impossibly deep places and I wanted nothing more than to get out of here. Alone. I pay my tab, ambling outside and slide into my old truck.

I light up a cigarette, tossing the pack on the empty seat next to me, and start to pull out of the parking lot, but not before mindlessly hitting a pothole. The glove box springs open, and a small yellow envelope tumbles onto the seat. My heart skips. I grab it quickly, shoving it back into the glove box, slamming it shut so hard I probably jammed it.

The contents of the envelope are pointless. It's just an extra key now, not a grand gesture with a bigger question.

Move in with me.

It was a big step for me. I remember the jittery feeling flowing through me when I woke up and decided it was time, drove to the hardware store and got that little brass key made. Complete with a pink keychain that was stupid as hell, but I knew she'd love it. I was going to ask her when we got back from New York.

"Fuck!" Slamming the steering wheel with my palm, I peel out of the gravel lot and drive home in silence.

I don't need any noise. The inside of my head is louder than my speakers could ever get.

CHAPTER FORTY-EIGHT

Audrey

My fingers hover over the phone screen, which is the only light in my small bedroom. It's quiet in the apartment besides the slight humming of the air conditioning, but I don't find peace in the stillness. I woke up an hour ago and immediately reached for my phone, scrolling through my messages. The family group chat was flooded with a string of unanswered texts from my parents, but that wasn't why I was still in bed, my eyes fixed on the screen.

I miss you...I know I fucked up. Can we talk? I type out. My chipped nails hover over the little send button. It would be so simple, a single tap to shatter the invisible wall that had grown between Rhett and me. One small action to cross the unspoken barrier which held us apart. But I couldn't do it now, nor the other fifty times I typed out some rendition of this message. I quickly deleted it, tossing my phone across the bed and bury my face in my pillow, shutting out the world.

But then I kick my legs out and I'm reminded of the empty spot at the end of the bed. My heart aches for Rhett, but there's a reason there. He knows why we haven't spoken, but not Mabel. My heart pounds against my ribs thinking about how she's probably looking for me everywhere, and no one can explain why I'm not there. A fat tear soaks into my pillow, dampening my cheek, because all I can think about is her tin of homemade treats, the ones she loves, are going to run out any day now.

I never imagined the day that I stepped onto that grassy yard, crouched down, and pet that drooly bloodhound would mark the beginning of something I'd one day lose. I never thought my heart would shatter knowing I could never go back—never to that place, never to her.

Penny moves on the other side of the bedroom door, and I know I can't stay here all day. I ungracefully roll out of the bed, slide on pink slippers and shuffle into the bright kitchen where I find her blending a smoothie.

"Well, hello sunshine." She smiles as I drop onto a stool, groaning with my head in my hands.

"Hey Pen. Off to Pilates?" I ask groggily.

Her long, blond braid whips around as she faces me, pouring her green drink into a to-go cup. "This morning is actually spin class. It's Monday," she adds gently. "You know it might be good for you to get back to the gym. Nothing gets you out of your head like sweating and deep breathing." She tilts her head at me, and I exhale, already tired from this day.

"Yeah. Yeah. Maybe tomorrow, okay?"

She nods, probably not holding her breath. "We still on for drinks after work? How's six p.m.?" Penny taps her freshly done nails on the countertop. Perfectly fresh nails with her new workout clothes. She is a glaring juxtaposition to me right now and it's not helping, even if I love her.

"Of course. Six tonight is good."

"Hey, you've officially made it past the first week." I know she means it as a celebration, like *oh look, you made it a whole week after getting dumped—again*—but there's nothing to celebrate. This past week has been hell.

Mustering up a grin, I avoid eye contact with Penny and walk to the coffee maker, turning it on. The front door closes behind Penny, and I go on with my day, like I've done all week.

One task at a time. If I pause too long, I'll fall back into self-deprecating talk and analyze every detail of this summer, wondering again and again if I could've done something differently.

My Realtor, Elena, called me last night, arranging a meeting this morning at a coffee shop near my old apartment. Apparently, I forgot to hand over the keys to the back garage, and the new buyer, who paid cash, is closing this afternoon. I let Ed know I'll be late today and decide to head out early, walking to the coffee shop. The walk is twenty minutes, giving me time to settle my thoughts.

As I walk, a notification pings on my phone. I have a meeting with Ed at noon. During lunch, of course, but rescheduling with him wouldn't be an option, I know that much. I'm on thin ice after backing out of the promotion. He's been giving me the cold shoulder all week, and his eerie silence is almost worse than if he flat out laid into me, telling me how irresponsible and careless it was to email him a resignation from a promotion he put his name on. I can't deal with more disappointment, even from him. Letting people down has become my entire personality as of late and it was becoming heavy.

The neighborhood coffee shop is loud with morning commuters, busy rushing from here to there, but the bitter aroma of espresso and chatter distract me from my thoughts. Elena's arm shoots up, waving enthusiastically, instantly catching my attention. She's seated at a small table near the wall of windows

"I'm so sorry for this, I can't believe I forgot to double check I had all the keys!" Her auburn curls shake around her face as she pulls an envelope out of her bag. I wave it off, truly unbothered. I would rather be anywhere but my office today.

There's only one place I want to be today, and it's not a place I'm sure I'll ever see again.

"Here you go." I set two silver keys on the table between us and Elena snapped them up, placing them in a tiny envelope. Her beaming smile is nearly contagious, and a quiet sense of pride wells up in me. Taking a chance on her felt right, and it paid off. I'm free of that house, and I have more cash than I know what to do with. But I'm not necessarily in a rush to use it; when the time is right, I'll know. At least that's what I keep telling myself.

One step at a time.

"Well, that was simple!" She clasps her hands together, but I have no desire to move and contemplate sitting here for a while, pretending my meeting took longer than it really did. No one would be the wiser. I could even treat myself to a lavender cappuccino.

Though what I'm craving is homemade coffee out of a chipped mug in a farmhouse kitchen, served by a man who calls me darlin'.

"I was worried you might have forgotten them intentionally...cold feet or what not." Elena scrunched her eyebrows, watching me closely as she placed her bag in her lap.

"Oh gosh, no." I pause briefly. "That house was never going to be my home."

Elena pinches her lips together, giving me a curious look.

"It's a beautiful house. The family who bought it is very excited."

Despite what my mother, Jackson, and everyone else thinks—that I'm ungrateful—I'm honestly glad to hear that. I want someone to find happiness there. Maybe it would prove not everything I touch turns to ruin.

It was always meant to belong to someone else, to be the vessel for another family's dream.

"That's wonderful." I grin and nod, but Elena hesitates, mouth hanging slightly open before speaking.

"May I ask what is next for you? Are you going to look for a new house, or maybe rent an apartment in the city for a while longer?" It's not unreasonable for her to ask me this as my Realtor, and it's not like I haven't been thinking about it. I just don't have an answer.

"I'm not entirely sure yet. My friend hasn't kicked me out so..." I reply with a small laugh. "I'm taking it day by day. Where I want to be, what I want it to look like."

Elena smiled kindly at me, accepting the answer.

What I don't say is when I conjure up images of home, it's not a building I see.

It's a feeling, it's a person.

It's...the man across the street.

Elena starts talking about a new development south of town, but her words are drowned out by the thumping of my heart. A white pickup truck I know too well parks across the street and out steps Rhett. Blue jeans, work boots and a gray t-shirt span across his broad chest. He rounds the truck, running a hand through his ruffled dirty-blonde hair, and I stare like it's a person who's come back from the dead. My breath grows shallow, my heart caught in my throat as Rhett pulls out a toolbox, unaware of my eyes on him, unaware my heart is screaming at me, begging me to move, to do something. But I stay clutching this wooden chair like it's my lifeline.

His blue eyes glance both ways across the busy city street before jogging across to the sidewalk. His brow is furrowed low, the face he makes when he's thinking. The face I fell madly in love with. Of course, he looks good. Like, really good. Like he hasn't lost sleep or woken up at 6 a.m. every day because he needs to type out messages he'll never send me.

Elena asks a question, but I don't answer, my mouth bone dry as Rhett steps onto the sidewalk, looking like he is going to walk directly into the glass, before he turns abruptly. He didn't see me. His eyes never met mine, his face didn't falter, his eyes didn't mist over like mine right now. He didn't see me.

I want to bang my hands on the glass and force him to stop and look at me.

But then what? What would I say?

All the things I'm too scared to even send in a text?

What would I tell him that he doesn't already know?

You lied to him. You ruined everything.

"Audrey." I jerked my gaze back to Elena, her brow furrowed as she followed my eyes out the window, landing on Rhett's back. He was walking away, further and further away, and I was glued to the seat.

"I'm so sorry, I thought I saw someone I knew." I attempt to smooth my expression, but the room feels like it's spinning. Part of me wants to sink further into the chair and hunker down here for the foreseeable future, and part of me wants to run down the sidewalk after Rhett.

"No worries, I have to get back to the office with the keys, but I'll call you when all is said and done. Congratulations on the sale!"

It takes a moment for her words to register, but I smile with tight lips and stand up, walking with her to the coffee shop door.

We shake hands, and my feet begin to move down the sidewalk towards my office building, back to my windowless, gray office. I walk, but I'm not sure I'm really moving.

My heart is still back at the coffee shop, wondering if I really saw him at all.

Chapter Forty-Nine

Audrey

I lightly rap on Ed's door and hear his gruff voice on the other side. His large corner office feels abnormally warm as I cross it, slipping into a chair across from his desk. His eyes stayed glued to the computer screen until I've been sitting for nearly a minute with my hands in my lap.

The tense energy stirring in the room puts me on edge, my foot shaking annoyingly as I try to brace myself for whatever conversation is about to happen.

"Audrey," is all Ed says, swiveling in his leather chair to face me with yet again another unreadable expression.

"Ed, how are you?" I asked, knowing he wouldn't really answer. It was just a formality.

"Listen, I've been going over your portfolio. You haven't signed on a new client for nearly six weeks." Disappointment hangs in the air between us, and I try to swallow the rising lump in my throat.

"Yes, I know. I'm sorry—" I don't know what I was going to tell him, but he doesn't give me the chance either way.

"Your father and I go way back. *Way, way back.* You know that."

I nod, brows creased, not sure where this is going, but know it's probably nowhere good. "If you were anyone but Samuel's daughter, you'd be out of this company already. You need to show me you want this."

I freeze, my breath caught in my throat, the weight of this moment crashing over me. Then a hopeful thought creeps up in my head, one I suspect I've secretly had for a while.

I want him to fire me. I need him to. I want him to give me a way out, to sever the last thread that binds me to this empty, hollow life I've created.

"I'm not going to fire you, Miss Elson," he exasperates, like he read my innermost confession. "But I'm going to transfer you to our auditing team. It will require up to 30 percent travel, and there will be a minor pay cut, but I hardly think that's worse than being fired. Wouldn't you agree?"

My gaze shifts from Ed's face to his hands, then to my own hands. It feels like several minutes pass by before I muster up the courage to speak, but in actuality, it's merely seconds.

Mere seconds for me to decide to change the trajectory of this year.

Of my life.

"Thank you, Ed, for this second chance. In truth, it's probably more than I deserve. But you don't need to do this because of who my father is." Ed sits up straighter, his face creased with confusion. "The truth is, I haven't been giving my full attention to this job. There's someone else out there who dreams of working here, who's worked really hard and deserves it, though."

"What are you saying, Miss Elson?" His tie strains against his reddened neck and I stand up, inhale deeply, extending my hand towards him.

"Consider this my official resignation notice."

He goes silent, staring at me with a stiff jaw, and I wait, giving him a few more beats to gracefully accept my handshake, but he doesn't move, so I drop my arm.

"You had real potential." He finally breaks the silence and I nod, not disagreeing.

"You're right. And it's time I finally use it."

I respectively turn on my heel, and leave the office, knowing there's nothing more to add. Once I'm inside the safety of my own office, I lean against the closed door.

My heart races faster than I can handle, but for the first time in a long time, my face breaks into a smile. I don't know what comes next, but for once, that doesn't scare me. Whatever I decide, it will be my choice.

I swear, I floated on a cloud into the Irish pub a block from Penny's apartment. They have the best happy hour specials, but more specifically, they have a curly haired Irish bartender Penny has this flirty thing with. I don't question it, because he keeps our drinks flowing even when the bar is slammed. So, when I walk in and see Penny sitting at the bar on the green leather stool, her elbows on the counter, laughing at whatever Richard the Irish bartender said, I smile, too.

"G'day, Audrey!" He flashes a crooked grin my way and sets a napkin down next to Penny. We aren't here *that* often, but he always remembers my name.

"Hey Richard! An Irish mule for me, please...with a shot of whiskey on the side."

Penny turns in her stool to look at me with wide eyes.

"I'm celebrating," I exclaim loudly, placing clasped hands in my lap.

Richard eyes us while mixing our drinks mere feet away.

"Okay...and what're we celebrating tonight?" Penny cocks her head at me.

I slam my palms on the mahogany bar top. "I quit my job today!"

Richard pauses the pouring of whiskey, while my best friend's jaw drops open. Pulling my hands back in my lap, I add, "And I officially sold my house."

Richard chuckles, shaking his head, and slams down three shot glasses in front of us.

"I don't get you American lasses, but this calls for a round of shots!"

Penny grabs my arm.

"I literally saw you less than seven hours ago. What in the *actual fuck* happened today?" She stares at me, not seeming to breathe.

It probably appears like I have finally snapped in her mind. I got dumped a week ago, sold my multi-million dollar home today without ever spending a night there, and quit a coveted job that paid damn well. But I didn't lose my mind.

"I learned how to say no today," I simply replied, as Richard fills the shot glasses with Jameson. Even though Penny doesn't take her eyes off me, waiting for elaboration, she grabs the shot with us, shooting it back.

As the burn of the whiskey wears off, I tell Penny about seeing Rhett this morning. I still hadn't unpacked everything it made me feel, and maybe that would take some time. But it had shaken something in me. Something that made me finally stand up to Ed and say no.

Penny was empathetic, never judging, just listening.

"So that's it, huh?"

"That's it, Pen."

We didn't talk much more about it, and I was grateful for that. We fell back into old ways, chatting about anything and everything random. I also asked her if it would be okay to keep living with her for a bit longer. She was more than okay with that.

We ended up staying, ordering appetizers, and laughing as Richard entertained us with horrible puns.

I didn't even realize how bad I needed this.

"Okay, so I'm sorry to bring the mood down but I have to tell you something," Penny starts, and I pause, nervous butterflies filling my stomach.

"This day is already one for the books, so just tell me."

"Maybe it's more of a request...but I need my rhinestone cowgirl boots back. I have a date this coming weekend, and I want to dazzle him with my unpredictable personality and insanely perfect legs." Penny sucked her drink through the tiny red straw, waiting on my answer as my fingers dug into the seat cushion beneath me.

I exhale a tiny laugh. "Okay, so the funny thing is, they are actually at Rhett's house." Penny blinks, unfazed by my words because she already knew that. "But I will buy you new ones. Just tell me how much they are, and I'll send you the money. Or we can go shopping! I want to pick up a few new things." Penny's strained smile makes me stop talking.

"That's so generous but I really need *those* ones." Penny swirls her straw smugly in her glass. "They are my favorite shoes. I wouldn't ask this of you if they weren't important. I got them in Nashville for a concert and they aren't replaceable."

I cringe, covering my face with my hands.

"You weren't going to leave everything at his house *forever*, right?" she asks, and I have to look away from her prying eyes.

"No, not *forever*. But he hasn't texted me about getting my stuff...and I haven't texted him asking for it either."

Penny sighs. "This is insane Audrey, you realize that right? One of you is going to have to be the bigger person. You need closure." She pauses, then murmurs. "And I need those boots back."

"I know, I know. But it's complicated, Pen. I still love him. Even if he never talks to me again, I know a part of me will always love him." My voice shakes, and the high I felt walking into this pub thirty minutes ago has completely vanished.

"I know you love him. And I have a feeling he still loves you."

"Ha—no. If he did, he would've called me, he would've talked to me." I turn away from Penny, quickly dabbing my eyes. Exhaling slowly, I try to steady my racing heart. "But I will text him. I will get your boots back. Promise."

Throwing her arms around my shoulders, Penny squeezes tight. "Thank you! And hey, this may open up communication between you two, who knows?"

I hesitate, unsure how much I want to unload in this very public bar. But no one warned me finding yourself could hurt this much, or that self-discovery comes with grief. And grief comes in uncontrollable waves.

"I think he was right, Pen."

"Hmm?" She turns so we are facing each other, knee to knee.

"When I first met him, I didn't know what I wanted. I just knew I wanted to feel *wanted*. Was that so wrong?" I asked as tears well in my eyes again. Penny shakes her head, waiting patiently, as I rub my thumb across my trembling lips. "It didn't take long to fall in love with him though. And I started to fall in love with who I was when I was with him...and for some reason that scared me."

Penny places her hand over mine.

"I want to be that person all the time. Even if Rhett doesn't..." I pause, suddenly aware finishing that sentence would break me in a way I wasn't ready to confront. If Rhett never spoke to me again; it would shatter me. "I can't go back to how I lived before. I want to be this version of me...for *me*." I nod, sitting up straighter on the stool, feeling a metaphorical weight lift off my shoulders as I meet Penny's shining gaze.

"I've loved every version of you, but I have to say, this one's kinda my favorite."

We both chuckle, at the absurdity of us crying in a pub at six o'clock on a Monday evening. Right on brand for our friendship.

"So now what?"

"I think it starts with me getting back your rhinestone boots."

Chapter Fifty

Rhett

It's a known thing among locals that there are twelves seasons in Roseville. After summer comes second summer or as my Meemaw used to call it: *hell's front porch*. And as the middle of September approaches, we're in the thick of it. Sweat runs down my jaw, dripping onto the instructions in my hands.

I hate instructions, I always have. They are insulting. *It's a dog door*. If I can't figure out how to install this on my backdoor, then what kind of carpenter am I.

After staring at the instructions for nearly fifteen minutes, with no progress to show, I throw them to the ground. The sound of an engine reverberates in the distance as Mabel's ears perk up, but she remains a puddle in the grass under the shade of the magnolia tree.

Before I can make it around to the front of my house, my mom comes flitting around the corner, a box in her arms, and smiles under her large sunglasses. It looks heavy on her small frame, so I wipe my brow and rush toward her, lifting the box from her arms.

"I didn't know you were coming over." I squint against the afternoon sun.

"Well, I didn't think you'd be home in the middle of the day on a Tuesday," she muses, making no attempt to hide the implication in her tone. "I'm just dropping off some veggies. I texted you last night letting you know."

I usually have all my consultations on Tuesdays, and it's busy season for the folks who want work done before the holidays. But I've had my phone off for three days now.

Good for business, I know.

But the temptation to call *her* has been strong lately. I spent the morning pushing all her clothes into one closet, so I don't have to look at them anymore. I can't even open my kitchen cabinets without seeing a stack of fancy mixing bowls. It's not like she asked to get anything back, but I couldn't just throw it out. Ky said I was torturing myself, but if that was true, so be it.

I never claimed to be the man who made all the right choices.

"I haven't checked my phone Ma, sorry. Been busy, but I appreciate you bringing this all over." She followed me as I led the way into the kitchen, resting the box on the island. I sift through the food mindlessly.

"You know it's only me here, right? I can't possibly eat all of this."

"Well, I figured you could cook something if you have someone over or something...you know..." She scanned the kitchen, surely searching for a sign that Audrey was back. She hadn't pried since I came back from New York. But her indirect commentary was almost worse.

"Party of one here. But thank you, I'll figure it out," I added quickly, guiding her back outside where I kneeled on the ground next to my project. "Sorry, I need to get back to this."

"What are you trying to do?" My mom stood in the shade of the house, hands on her hips and feet planted solidly on the ground. I have a feeling she isn't going to be easy to get rid of. Clearly, she has something to say to me.

The sun continues to beat down on me, my blue t-shirt sticking to my back, only adding to my agitation by the second. I push my damp hair back, feeling as disheveled as I probably look.

"I'm installing a dog door." I know I'm being short, and I hate that. But I had my phone off for a reason. I want to be alone. I'll be myself again by Sunday dinner, but right now, in the middle of the week, I just want to avoid responsibility and be an asshole in the privacy of my own home.

"I can see that. Well, it doesn't look like you're getting very far." She points out the obvious and I bite my cheeks before I say something rude.

"Ma, is there a reason you stopped over? I'd love to chat more, but I need to concentrate." I muster up a half-hearted grin, with the crumpled sheet of useless directions in my hand.

"Honey...it's none of my business, but it's clear you're rattled by whatever happened between you and Audrey."

There it is.

"Everything is fine. I'm busy with work, you know this is a busy time of year."

She places her hands on her hips, cocking her eyebrows, unsatisfied with my bullshit answer. Pushing myself up from the ground, I face her, staring into eyes that look identical to mine. "It didn't work out between us, okay? Sometimes things don't work out." I sigh, shoving my hands in my pockets. "We were just two people who crossed paths and had a thing. That's it. That's all it ever was, all it was ever going to be. I'm sorry if you and Desi thought otherwise." I turn away from her knowing eyes, done with this conversation.

Done thinking about this.

Done talking about it.

Done trying to get my heart to believe the bullshit my mouth is spewing.

"Do you really believe that, Rhett?"

My heart somersaults in my chest, but I stand there, stubborn and pissed off. Thinking about the closet full of Audrey's stuff inside my bedroom, and how she should be here, right now.

"I think you loved her." My mom looks pointedly at me, sighing softly. "And baby, she loved you, I know she loved you. Whatever she did, or you did, whatever happened…just make sure you're willing to throw everything out over it."

"I don't want to talk about this." My voice is gruff as I start walking away.

"This is the last thing I'll leave you with, okay?"

I'm forced to turn and face the woman who raised me, the one who sees straight through my angry facade. "In life, you only get one great love. If you're lucky, that's the person you spend your life with. And honey, life is short, so damn short." Her voice catches as she shrugs, and my throat tightens. "You can be angry and hurt, but don't waste time, Rhett. You already know the answer. You know if she is the one for you. That doesn't mean it's going to be easy. It means all the stuff you have to sort out between you is worth it."

I don't say anything back, the words caught in my throat, tearing away at every ounce of angry resolve I built up.

"Thanks for the food, Mom."

"Love you, honey."

"Love you, too," I add, and she quickly kisses my cheek, pats Mabel on the head and heads back to her car, leaving me alone to stand next to my house in the blazing sun.

"Alright, Mabel, let's get this damn door installed." I kick aside the directions and grab the drill.

An hour later, there's a hole in my door. Well, technically it's a door. A swinging dog door I already know Mabel is going to abuse. This was never part of the plan either.

But a few nights ago, I found myself scrolling through my phone, when I came across photos of me and Audrey. A random night in late July. We were rocking on the front porch swing, her legs across my lap, when she looked up at me and said "You know what would make me happy right now? Strawberry ice cream." That's all she had to say. Minutes later, we were bouncing down the old country road to the pink ice cream stand my mom used to take me to after my baseball games as a kid. Audrey got strawberry ice cream on a waffle cone, smiling ear to ear, as we sat at the edge of the field on the back of my truck.

I remember everything.

The way a summer storm came out of nowhere, soaking us in seconds. Kissing in the cab of the truck while the rain pelted the window. The white sundress, her hair falling around her face, the way her lips tasted like sugar. I felt like the luckiest man in the world that day.

We waited out the storm together, my arm lazily draped around her as she leaned into the crook of my chest. We drove home in a happy daze, only to find Mabel sitting on the front porch, soaking wet. Audrey nearly jumped out of the truck before I could even put it in park, running across the front yard to Mabel, who was completely fine. She probably rode out the storm under the porch. But I should've known better. Audrey quickly became Mabel's mother the moment she met her.

Minutes later, Mabel was on the kitchen floor, wrapped in towels as Audrey spoke sweetly to her, feeding her blueberry biscuits. I said nothing because those two were in their own world. 'Girls Club', Audrey jokes. We spent the next hour sitting on my couch, researching the best dog doors, because god forbid Mabel ever get stuck outside again. Audrey found one she thought was perfect. It was high tech, way too expensive, and completely unnecessary.

"Rhett, you have to get this." She'd shoved the phone in my face, her arm still wrapped around the sleeping hound dog.

"Mabel doesn't need a seven-hundred dollar dog door." Mabel lifted her droopy eyes my way as I said it.

Audrey set her phone down. "Okay, let me buy it for her then. You can install it, right?"

I stared at her with wide eyes. "Of course I can install it! But no, I'm not letting you spend your money on that. I'll build her one, and it will be even better." I wasn't rolling in money, but business was steady over the summer, and I was comfortable. But I still didn't need to spend that much on a dog door.

And I never truly knew how much money Audrey had. I knew it was a lot more than I'd ever see in my lifetime, but she didn't talk about it, she never flaunted it, and I never asked. She simply offered to pay for certain things, things she knew I wouldn't spend money on, like a *freaking dog door*. But I didn't want her to do that; not when I could build it myself. Or so I had thought.

Because here I am now, two months after that conversation, and I ordered the expensive dog door she wanted. That's the thing about Audrey. She plants herself deep, infiltrating every corner of your mind. Even when she's gone.

"Try it out, Mabel. Go on, go inside, girl." I instruct as my dog eyes the door skeptically, drool hanging from her jowls.

Out of patience, I step inside, grab a treat, and squat down on the other side of the dog door, calling her inside.

"Come on Mabel, I got a treat." I hold out the beef stick treat in my hand. It's a bit stale, I will admit, but it should do the trick. She's a bloodhound, she should smell this a mile away.

Mabel cautiously pokes her head through the door, nose twitching, eyes locked on the treat in my hand. Eventually, all four of her clumsy and muddy paws are inside the kitchen, where she turns her nose up at the beef stick, and lets out a small huff.

"You too good for store bought now? It's pure protein, it's good for you." I wave it around like a mad man trying to talk reason into my dog. I try to give the treat to her again, but Mabel lets out a loud bark, eyes locked on the tin on the counter.

The tin that's been empty for two weeks now.

"Those treats are long gone, dog. It's just me and my beef sticks. You're going to have to deal with that."

Mabel grumbles the only way a dog can, turning around and waddling into the living room, before she drops herself dramatically on the floor in protest.

"Whatever, you'll get used to this. Things are going back to how they used to be!" I holler and toss the treat into the trash. Then I get in the shower, turning the water as cold as it can go to shock myself out of thinking about *everything*.

CHAPTER FIFTY-ONE

Audrey

Penny and I curl up on opposite ends of her pink velvet sofa, with a smorgasbord of snacks and charcuterie in front of us, and a 90's rom-com we'd seen a hundred times playing on the TV. I type out a text, read it, and delete it, grabbing more snacks, avoiding the inevitable. All while secretly hoping Penny will just let me buy her a new pair of boots.

Penny grunts, ripping the phone from my hands while balancing a very full glass of wine in her other hand.

"Dude, you have to just send it." She swipes my screen. "Let me see what you're working with." She stares at my screen for several seconds while my patience wears thin.

"Nothing sounds right. Like, '*Hi it's me, your ex-girlfriend. I left half of my possessions at your house, but I just need to pick up one item. Burn the rest*'."

"Oh my god, you can't let him burn your Celine bag!" Penny gasps and I wince. No, I'd never let him burn *that* bag.

"Penny, focus! He's not burning my stuff. Unless he already has? Maybe that's the reason he hasn't reached out." Our heads jerk toward each other, eyes wide. "Okay, give me the phone. I'm going to send him something cordial and professional."

Plucking the phone from her hands, I type out something I'd send a coworker and hit send. Quick enough that I can't even think about it. She hovers over my shoulder.

> **Audrey:** Hello Rhett. I apologize for bothering you with this, but I am in need of the rhinestone cowgirl boots I left at your house. They belong to Penny. Could you kindly put them on your porch, and I'll pick them up tomorrow? Please let me know a time that is convenient for you. Regards, Audrey.

"You signed the text with your name…" Her mouth is open as she continues to stare at my phone.

I flip the phone over, placing it beside me, and pick up a cracker with cheese. "Yeah, I know. But what if he deleted my number? He'll need to know who's texting him." As the words leave my mouth, regret creeps right in. *This is a disaster.*

"Because a lot of girls leave their boots at his house…" Penny teases, but the vibration of my phone has us both jumping in our seats. A wave of nausea rolls through me, my hands growing clammy.

"Read it, I can't."

Penny reaches for the phone, and I lower my face into my knees as she reads it aloud.

"I'll put them on the back patio at 8 a.m."

I wait in silence, with bated breath, for Penny to continue.

Surely, there has to be more.

"That's it? That's all he said?" I croaked, glancing at my best friend.

"Sorry, babe." Penny frowns sympathetically, and refills my glass, handing it to me silently. I take a mindless sip. I really thought he'd have something to say after all this time.

It's been three days since I quit my job. Technically, I had given my two weeks' notice. Even though I hated the place, I wanted to do the professional and right thing. I was finishing out the two weeks remotely, deciding not to show my face in a place where people saw my last name and decided they already knew everything about me.

Those days were decidedly behind me.

I knew it was only a matter of time before my parents found out about my shameful resignation from the firm, so I had decided to call them and rip off the bandage.

My father barely said anything when I told him, but the disappointment seethed through the phone. Not one bit surprising.

My mother, however, reminded me quitting in such a fashion was clearly a violation of unspoken family rules. I stifled a laugh and kindly thanked them for helping me get that job, and finished the call letting them know there would be no further discussion about my career.

But that's behind me, and it's a new day. An early morning thunderstorm woke me right before my alarm at 6 a.m.; the lightning bright enough to cause flashes of light through my blackout curtains. Rolling over, I pull the covers off, reaching for my phone.

I don't know why I'm still expecting something that is never going to happen.

Hope is a bitch.

Slipping my feet into slippers, I throw my silk robe on and trudge out to the kitchen. I move through the kitchen, letting the heavy rain be my only soundtrack. Within twenty minutes, I have the dough formed and the oven preheated. Using a heart shaped cookie cutter—I left my bone shaped one at Rhett's—I cut out three dozen blueberry dog biscuits.

Just because Rhett and I aren't together doesn't mean Mabel should suffer.

While they baked, I quickly showered and threw on shorts and a college sweatshirt. I second guess my outfit choice, wondering if I should try to look nice, but the truth smacks me as I ruffle through my dresser drawers.

You're not going to see him.

I knew him well enough to know he wouldn't be home this morning. If he was avoiding me through text, he'd surely go out of his way to avoid me in person.

The blacktop of the highway greets me as I leave the city. It's me and a few cars heading out this way. Everyone else is leaving the country, commuting into the city for work. It only adds to the bizarre, anxious tightening in my stomach. With every streetlight, stop sign, and cornfield passed, my heart hammers harder and harder.

Then the old familiar oak tree comes into view, the one with the tree swing that greets you as you pull into the long gravel driveway. I turn down my music, like that will help me as I drive slowly past the white house, stopping in front of the garage. My hand lingers on the shift knob as I put the car in park, wondering how the hell I got here.

How *we* got here.

I'm frozen in my car as memories from the first night I met Rhett come rushing back to me. It feels like a distant memory now. He might have thought he was just being polite, but now all these months later, I can see that night for what it truly was.

He saved me, but I don't think he knows that.

Maybe that's only just for me to know, but that makes it hurt worse. Because I never got to thank him properly. Thank him for being the first man in my life to see me for me; not for my family's name or the number in my bank account.

Just then, a clumsy dog comes barreling around the corner, her ears flapping wildly as she rushes toward the car, pulling me from my cloudy thoughts.

"Mabel!" I yell, leaping out of the car as fast as I can to greet my sweet girl. She whimpers and curls around my bare legs, her body wiggling with uncontained excitement. She eventually succumbs to rolling over, exposing her belly. I kneel in the gravel, pushing my fingers into her warm, brown fur.

"I missed you so much." Her heart thuds under my palm, and as I reach behind me and snatch the treat container out of the car, she hops up, nose in the air.

"You didn't think I'd show up empty handed, did you?" I pull a freshly baked treat out, and Mabel sits and gently takes it from me, galloping to the backdoor where she eats it in two bites. My eyes follow her to the paper grocery bag sitting on the steps.

Penny's boots.

There's no truck to be seen, only Mabel, manning the house all by herself. As I walk over, Mabel comes back to me, butt wiggling, and I place a hand on her head, scanning the backdoor.

"He did not," I mumble in disbelief, eyeing the dog door. The expensive one I picked. Tears prick at my eyes, but I quickly wipe them away.

"Men are unbelievable." Grumbling, I grab the boots from the steps but pause when I see the treat container in my hands. I can't leave it outside; Mabel will find a way to get to it, even if I set it on the table. I glance at her, her gaze fixed on me and wonder if I could just put it in the kitchen instead.

But it's not my house. It's not my home to come and go as I please. Even if I had wanted it to be, even if I had silently said in my head this *was* home.

Now I see how careless that was of me.

Mabel pushes by me, effortlessly going through the doggy door. *Little show-off.* I smirk, conflicting feelings clouding me. Rhett installed the door. That means life went on without me here. And of course, I knew it had.

I have to go inside, though. For Mabel.

Just set the treats down and leave. It'll be tempting to take some of my things, but I didn't bring anything to pack them in and doing that would only betray his trust again. Something I've already done enough of. If I want to hold onto any hope for the future, I need to start rebuilding now.

Pushing my weight into the door, which always sticks, I silently thank Rhett for leaving it unlocked. The overcast skies outside darken the small kitchen, and it's quiet enough that I can hear my heart thudding in my chest.

The sound of the ceiling fan whirling in Rhett's bedroom draws my attention to the cracked open door, but I refuse to step closer to it. I also try to ignore the lingering smell of cedar and musk that flooded me the moment I stepped inside.

"I hope you're taking care of yourself," I whisper, surprised by the tightness in my throat. Tears well in my eyes, so I quickly cleared my throat, and set the treat container down towards the back of the counter with purpose. Before I can second guess myself, I leave, slamming the door behind me. I snatch Penny's boots as a misty drizzle meets me, and my focus narrows as I pull my sleeves over my hands and hurry toward the car, rain speckling my skin. Then I hear a sudden whoosh, and when I turn, Mabel is running, trying to catch up to me.

I stop as she does, glancing at the gray storm clouds looming over us.

"I have to go, girl." Every word hurts to say as I look into her deep, honey eyes. "You be good, okay?" I bite my quivering lips and bend over, kissing the top of her head. Thunderclaps sound in the distance and she lets out a startled howl. "Go back inside Mabel, go on now." I try to nudge her back to the house, but she plants herself in the driveway at my feet.

She has the dog door now and will go back inside to safety, but if I don't leave, I know I'll be pulled back in. Staying isn't an option—it never was.

Scurrying to my car as rain releases from the cloud above, I toss the boots into the backseat and start the car with my heart in my throat. Mabel continues to howl, watching me through the front window. I punch the gas and spin the car around, speeding down the long driveway. Through my blurry eyes, I catch movement in the rearview mirror. The white house shrinks in the distance as Mabel trots after me, her pace quickening, faster and faster, chasing my car as I drive away.

"No, no, no! Dammit, Mabel," I plead inside the car, my heart cracking in two. The tears fall faster than I can whisk them away, my chest heaving with sobs as I continue to turn onto the street. Mabel stands at the edge of the property, howling for me to come back.

White-knuckling the steering wheel, I drive away, feeling myself unravel with every mile that separates us.

CHAPTER FIFTY-TWO

Audrey

Instead of turning onto the highway to head back into the city, I make a right at the stop sign, and head into downtown Roseville. I need comfort—of any sort—and I know where to get it.

Rain soaks the sidewalk, but inside the diner is quiet, the booths full of mostly older folks, who all look at me as the door chimes. It's weird to be here without Rhett, but he doesn't own this town. Or the booth.

"Just one?" A waitress about my age asks with a small smile. I nod, pulling my damp hair up into a top knot.

"I'm sorry, the rain got me good," I wince, apologizing as I slide into the red booth with water dripping off me.

"Don't even worry about it. How about a warm cup of coffee?" She turns over the white ceramic mug.
"Yes, thanks, and I'm going to get the classic waffle."

"Sounds good."

Once she walks away, I add cream to the coffee, breathing it in before sipping it, letting the warmth fill me. The chatter around me settles me a little, and I do everything I can to push the image of Mabel from my mind. I have to.

I take out my phone to text Penny.

> **Audrey**: Mission complete. Got your boots.

> **Penny:** Did you see him? And thank you. I owe you.

She did owe me.

> **Audrey:** He wasn't home. But Mabel chased me as I left, and now I'm in the diner in town, sitting alone in his booth, waiting for a waffle. Please tell me I haven't lost my mind.

> **Penny:** I think this is all necessary. It's part of healing. It's closure.

I shake my head, bringing the white mug to my lips. The thing is, I don't want to heal, I don't want closure from Rhett. I don't want this gaping wound in my heart to become a scar I look back on one day, like a distant summer fling.

That's not how I want to remember this summer.

I slide my phone back into my jacket pocket, at a loss for what to say next.

Music plays softly in the background, and I bring my focus to the quaint Main Street outside. A few people walk by the diner with umbrellas. I'm grateful for the rain. It made me slow down a bit today. The car across from the diner pulls out of its parking spot, revealing a boarded up shop I've never noticed before.

"One waffle. Anything else I can get for you?" The waitress comes back, placing my food before me.

"Thank you." I pause, the coffee mug halfway to my lips. I tip my head slightly toward the window. "Actually, maybe you can answer this. Do you know anything about that empty store front across from the diner?"

Her eyes follow mine to the window, where the rain has softened to a drizzle. Across the street, an empty retail space sits wedged between two busy storefronts. The awning sags slightly, its fabric stained and weathered. A faded 'For Rent' sign clings to the inside of the dusty windows, its edges curling from age. The sign is so bleached from the sun that the phone number is nearly invisible, just faint shadows where ink used to be.

"That place has been empty since I started working here...gosh, probably before that. So, at least six years." She shrugs her shoulders, turning back to me.

"Oh okay. Thank you." I smile as I savor my waffle, a nervous flutter igniting within me as my mind wanders off on its own. I eat in silence, my eyes trained out the window.

I linger in the booth, my coffee refilled twice, as a wild idea claws at the edges of my mind. It's relentless, impossible to ignore—a notion which would've been unthinkable just six months ago. Yet here it is, screaming for my attention, daring me to consider it.

Twenty minutes later, I find myself in my car, surveying the sad, neglected space. It's crying out for reinvention, for someone to show it love. It needs to be reminded that just because it's been empty for so long, it doesn't mean it's unworthy.

The right person simply hasn't come along to see its potential. Until now.

I hit a contact in my phone, and my Realtor's voice fills my car. "Hello, this is Elena!"

"Hey Elena, it's Audrey! I hope I didn't catch you at a bad time. I have a question for you and was hoping you could help me." I smile, my heart skipping a beat as I lean over my steering wheel to get one more good look at the empty store.

"Can you get the information on a property for me? The address is 308 Main Street in Roseville."

CHAPTER FIFTY-THREE

Rhett

Mabel hasn't stopped going in and out of the damn dog door every five minutes since I installed it two weeks ago. It's enough to drive a man crazy. I'm about to lock it through the app when I hear my name in unison coming from the driveway.

"Uncle Rhett!" Jessie and Jenna call out as they run clumsily in their pink rain boots towards me.

"What are you supposed to be, a unicorn or a princess?" I ask, pulling the wings attached to Jessie's back.

"I'm a fairy unicorn queen, obviously!" She flips her hair, and my sister strolls up behind them, carrying a casserole dish, rolling her eyes at me.

"Don't even ask. She hasn't taken those wings off for five days now, and I can't do a thing about it."

"Noted," I nod, going back to focusing on the grill in front of me. It's finally cooled down outside with the start of October just days away. There's a slight breeze in the air that wasn't there a week ago, a promise of changing leaves, a slowdown from summer. I'm usually a fall person. I love the cool weather, when I am not drenched in blankets of humidity in my workshop or melting in my old truck. But an uneasiness has overcome me these last few days that I just can't shake. It's driving me fucking nuts.

"Thanks for hosting dinner here tonight, honey. My oven is still on the fritz." My mom saddles up next to me.

"It gives me a chance to grill. I didn't get to do that much this summer." I bite my lip, not wanting to open an invitation into that subject. "I'll stop by after my appointment Tuesday to fix it. It's probably the sensor."

"Whatever you say, baby. It gives me a break from cooking," my mom replies, winking at me. The girls run by, the dogs chasing them through the grass.

"What's different back here?" my mom asks, pushing her sunglasses up into her hair, which is piled messily on top of her head. The same way Audrey used to wear it. The thought flickers through my mind, uninvited, and I shove it away before it can take hold.

"I finished lining the garden with pavers, hauled some junk away, and started power washing the house. Me and Ky are going to paint it this Friday after work," I rattle off.

My mom's eyes grow wide, and she smirks, popping a blueberry from the salad into her mouth.

"Don't say it, Ma," I add, half joking as I turn to check the sizzling steaks.

"I'm not...I'm glad you're getting stuff done."

I turn off the flame, placing the steaks on a wooden board and bring them to the table, avoiding eye contact with the one woman who can read me like a damn book. "I had other priorities. I was going to get to it all eventually," I reply roughly.

"Why the sudden change?" Her voice is cool and light, but when our eyes lock, I know my irritation is glaringly obvious.

"You know," I mumble, and she offers me a small shrug and sad smile.

"Dinner's ready!" I call to the girls who come running towards us, pink blurry visions of messy blond hair and fairy wings. Mabel's on their heels, hopeful she'll get a trim of meat.

"How's work going Rhett, you busy again with new clients?" my sister asks. Both she and my mom are watching me closely as I slice into my steak.

I feel like an ant under a magnifying glass and my shoulders grow tense.

"It's going. I'm busy," I add slowly, knowing what she's not saying.

You barely worked this past month. What the hell is going on? Are you back to normal or do we need to worry about you?

Desi smiles real big and says, "Good, I'm glad. Good to stay busy!" She was talking to me like I was one of her daughters and I groaned, barely audible enough for them to hear over the music playing. I also installed outdoor speakers for the workshop and movie nights outside.

Solo movie nights.

"Hey girls," I said, and the twins looked up at me from their dinner plates. "I have a whole new setup for the outdoor theater. Maybe one of the weekends your mom will let you come over and do a movie night." Their eyes light up, and they turn to their mom, toothless grins spreading on their small faces.

"Mom, can we, please?" they beg in unison.

My sister nods, "Of course." But then she turns her attention to me. "A real outdoor theater? That's pretty fancy for you, Rhett. Sounds like the perfect date night set up."

Scoffing, I point my fork at her. "Great Desi, you can borrow it anytime you want for a *date*."

"Mom, you have a date?" Jenna asks horrified and I laugh, but Desi doesn't think it's funny. Her eyes narrowed at me.

"I have no dates set for the foreseeable future. But you might, you never know." She pinches her lips together. She couldn't accept her big brother likes his solitude.

Or was trying to get used to it again.

Shit was finally getting done. She should be happy for me. I'm not at Bourbon Barrel drinking my paycheck away, bringing strangers home to my bed.

"Okay, let's change the subject, yeah? Cool, thanks." I flash a toothy, *shut the hell up* grin to the whole table, and my mom perks her head up.

"Oh! There's new paper in the windows of the old butcher shop."

"Huh?" I take a sip of beer, gazing at her.

"I was in town running errands today and saw a crew of guys going inside. There's paper covering the windows and the rent sign is gone. No one knows what's going in there, but I heard at the post office someone bought the entire space in cash. Rumor is it might be a bakery!"

My sister starts to respond to my mom, but her words are drowned out by the sinking feeling washing over me.

Every town needs a good bakery; it's just a fact, Rhett.

A low laugh booms from my chest as I bring the bottle to my lips, shaking my head.

"This is a cruel joke, right?" I mumble to the universe.

I take another cold shower after my family leaves and settle in for the night. Tomorrow will be a long day of catching up on invoices and drafting plans for a new client. As I pull a pair of shorts from the dresser, I pause longer than usual to examine myself in the mirror. My blue eyes look somehow duller, lacking their usual spark. My summer tan remains, a permanent reminder of the time I spend outdoors. Lately, I've been spending my evenings on the front porch with Mabel, staying out there until I'm fighting off sleep. It's far better than being inside, where the memory of Audrey haunts me at every turn.

Her ghost isn't just in the house but in everything I do. I used to enjoy simple nights alone, walks with Mabel along the meadow, it was all *enough*.

But that's the thing about *enough*. Once you get a taste of *better*, it's pretty damn hard to go back to *enough*.

"Alright Mabel, let's go," I call out as I walk through the house, hearing her groan from the couch. I set down my drink, glaring at her, reaching my hand into her treat bin on the counter.

What the hell is this?

There's a container I never noticed before. A glass to-go container full of the blueberry biscuits.

"How the hell?" I open it, checking to see how fresh they are, when Mabel suddenly appears at my feet, one ear flopped over the top of her head. "When did these get here?" I question her, scratching my head. They can't be that old. Audrey had to have brought them when she picked up the boots. The ridiculous rhinestone cowboy boots.

I shake my head, not wanting to picture her in my house. I throw one at Mabel, who catches it in the air. I snatch my beer, and march to the porch, letting the screen door slam behind me.

She is everywhere.

CHAPTER FIFTY-FOUR

Audrey

"**D**o you think the town will allow you to get a pink awning?" Penny asks with her hands on her hips, staring at the clapboard building I now officially own. The owner was so thrilled to get it off his hands that when I said I'd pay cash, he nearly threw the deed at me. There were two floors; the first was the shop and the second was an apartment, though no one had lived in it for a while. First, I needed to get this bakery up and running, then I would turn the top into a livable apartment, perhaps for myself.

"Pink?" Furrowing my brow, I looked at my best friend who nodded, chewing her pink lip, probably redesigning the entire thing in her mind. "I was thinking I'd do a neutral palette."

It was Penny's first time seeing the space. "Okay but hear me out. Neutral palette, very minimalistic and aesthetic, with pops of pale pink. I think it would be beautiful."

I stare at the building, trying to visualize what she's saying. "Okay..." I nod slowly, a small smile on my face. "I can see it."

Penny looks pleased with herself as I lead her inside the construction zone. Brown paper still lines the front windows. I want everything to be a surprise to the public on opening day. However, the town gossip mill was already going wild with speculation. But I'm good at keeping secrets.

"Oh my gosh, this is...wow." Penny slides her sunglasses down her nose, peering around the empty shop. I knocked down the interior walls and removed the thick plaster from the side walls to expose the hundred-year-old brick.

"I found someone who is going to restore the original pine floors and the tin ceiling tiles. I want to preserve as much history as I can." Pride swells in my chest, along with a dash of overwhelm. This business was so out of my element, but I was taking it day by day, figuring it out as I went.

"I'm so excited for you, Aud. This is seriously going to be so cute! People are going to make the drive from the city once they taste your cookies."

"I can't believe I bought a building, Penny. Who am I?" I let out a small laugh, feeling slightly lightheaded as I consider the tasks ahead of me.

"I can't think of anything more perfect than this for you. I mean it. You're going to transform this place and bring people together in this community. You were never meant to sit behind a desk crunching numbers or whatever you did." We both laughed because no matter how many times I explained it, Penny never understood my financial job. We walk around a bit more, as I show her some inspiration images for the space.

"Do you have a name yet?" she asks.

"I thought of a few, but none really fit. I'll know when it's right."

The contractor and his crew arrive as Penny is heading out, so I thank her for coming and hug her goodbye. I plan to stick around. It's finally a renovation project that I'm fully invested in.

By noon, the framing of the walls takes shape. I step outside for a breather, letting the warm sunshine wash over me. The air somehow feels different here; crisp, clean, as if it carries a kind of clarity I hadn't noticed before.

Main Street is calm, the quiet broken only by the faint chatter of mothers pushing strollers, and the shuffle of customers filtering in and out of nearby businesses. I settle onto a bench along the sidewalk and people watch. I'm still waiting for the fact that this will be the view from my new 'office' to sink in. A few feet away, an older gentleman stops, leaning heavily on his cane. He stands there for a moment, his gaze fixed on the papered windows of my shop.

"Good afternoon." I put my phone down and smiled at him. He nods at me, still leaning on his cane.

"Do you know what they're putting here?" His gentle eyes are full of curiosity. I bought the building under my LLC, so it hasn't publicly been announced I'm the owner yet.

"I've heard it's going to be a bakery," I say, waiting for his reaction.

"Hmm." His lips twitch into what I think is a tiny smile. "I hope they have cinnamon rolls." He turns to face me. "My wife, Glenda, loves them. She's in a wheelchair, so it's hard for her to go places, but I used to get her a cinnamon roll every Sunday after church. She'd love it if I did that again. Maybe this place will have them." He shrugs and an unexpected lump forms in my throat.

Pinching my lips together to prevent the tears from spilling, I clear my throat. "I bet they will have cinnamon rolls. When this place eventually opens, you'll have to bring Glenda in. I bet she'd love it."

"Alrighty miss, I will try." He smiles, nodding at me and continues slowly down the sidewalk.

My heart doesn't recover from the interaction right away, so I close my eyes and let the early fall breeze blow across my face.

I hope someone loves me that much in fifty years.

What happens next isn't a decision. It's an unstoppable pull, something I can't fight. I break into a jog across the street, slide into my car, and grip the steering wheel, driving down Main Street, leaving the bakery behind.

My heart thunders, each beat reverberating in my chest as I cross over the railroad tracks.

The narrow road, lined with cornfields, feels endless, but there's no time to think. I let my heart guide me toward the one person I can't bear to be without for another second.

The large oak tree comes into view as my tires slide into the driveway, kicking up gravel as my car skids to a jolting stop right in front of the house.

Don't think. Don't think. Just tell him exactly what you feel.

Rhett's truck sits in front of the workshop, and the barn doors are wide open. He's so close, he's right there.

My feet hit the ground with a quick, steady rhythm, and I don't bother shutting the door behind me. Each moment feels more important than the last as I make my way toward the back of the house. My body moves instinctively here, my feet on the soft grass, as the quiet rush of adrenaline fills me.

"You tryin' to get yourself killed out there?" Rhett's voice echoes across the yard, halting me in my tracks. I stumble forward, my green rubber boots slipping on the grass as I grip the fabric of my blue cotton dress, fists clenched at my sides.

My heart hitches in my chest as I turn to see Rhett standing at the edge of the meadow. His favorite baseball hat on his head. The worn white cotton shirt spans across his chest, a rag in his grip.

The yellowing leaves, tall dry grass, the blue sky; it all fades behind him. Because all I see is him.

My throat goes dry, and my eyes sting. Blinking away the water collecting on my eyelashes, all the emotions I'd suppressed for weeks bubble to the surface.

"I need to say a few things," I start, well aware I'm shouting across the yard, but I can't get my feet to move, so Rhett takes a few steps toward me.

From behind him, Mabel comes barreling through the tall grasses, right into me. Her nose finds my hands, and I run my hand down her back, but I can't take my eyes off the man slowly approaching me. He doesn't stop until he's so close that I have to tilt my head back to look at him, straight into his icy, blue eyes. The eyes that warm to the color of the sea for me. He wears a few days of unshaved stubble, lining his square jaw, his narrowed eyes gazing down at me.

"Audrey, what are you doing here?" His voice is low, rough, strained. My name on his lips giving my heart the courage to say what's etched on the surface of my skin.

"You were wrong, Rhett."

He cocks his head, lips pulling back to reveal a smile that causes my lungs to squeeze. He might be the most stubborn man I ever knew but I was not going to let him get away without hearing everything I had to say.

"You been holding onto that sentence for a month now?" he growls, but I catch a sparkle in those eyes.

"Yeah, I have." My voice gains confidence as he drags his eyes painfully slow over me.

"You going to tell me what I was wrong—"

I cut him off, stomping my foot in the grass, pushing my finger into his hard chest.

"I liked those creaky stairs," I state loudly, and Rhett goes still. "And I like your senseless old truck, and the way you say my name." I choke out my words, as tears start streaming down my face with every admission, but I can't stop. "And I like the way you dance, and the way you pretend you don't care about anything. I know you care."

I gulp in air, shaking my head, but Rhett wears a small, crooked smirk. "You think I want a big life, but I don't want anything but this. I just want this. I want your loud, crazy dog. And your family. And you."

"Audrey…" Rhett's eyes cast down, his head tilting towards me, and I want to run my thumb across those full lips. I yearn to bury my face in the space between his neck and shoulder where I fit perfectly, but I haven't told him everything yet, and I need him to know all of it. Even if he never wants to see me again, even if he tells me to leave and never come back.

I need to tell him the truth, every piece of it.

"I did think, at first, this thing between us was going to just fizzle out. I thought I could move on from my old life and use you as a bridge. But what I didn't know…is you would become the most important thing to me."

He bites his lip, his eyes growing the slightest bit misty.

"I quit my job Rhett, because you were also right about that. I thought I knew what I wanted, I thought I knew exactly what my life was supposed to look like." His touch surprises me, sending a shiver down my spine as he gently nudges my face up to his. I can't breathe but I have to go on. I have to get it out.

"I waited to tell you all of this because I needed to be someone you deserved. I needed to be who *I* deserved. I needed to get to know myself first." His eyes focus on me so intensely that I fear my legs may collapse, the columns of my throat growing weak, but I continue as he waits silently.

"But Rhett...what I discovered was the more I got to know me, the more I missed you. Because without you...I'm not me." Hot tears spill down my face, and his hand cups my jaw as his thumb gently brushes a tear away.

"I know I hurt you, and it kills me every day, but it doesn't make it any less true that I'm in love with you. I love all of you and—"

This time he doesn't let me finish my sentence before closing the gap between us, his fingers sliding into my messy chocolate hair, gripping me tightly to him. He pulls me close, holding me against his chest, and as our lips meet, a wave of warmth floods through me. I remember what it feels like to be so safe that I can simply let go and melt into him.

Mabel lets out a howl and the world grows smaller around me, until it's just Rhett and I. He grabs the back of my thighs, lifting me up, never letting us part as he kicks the back door open, carrying me into the house.

Our fingers trace the contours of each other's clothing, pulling at the fabric with a quiet urgency, revealing the warmth of our skin beneath. There's a fire burning rapidly between us, one I hope to never put out.

But as my hands hold the man I love close, his eyes never leaving mine, he pauses, pulling back slightly.

"I love all of you, too, darlin'. Will you please come home?"

My eyes well along with my pulsing heart, and I silently nod, pulling him back to me, feeling every piece of who I was, and who I am now, welded together by a man who feels like home.

Epilogue

Audrey - 5 months later

My tan wool coat swings around me, as I smile at the people gathering on the street in front of me. They closed down Main Street for this. For me and my little bakery. It felt extremely cliche to open a bakery the week of Valentine's Day, but I didn't want to delay it any longer. Everything has been leading up to this moment.

Scanning the crowd, my eyes fall upon my favorite people. I can't hear what Penny and Rhett are talking about, but she is laughing at whatever he said—even if she still calls him Red. Renee and Desi are planted beside them, waving and giving me the thumbs up. The attention is intoxicating in the best possible way. I can feel the love surrounding me today, and I'm deeply grateful for the life I've built here.

It's been a long five months. Five months of learning what it means to rebuild...both a building and a relationship. Rhett spent many nights with me in this bakery, helping me set up, grabbing my shoulders to remind me to take deep breaths when I was decidedly in over my head. And of course, always up for it when I suggested we take a break for waffles and coffee across the street.

I also had finally given Penny her space back, but we had a standing weekly dinner date where I filled her in on life at the farmhouse, and she filled me in on her ever-evolving career and dating life.

It had taken about two seconds after coming back into Rhett's life for him to realize I meant it. I loved all of him, I wanted all of him. Even though I told him I loved everything in his life exactly as it was, he continued to fix up the house. I made him promise to never get rid of all of the quirks I'd fallen in love with last summer and he agreed. It was perfectly imperfect, just how I preferred.

It wasn't all sunshine and roses though; nothing ever is. There were hard days. Many hard days between that Monday in October and this crisp February morning. We butted heads on many things and had days where we needed some space. But every single night we came back together, choosing each other, again and again. That was what mattered. Our love was bigger than any of the pain.

Mabel also forgave me for leaving, and I promised to never stop making her treats. I got so good at baking her different kinds of biscuits, I decided to dedicate an entire case in the bakery to dog treats.

It all seems picturesque, right? Me, the big city girl falling for the man with the truck and white farmhouse. I left my corporate job for small business ownership. But none of those details really mattered, I realized as I looked at the crowd, my eyes locking with Rhett's.

It wouldn't have mattered where we were, who we were, or what jobs we held. It wouldn't have mattered what zip code we lived in or the legacy of my family.

Because I was always meant to be *this* version of Audrey. It just took some time to find her.

And Rhett Anderson...he was always meant to be the love of my life.

It just took a bit of unraveling.

"Are you ready?" The mayor saddled up next to me, a smile on her face as Penny wove her way through the crowd to hand me a pair of giant pink scissors—she insisted I needed them— and I nodded at the mayor. A large ribbon divides us and the crowd of my new hometown.

"Thank you to everyone who came out on this chilly winter morning. I am so grateful for the way this community has rallied around me and supported me all these months while I make something I think will be truly special." I smiled wide, as I cut the ribbon on a new adventure.

"Welcome to Mabel's Bakeshop!"

Also by Katherine Bitner

The Hometown Series:
Unravel Me

Stand Alones:
Strayed
The Way You See Me
Time to Bloom

Afterword

This book was a labor of love...I remember driving in my car, listening to music when a song came on that inspire a thought. What if *she* was the rich one, the one who was unsure and finding herself, and he was the one pining for her? I had the first chapter in my head for months before I finally took the dive into this love story. And my gosh, do I love it.

So many thanks to my friends, who are also authors, who listened to my fears, my excitement and helped me with my several (LIKE TONS OF) plot holes. To Danielle and Haley who gracefully listen to my ranting voice memos, and Rachael for keeping me on track with your structured writing sprints at coffee shops all summer long. And to all my beta readers, my editors, and the entire bookish community that kept encouraging me when I was derailed by self-doubt. None of this would exist without you. Grateful doesn't even cut it.

Thanks to my sister who did the character artwork for this book, and told me she prefers fantasy books, but is proud of me none the less. I'm sorry I don't have a brain for fantasy, but maybe one day! And to my husband, Brian, for giving me first hand experience at how a gentleman acts, for answering all my questions about vintage trucks, and for looking amazing in Levi jeans. Oh and thank you for letting me play this books playlist on every drive we went on for the last year. You're a trooper.

Much love. Until next time, Katherine

About the author

Katherine Bitner is the author of contemporary love stories that will rip your heart open…and stitch it back together in the end. Most of her books feature a dog – because her rescued pit bull, Wilbur, insisted.

Katherine loves talking to readers, helping new authors, and rewatching her favorite comfort show – The Office – from her sofa in North Carolina. If you like gritty characters, dramatic storytelling that pulls you in, and a theme of women finding love and themselves, you're in the right place.

Find her on the socials – she is on them way too often (when she should be writing)